FATE & FANG

FATE & FANG

THE BOUCHERS
BOOK THREE

NICOLE JACQUELYN

Fate & Fang
Paperback Edition

Love N. Books Press
An Imprint of Wolfpack Publishing
1707 E. Diana Street
Tampa, FL 33610

www.lovenbookspress.com

Cover design by Jennilynn Wyer Designs
Edited by My Brother's Editor

Paperback ISBN 978-1-969876-02-8
Ebook ISBN 978-1-969876-01-1
LCCN

To the readers who don't read vampire romance
but have found themselves reading about the Bouchers
anyway.

FATE & FANG

DANIEL

PROLOGUE

I stared at the small dip in the sheet between my baby brother's head and torso. It didn't matter that his body was shielded from view. Everyone in the room knew what had been done to his body.

Ezekiel had been tortured. Slowly. Agonizingly. Ripped into pieces like a slab of meat.

My baby brother, who'd driven me crazy since the moment he could crawl, was gone. He'd never again steal my motorcycle and bring it back beaten to hell. He'd never call me over and over again until I agreed to go with him to Egypt or India or Amsterdam on a whim. He'd never steal the edge piece of my mother's brownies off my plate again, never tackle me from behind on the sparring mats, never grin at me mischievously right before he did something completely unhinged.

I wasn't sure what death entailed. No one was. It was impossible to know if the end came quickly, like a snap of the fingers, or if it took a while, like drifting to the center of a lake when your raft came unmoored, but whichever it was, I prayed that it had been peaceful. Zeke deserved that much after what he'd gone through.

It felt as if a piece of me had been torn away, and the space left empty gaped wide, the edges ragged.

Rage on a level that I'd never felt before rose in my chest until it felt like I could open my mouth and breathe fire. The room flickered, a red haze clouding my vision for a moment and then disappearing again.

My brother Chance gripped my bicep, giving it a squeeze in warning.

"You have all that you need from him?" my father asked the commandant of Vampire Command.

I'd fought for Arthur Carruthers for years. Bled for him. Killed for him. I'd answered every call and followed every order.

Now, I could barely look at him.

I was *done*.

I ignored Arthur's response and everything that followed as I put one foot in front of the other, following my father and brothers out of the morgue. It took every piece of focus I had to climb the stairs and walk through the nondescript building, passing the Vampires working their administrative jobs like the world hadn't just crashed down around us.

They'd known Zeke had been captured. I would've bet every dollar in my accounts that they'd been on their little computers, their fingers flying over their keyboards, searching for any kind of information that would help them get my brother back. They'd analyzed the odds, called in favors, searched records for his team's strengths and weaknesses, and planned and replanned the rescue mission.

But not one of them had called any of his brothers.

I wished every one of them dead.

The flight home was a blur, and the freedom I usually felt with my hands on the controls and nothing but air and space around me was absent. The only thing I felt was relief that I was closed into the cockpit, away from the grief of the others.

I already knew how things would play out. My mother's devastation would be overwhelming. My father's rage would rattle the earth. Ambrose would grow more protective and desperate to find answers. Beau's disillusionment with the world would grow, and he'd become more distant than he already was. Chance would be unable to contain his need to say the most offensive thoughts that popped into his head, an impulse he'd barely contained before.

None of them would recover. None would ever be the same.

I would have to be the calm in the center of the storm.

I was used to that.

I was the easygoing brother. The hard-to-rattle brother. The kind brother, the friendly brother, the never-caused-a-moment's-worry brother.

Since the day I turned six years old, I'd trained myself to be all of those things.

I used the silence around me to find the peace I needed. By the time we touched down on the private landing strip at home, I had pushed down every bit of emotion, every agonizing vision of what Zeke had gone through, the urge for vengeance, and the pulsating rage into a small box in the back of my mind.

Only a hundred years of conditioning kept that

box from breaking open as I stepped through the cockpit door and realized what my brothers were discussing.

"Do we really believe that this wasn't a targeted blow?" Chance asked, his eyes landing on each of us quickly, like he couldn't figure out where to look.

"Fuck no," Beau replied darkly. "They knew what they were doing."

"They were trying to figure out what would kill him," I said quietly. It was the only thing that made sense. "Worked their way through—"

"Enough," my father barked, his hand slashing through the air. "That's enough."

It felt as if all the air had been sucked out of the plane. My ears rang.

"Fuck," my eldest brother Ambrose breathed, looking out the window. "Mom's coming."

Straightening my shoulders, I shoved the rage even deeper.

Rage would help no one.

As soon as I knew red wouldn't cloud my vision, I helped open the door and let down the stairs.

Our mother watched us disembark with her hands over her mouth, her eyes frantically searching the spot behind each of us. Waiting. We filed out one by one, and when she caught sight of my father bringing up the rear, she collapsed to her knees.

He vaulted over the railing before I'd reached the bottom stair, gathering her into his arms as she pounded her fists against his chest.

I looked away.

Following my brothers, we left our mother and father standing on the runway, the sound of her screams like knives digging into my spine with every step.

Our father would take care of her. As her mate, that was his right and his most sacred calling. Soon though, she'd need us. As her children, she would crave our presence, even while it hurt her, because four of her sons could never fill the space where once there had been five.

Without a word, we parted as soon as we reached the house, each of us going to our own little apartments. Our mother's wailing rang in my ears until I closed myself inside.

Closing my eyes, I let my legs buckle beneath me, sliding down the wall until I landed on my ass.

Ezekiel, you asshole. If you're out there somewhere, just know that I'm going to beat your ass when I get there. This is because we never let you go first, isn't it?

Letting out a shuddery breath, I opened my eyes again. It was almost as if I could hear his annoying laughter.

I'd never encountered an issue that I couldn't solve—sometimes with plain logic, sometimes with brute strength. Every problem had a solution. It was as simple as that.

There was no solution for Zeke's death. No way to move past it or get around it.

I slammed my fist against the rug, making the flooring beneath it groan.

The only thing I could do moving forward was protect the rest of them.

I stared at the back of my couch, my thoughts racing.

Vampires weren't immortal like the myths that

humans threw around. Though harder to kill than humans, it was still possible to end us. It wasn't until we'd completed a mating bond that immortality set in. After that, the only way to end our lives was decapitation, and that was nearly impossible to manage on a fully grown and mated Vampire.

Pushing myself to my feet, I brushed my hair back from my face and smoothed down my beard.

That was the solution.

I couldn't bring Zeke back, but I could save the others.

They needed mates.

But first, I was going to take out every single human that had anything to do with Zeke's death. I wasn't sure where to begin, and I wasn't sure how I would do it—but I was very good at solving problems.

CHAPTER 1
ROSEMARY

I was surrounded by handsome men, and while normally that would've been a dream of mine, the split in my lip stung like hell, the ropes around my wrists and ankles had chafed the hell out of my skin, and the men were staring at me with an intensity that didn't feel particularly sexy. I tightened my grip around the broken bottle in my hand. It wasn't much as weapons went, but assuming they didn't shoot me before I could move, there was a good chance I could take at least the little one in hand-to-hand. He'd seemed pretty non-threatening when my kidnappers had dropped him in my room like a trussed pig, but that didn't mean much. I'd met plenty of men who seemed okay at first and turned into monumental assholes later.

They got bonus points for untying me, but that didn't mean I trusted them.

"Whoa," one of them said, his head jerking back in surprise. "We're not going to hurt you."

I looked at each of their faces. They were dressed

head to toe in black fatigues. Each one had an earpiece. There was a definite family resemblance. Two of the men were clean cut—short hair, fresh shaves, chiseled jaws. The one talking to me was a little rougher looking with scruff and longer hair. The only one who didn't match the set was the guy who'd been tied up at my feet for the last hour or so. He was smaller than the others, and his coloring was all wrong. Thoughts raced through my head so fast I could barely catch them.

"What the fuck is going on?" I asked flatly. My mouth snapped shut when another man stepped into the room, and my stomach swooped.

I'd seen him before. I'd recognize the warm brown eyes anywhere, though the last time I'd seen him, they'd been twinkling with laughter. His beard was trimmed shorter, and his hair was longer, pulled back in a knot at the base of his neck. I stared at the tattoos on his throat. His Adam's apple bobbed as he swallowed.

"I know you," I said, trailing my gaze upward until I met his eyes. "How do I know you?"

"No fucking clue," the man replied, his voice deep and raspy. "You planning on using that?"

I glanced down at the bottle still gripped in my fist. "If I need to."

"How far do you think you'd get?" he asked casually.

Not far enough.

"You'd be surprised," I replied, staring. He was more beautiful up close. His lips formed a cupid's bow, nearly hidden by his mustache, and his jaw was so strong that even his beard couldn't disguise it. High cheekbones that were flushed with color. And those eyes.

"You remember where we met yet?" He smiled, his eyes crinkling at the corners.

Yes. I did.

"No one here is going to hurt you," the man said, flipping his pistol around so he could hand it to me. "Take it."

I reached out and wrapped my hand around the grip. It was larger than I was used to, but beggars couldn't be choosers. I felt the muscles in my neck relax a little.

"Bullseye," I told him, searching his face for any recognition.

He shook his head slowly, like he didn't understand.

"The gun shop. That's where I saw you."

"I haven't been there in almost a year," he countered, tilting his head.

"I know." I licked my lips and winced as my tongue found the cut. "You came in with another guy. He looked like you, but his hair was shorter."

My cousin had whispered that he wouldn't have minded being the meat in that particular sandwich, and I'd nearly choked on my tongue.

"My brother Zeke."

His brother? I looked around the room again. The other men resembled this one, but none of them was the one from before. I may not have remembered where I'd seen him at first, but now that I'd been given some context, I would've recognized the missing brother.

"He's not here," the man said, his eyes roaming all over my face like a caress. It was like he was cataloging my features. "These are the rest of my brothers. Ambrose, Chance, Beau, and Charlie."

I looked away as I felt my cheeks heat. Their stances had relaxed fractionally, but every single one of them was staring at me like I'd grown two heads. Even the little one, whose lips had pulled up in a small smile. He didn't fit in with the others.

"Zeke's mate," the man across from me said.

I looked back at him. "You're Vampires?"

"Yes," he replied simply.

That made sense. Jesus, it made perfect sense. I wasn't sure why I hadn't seen it the minute they'd busted through the door. The only thing I could blame it on was the lack of sleep and any kind of brain food over the past week. It wouldn't have killed the idiot kidnappers to bring me a piece of broccoli, for god's sake.

They'd come for their brother's mate, that was clear enough, but every Vampire I'd ever known had been just as good at disappearing as they were at completing an objective. Half the time, no one knew they'd ever been there in the first place. So why were they still standing in that little room staring at me?

The beautiful Vampire standing across from me was calm. Patient. His gaze was soft and warm and hopeful, but it wasn't weak. No, there was intensity there, a thrum of something I couldn't quite pinpoint, but felt close to *possession.*

He'd handed me his pistol without hesitating for a second, and while I knew that Vampires lived through most injuries, it still wasn't pleasant for them to be shot. It was as if he'd known I wouldn't use it. Why?

Sweat dripped down my spine. I didn't like puzzles that I couldn't solve.

A memory of my dad looking at me over his glasses

played in my head. *Don't overthink it, Flower. The simplest answer is usually the correct one.*

Okay, so the simplest answer to why this Vampire was looking at me like I was some kind of supermodel, even though I hadn't showered in a week...

But that would mean—

"I'm your mate?" I asked, bracing myself for his laughter.

"Yes." He brushed his tongue along his bottom lip, and my stomach flipped.

"Shit," I whispered, dropping my arm down limply at my side. Only years of training kept me from dropping it as shock made my limbs go numb.

The Vampires burst into motion.

"So you don't know who Finau is, then," the scruffy one drawled.

"I've never even heard that name," I replied, watching as he nodded thoughtfully.

"Why were they holding you?" the beautiful Vampire asked as his brother left the room.

"I don't know," I replied, clicking on the safety of the pistol. I rounded the desk and tried to hand it back to him.

Vampire lore was legendary. People discussed them ad nauseam, and I'd heard every harebrained theory there was. Most of it was bullshit, but sometimes humans stumbled onto a piece of truth.

Like the fact that if I were this Vampire's mate, I was suddenly the safest I'd ever been in my life.

"Keep it until we're out of here," the Vampire said, his gaze still roaming all over me.

I nodded and adjusted my grip.

I followed him across the room as his brothers

started yelling from the main part of the garage where I'd been held.

"Shit," he hissed as he picked up speed.

"Wait," I called, jogging behind him. My legs protested as the muscles stretched and tightened, but I refused to acknowledge it.

"You okay?" he asked, jerking to a stop in the hallway.

"What's your name?" I asked, pausing a foot away.

"Daniel Boucher." His gaze was warm as he shot me a soft smile.

I barely stopped my mouth from dropping open. Everyone had heard of the Boucher brothers. Their names were legendary in certain circles, and I'd spent the past five years hearing about their exploits.

"You gonna tell me yours?" he asked as he started moving again.

"Rosemary Whitlock," I replied, watching for any sense of recognition. None came.

"Nice to meet you, Rosie," he said as we exited out of the hallway to find his brothers barking at each other.

Panic seemed to pulse inside the building like a living thing as I followed the group toward the doors. I wasn't sure where we were going, but I would've followed the devil if it meant I could escape the four walls of my prison. Armed intruders breaking in to kill my captors was the perfect cover, and I nearly sighed as I took in a lungful of fresh air outside.

From what I could gather from the shorthand they spoke, their home had been attacked while they were away. No one said it out loud, but from their sharp movements and the speed at which we reached their cars, there were very important occupants at home.

Daniel threw open the back seat of a nondescript sedan and gestured for me to climb in. As soon as I was seated, he threw himself into the driver's seat. Seconds later, we were speeding toward the end of the block and flying around the corner. I buckled my seat belt as I watched his brother in the front passenger seat, his body strung tight as a wire as he leaned forward, like that would make the car move faster.

"They're really good drivers," the not-brother said from beside me as he buckled his own belt. "Lots of practice." He didn't sound confident.

"I'm not worried," I replied, watching as we sped through red light after red light and then swung onto the freeway.

"I'm Charlie," he said, glancing at me and then back out the front windshield.

We were going so fast that it was nearly impossible to look away from the road ahead of us. It was instinct, the urge to see where we were going.

"Rosemary," I replied.

"Pretty name."

"Sorry I didn't untie you back there," I said distractedly. "That looked uncomfortable as hell."

"How could you have?" Charlie asked skeptically. "You were tied to a chair."

"Right."

With a small jolt, I remembered hearing about the death of one of the Boucher brothers. The youngest one. That's why he hadn't been in the garage with the others. It had been pretty big news for a minute because the highly trained Vampire had been kidnapped and tortured. I tried not to look at Charlie again. I'd never met a human who had lost their mate before, and I didn't want to stare like some creep.

Forcing myself to look away from the cars we were passing, I pulled the magazine out of the pistol in my hand and checked the ammunition. The weight of it assured me it was loaded, but I had a feeling that I'd need to know exactly what I had to work with. Whatever situation we were walking into was bad. The brother in the passenger seat—I couldn't remember which Boucher he was—kept calling for a man named Sven through his comms.

Eventually, Sven stopped answering.

My stomach was in knots by the time we turned off a windy road onto a long private driveway lined with old growth. My skin was damp with clammy sweat even though the night around us was cool. I was pretty sure I had a fever, but I'd deal with it later.

Absolute carnage greeted us as we pulled up in front of a massive house.

"Oh my god," I mumbled under my breath.

There were bodies everywhere. Lying in the yard. In heaps on the front porch.

"I'm coming with you," Charlie announced. Bravely, I thought. His voice shook a little, but he'd still said it.

"No. Keep watch," the brother ordered. He jumped out of the car while it was still moving.

"Fuck! Ambrose!" Daniel yelled in frustration.

Right. That was Ambrose Boucher. I should've known he was the oldest. Something about the way he carried himself indicated that he was used to being in charge of the others.

We slid to a stop in the gravel as I unbuckled my seat belt and clicked off the pistol's safety.

I'd inadvertently stepped into a situation that was clearly fucked and none of my business, but I wasn't about to cower like an infant. I refused to be caught unaware, and I sure as shit wasn't going to sit in the car.

"Stay here," Daniel said as he threw open his door, leaving the car running.

"Not a fucking chance," I argued, following him.

Distant shots had us both snapping our heads toward the east side of the property.

"How good are you with that?" Daniel asked, nodding toward the pistol.

"Very good." I'd been training since I was eight, but that wasn't information that needed to be shared at present.

He watched me for a moment, tilted his head sharply from side to side, and finally nodded. "Stay close."

We quietly jogged across the expanse of lawn and stepped into the trees. I stayed near Daniel, but chose my own route as we picked our way through the foliage, our steps nearly silent. The trees were so thick above us that what little moonlight we'd been using to see had all but disappeared. My eyes adjusted slowly to the dark, but I'd been in worse places at night. Using my other senses and pure instinct, I rounded bushes and picked my way through ferns as the sound of a struggle came from somewhere ahead of us.

When we finally found the three men, the differences between them were stark. Two of them were wearing camouflage tactical gear, their faces painted so dark that only the whites of their eyes shone in the dark. The other was in plain black, functional work pants and a long-sleeved shirt, and he was kicking their asses like it was nothing. The fluidity and speed of his movements were instantly recognizable. Another Vampire.

"Did all of you make it back?" he asked casually as he snapped the neck of one of the men, letting him drop silently to the forest floor. The other man roared and dove for the guy in black.

"Even brought home an extra," Daniel replied calmly.

"No shit?" He elbowed the camouflaged man in the throat and then turned to us as the man went down, clutching at his neck. In the light, I knew his face would've been mottled with color as he struggled for air that never came, but in the dark, he just looked like a formless shape writhing on the ground.

"Rosie, this is Josiah," Daniel said quietly as we walked further into the woods.

"Hey," I whispered, scanning the darkness for anything out of place.

"Nice to meet you, Rosie," Josiah greeted.

"It's Rosemary, actually."

"Rosemary, then."

We quietly made our way around the property in a wide circle, and I'd begun to think that we wouldn't find anyone as we crossed over the long driveway. The night was silent, though, and that made the hair on the back of my neck prickle. My stomach and chest were still aching, and my clothes stuck to me damply, but I tried my best to ignore it. When I was home again, I could figure out what the hell was going on. I wasn't sure how I would've caught something from the men who'd held me in that garage, but I couldn't rule out food poisoning from the cheap restaurants they'd frequented.

I needed to get home.

The Vampires on each side of me broke into a slow jog as we entered the trees again. They could clearly see or hear something that I couldn't. Taking a deep breath, I followed them, trying my best to keep my footfalls silent. It wasn't easy as I tried to match their speed, and eventually I stopped trying for finesse and just focused on not tripping on anything.

I smelled the blood before I saw what they'd been racing toward. There was a body lying on the ground while three others kicked at it.

"Motherfuckers," I breathed as I ran harder. My footsteps were clumsy and louder than they should've been, but my body didn't seem to be cooperating like it usually did.

Without warning, one of the men who'd been kicking the body spun toward us, and a spray of bullets thunked against the trees and bushes around me.

Dropping into a crouch, I ignored the fear that coated my skin and aimed. I couldn't see if I'd hit the man, but by the way he folded in half with an almost breathless wail, I was pretty sure I had.

In the time it had taken for me to shoot, the Vampires with me had closed in on the other men and made short work of taking them out. I rose and hurried toward them as they kneeled beside the body on the ground.

"Get up, you big baby," Josiah chided, making the body chuckle.

"Fuck off."

"Where are you hit?" Daniel asked as they helped him up.

"Shoulder and side."

"Sloppy," Josiah said, shaking his head.

"I thought there were two," he groaned as they helped him to his feet. "There were three."

"Can you walk?"

"I'm fine." He took a few stumbling steps and stopped short when he saw me. "Congratulations, Danny."

"Thanks," Danny said, hooking his shoulder under the injured man's armpit. "Rosie, this is my cousin Matthias. Josiah's brother."

I could've guessed that myself. When both Vampires were facing me in the dark, I could barely tell the difference between them. The shapes of their faces and the way they held their bodies—even with Matthias wounded—were nearly identical.

Josiah ran to make one more check on the perimeter of the property while we helped Matthias to the driveway. Our shoes crunched on the gravel as we trudged toward the house, but since neither of the Vampires seemed concerned by the noise, I wasn't either. I still scanned our surroundings like a hawk, searching for anything out of place as we made our way toward the house. It took so long that by the time we reached the cars, Josiah was already there and barely out of breath.

"All clear."

Charlie climbed out of the car, his face practically gray.

"Shit," Josiah said, moving toward him. "You been there this whole time?"

"Danny asked me to stay," he said, glancing toward us. "I wanted to get out, but no one left me a weapon, so—"

"Dammit," Daniel muttered. "My bad, Charles."

"I didn't want to get in anyone's way," Charlie replied, glancing toward the house. "But—"

"Go," Matthias ordered tiredly, jerking his head toward the house.

Danny transferred Matthias over to his brother just as the scruffy Boucher rounded the house. Not Danny or Ambrose, so it must've been either Beau or Chance.

"Shit, Matthias," the Boucher brother grimaced. "How bad?"

"Not bad," Matthias answered as Josiah helped him up the steps. "The women?"

"Alive."

"Good news," Josiah said, stepping over a body.

My stomach cramped suddenly, and a fresh wave of sweat beaded on my forehead.

"I realize that you're dealing with some shit," I said on a wheeze, wiping my face with the sleeve of my shirt. "But if I could borrow a car? I need to get home."

Danny's gaze swept over me. "I'll drive you."

"You don't have to—"

"What can you tell us about the men in the garage?" his brother interrupted.

"Chance, now's not the time," Danny chastised.

"No better time," Chance countered. "Details while they're fresh."

"Well, the rat-faced one was partial to Thai food," I replied tiredly. "And the one with the beard and the huge mole next to his nose liked gas station fried chicken."

Chance just stared at me.

I had no idea how much they already knew, so I had no clue how much to tell them. If they were already dealing with the human militia, then they'd clearly stepped in shit already, but that didn't mean that I was authorized to start blabbing. Loose lips sink ships and all that.

"I don't know anything," I lied. "When I got home from work on Thursday, some guys threw a bag over my head." I gestured at myself. "It took three of them to get me into the van. There must've been something on the cloth because I passed out, and when I woke up, I was in that chair."

"Did they say why they took you?" Daniel asked doubtfully.

"They didn't really say anything. They fed me and took me to the bathroom three times a day. Like clockwork." I huffed. "I'm pretty sure they set an alarm so they didn't forget. It worked in my favor, though, because at least I knew what time of day it was."

"And they didn't fuck with you?" Chance asked.

"They pretty much ignored that I was there."

"You seem very calm about all this," he said slowly.

I forced my body not to tighten as Chance glanced at Daniel.

"I'm good in a crisis," I replied flatly. "But I'd like to go home now."

"I'll take you," Daniel said.

He and his brother had some kind of silent conversation. Eventually, Chance shrugged and turned back toward the house.

"Let's go," Daniel said, throwing open the passenger door for me. I brushed past him as I climbed inside, and everything inside me lit up like the fucking Fourth of July. Swallowing hard, I primly pulled on my seat belt as he shut me inside.

I hadn't showered or brushed my teeth in a week. My hair was tangled. The thighs of my jeans were crusty from the food I'd spilled while trying to both eat and hold the paper plate steady a few days before. I stank. I stank so badly that even I could smell it, and I'd been sitting with it for days.

"Where am I going?" Daniel asked as he got into the driver's seat.

"I-5 south," I replied, pressing my arms against my sides.

The car was quiet as we turned in a circle and headed back down the tree-lined drive. I'd moved past the point when my mind raced and slid deep into the territory where everything quieted. As soon as I got home, I could decompress and figure out how in the world I'd crossed paths with the Bouchers. First, a shower, then something to eat, and then I could process.

My hands began to tremble with the inevitable adrenaline crash.

We raced toward the freeway in silence, and I watched how the dashboard lights lit up Daniel's face. Things were clearly fucked, but he'd still agreed to immediately take me home. He'd left everything behind in order to do what I'd asked, and I couldn't figure out why it had been so easy. Was it because I was his mate?

No, I couldn't think about that yet. I needed to bathe first. Then eat. Then, I'd go over everything that had happened.

Reaching forward, I opened the dash, made sure

that I'd flicked on the safety, and set Daniel's pistol inside. As I sat back, I flexed my fingers. They were stiff from how tightly I'd been holding it.

I wrapped my arms around my waist and tried to ignore the ache in my chest. I was twenty-three, and I had no history of heart problems in my family. I *wasn't* having a heart attack. It was probably just a symptom of an adrenaline crash.

Why the hell was it so fucking hot in the car? The heater wasn't even on beyond the window defroster. I grit my teeth, knowing that I must just be radiating BO from how badly I was sweating. I considered rolling down my window even though it had started to sprinkle rain.

"I know you're lying," Daniel said quietly, his voice breaking the silence like a slap.

Shit.

CHAPTER 2

DANIEL

Rosemary was too calm.

She'd followed me out of the garage she'd been held in too easily.

She handled a weapon like she'd been born with one in her hand.

At no point had she complained, hesitated, or behaved as if she was scared.

It didn't make any sense. I was missing something.

Hearing her voice had felt like the final piece of a puzzle falling into place. Stepping into that room and seeing her face had felt like the pinnacle moment of my life. There she was. The woman I'd been waiting a century for. My mate. The other half of me.

She was a mess. Her hair was a rat's nest. Her clothes were dirty. She smelled.

She was also perfect. My height, muscular and strong, long brown hair, and hazel eyes that missed nothing. Pouty lips. If I could've chosen what she looked like, I wouldn't have imagined anything different. She carried herself like she was used to commanding every room, unwilling to make herself smaller for the benefit of others. Her confidence hadn't been shaken even after being held for days in a broken-down garage. I liked that.

She was also lying through her teeth.

"Lying about what?" Rosemary asked, staring out the front windshield. Her voice didn't shake. Her expression didn't change.

"Not sure yet," I replied, switching lanes. "Why don't you tell me?"

"I haven't lied to you."

"I find that very hard to believe."

"Not sure what to tell you."

I glanced over at her profile, and something twinged in my chest. I reached up to press the heel of my hand there. Gods, she was beautiful.

"Take the next exit."

I nodded as I changed lanes. I wondered where we were headed. She'd said she wanted to go home, but it made little sense that she'd show me where she lived.

She'd been kidnapped, seen multiple dead bodies, shot a man, and she hadn't once asked to call the police. I wrestled with the urge to pull the car over and grill her for information. Who the hell was she, really?

"Left at the next intersection," she ordered as we pulled off the freeway.

"You realize that you're going to have to come clean, right?" I asked, following her directions.

Gods, I wanted to reach for her. It felt like everything was spinning. Euphoria that I'd finally found my mate was juxtaposed with the reality that she had something to do with the humans that were targeting Vampires and their mates. We'd found her in one of their hideouts, and she'd come out swinging. I didn't believe that she'd been with them—the universe couldn't be that cruel—but she was involved somehow.

She'd immediately recognized that she was my mate.

My head throbbed.

"Now, right," she said, pointing.

I turned onto a two-lane road and slowed as we rounded a curve. We were headed into a less populated area, leaving streetlights behind, and for a moment, I wondered if she was leading me into an ambush of some sort. My gaze shifted toward the dash where she'd stored my pistol, and I discarded the idea.

"I need a shower," she mumbled. "Then we can deal with"—she waved her hand around—"whatever."

My phone vibrated in my pocket, and I pulled it out. I'd left our home, prioritizing my mate above the mess I'd left behind, and while I knew everyone would believe I'd done the right thing, guilt still lay heavy on my shoulders.

"Still have your head?" my brother Chance asked when I answered it.

"For the moment."

"Where'd she take you?"

"Track me," I replied vaguely. "How's it going there?"

"We didn't lose anyone," Chance said with a sigh. "Lucy isn't great, but Ambrose is with her. Mom's going to be down for a while."

"Matthias?"

"He'll be fine."

Chance hesitated, and my gut clenched.

"What?" I barked.

"Uncle Sven hasn't woken up."

"At all?"

"It was a partial," Chance said quietly. I could hear him moving. "He's alive, though."

"Shit."

"You know they have to take our entire head," Chance reminded me. "He'll be fine. Oh, and Dad's awake."

"How's that going?"

"He's surprisingly calm."

"So not tearing down the house with his bare hands?"

"Not yet, anyway."

"What about Reese?" I asked. I hadn't seen my brother Beau's mate at the house. There was a very good chance that they'd been together long enough that her immortality had locked in already, but it was impossible to know for sure.

"She and Aunt Alice are fine. Did you know she could shoot?"

"What?"

"Oh, yeah," Chance said in amusement. "Little sister is a damn sharpshooter. She took out all those men in the yard with a rifle."

"No shit?"

"She's got nothin' on Lucy, though." Chance laughed darkly.

"What do you mean?" Our oldest brother's mate was fierce, but not especially intimidating.

Rosemary pointed to the right, and I slowed to take the turn.

"She took out almost as many with a pistol in the

front room," Chance said. "We found her unconscious on top of a guy twice her size. She took him out right before she passed the fuck out from blood loss."

"Gods," I breathed.

"Snapped his neck."

"What?" I barked incredulously.

"Moral of the story—don't fuck with Lucy." Chance hummed. "Or Charlie."

I huffed in agreement. Ambrose's mate Lucy was Charlie's sister. It was unheard of that Vampires in the same family mated a pair of siblings, but when we'd gone searching for Zeke's mate, Charlie, Ambrose had taken one look at Lucy and known instantly. In a twisted way, it made sense. The Gods had known that one of the Franklin siblings could never live forever without the other. Charlie would never survive immortality without his sister by his side.

"All good here," Chance said. "Mostly. Take care of your shit. I just wanted to check in."

"Appreciate it."

"You weren't even thinking of your poor family, were you?" my brother accused, laughter in his voice. "Mating heat strikes again."

"Fuck off."

"I'm just fucking with you. We're good, Danny boy. Let us know that you're not dead when you come up for air." He hung up without saying goodbye.

"Love you too," I muttered under my breath, dropping my phone on the dash.

"Everything okay?" Rosemary asked as we made our way through the woods. We were in the middle of nowhere.

"Everyone's accounted for," I replied.

"That's good."

"No questions?" I pressed. "You're not curious what the hell you stepped into?"

Rosemary pressed her lips together and seemed to straighten.

"Who the fuck are you?" I asked, keeping my tone as light as I could make it.

"Turn right at this driveway," she said instead of answering the question.

The long gravel road was pitted with holes, and I had to slow to a crawl as we jerked and jostled from side to side. At the end was a small house, more of a cabin, really. Almost every window was lit.

The hair on my neck prickled as I parked out front and followed Rosemary out of the car. Something wasn't right.

"Come on in," she griped as I followed her up the steps to the small porch. She threw open the front door and called out, "I'm home!"

My hand had already reached for the pistol at the small of my back when the sound of scrambling paws reached us. Following closely behind was the sound of wheels squeaking across the floor.

I dropped my arm as an old gray bulldog came running into the room, his tongue hanging so far out of his mouth it nearly reached the hardwood.

"Hey, Thunder," Rosemary said tiredly, crouching down to catch him before he ran into her legs.

"Where the hell have you been?" a voice barked as an older man in a wheelchair appeared in the doorway.

"Hey, Pop," Rosemary said, rising back up with a groan.

"Who the hell are you?" he asked me.

"Pop, this is my mate, Daniel Boucher. Daniel, this is my father, Gary Whitlock."

"Well... shit," the man said, his shoulders dropping.

"Yeah," Rosemary said, lifting her arms and then letting them fall. "Surprise."

"Good to meet you," I said, stepping around my mate to shake her father's hand.

"Your mate is a *Boucher*?" Gary said, looking over at his daughter, his eyebrows raised.

She gave a short nod, and her father scoffed.

"What am I missing?" I asked, looking between them. It seemed as if they were having a full conversation without saying a word.

"I need a shower," Rosemary announced. "Pop, you'll entertain Daniel, right?"

"Rosemary—" I couldn't stand the idea of her out of my sight.

"Go on, Flower," her dad ordered with a jerk of his head. "You stink."

"Well aware," she mumbled as she walked toward him and kissed the top of his head as she passed. "And I'm starving."

My heart raced as she disappeared from view, and I barely kept myself from following her. If her father hadn't been blocking most of the hallway, I probably would've. I stared in the direction she'd gone, my mind racing.

What the hell had I walked into?

"Sure you got questions," Gary said, turning his wheelchair around. "Come on. We can talk while I make her somethin' to eat."

I followed him into the kitchen. The house was clean but clearly lived in. The floors were scratched from years of use, the door jams were gouged at the height of Gary's wheelchair footrests, and there were random knick-knacks and framed photos everywhere. Inside the kitchen was an entire row of well-worn cookbooks. Almost every one of them had little notes peeking out of the top.

"Can I get you somethin' to drink?" Gary asked as he moved toward the fridge. "We've got beer, milk, and water." He glanced at me over his shoulder. "Don't keep hard stuff in the house."

"No thanks," I replied cautiously. I couldn't figure him out. The man was as calm as if I'd just brought his daughter home from a date, but from everything Rosemary had said—she'd been missing for a week. What kind of father didn't care that his daughter had disappeared?

And why the hell hadn't he reacted when she'd told him we were mates?

"I can hear your mind spinnin' from here," he said in amusement as he pulled various items from the fridge. "Sit down. She'll be a while."

I walked further into the kitchen and sat down while he gathered things for what looked like a sandwich. When he'd piled everything he needed onto his lap, he brought it all over and set it out on the table.

"First things first, I've heard of you," he said conversationally.

"You have?" I asked flatly.

Gary nodded and pulled out a pair of reading glasses. He put them on the end of his nose and got to work on the sandwich.

"I wasn't aware that humans talked about us," I countered.

He let out a rough chuckle. "Well, you've got me there." He pushed up the sleeve of his flannel and flexed his wiry forearm. "You know what that is?"

In the center of his arm was a faded tattoo. Even with the lines blurred by age, it was instantly recognizable. The outline of the United States was innocuous unless you looked closer and realized that Florida was too pointed at the bottom, and there was a mirror image on the opposite side. As if the United States had fangs.

"You worked with Command?" I asked in surprise. There had always been humans who worked alongside Vampire Command, but the list was small and highly guarded. Only the highest levels of security clearance were given the opportunity, and not all of those humans passed the psychological tests that our Command required.

"For thirty-four years," he confirmed. "Not so long as you"—he glanced at me over his glasses—"but for a fair bit."

"How did you end up here?" I asked, glancing around the room before I realized what I was saying.

Gary chuckled as I internally kicked myself for insulting the man. Humans who worked for Command were paid very well, both because the work was highly dangerous and because it inspired loyalty. There wasn't anything wrong with his house, but if he'd worked for them for thirty-four years, he could've bought himself a private island somewhere.

"I own a thousand acres," he said after a moment. "And this house suited me and my wife just fine."

"I apologize—"

He waved me off.

"My wife was sick," he said, carefully assembling the sandwich. "Experimental treatments don't come cheap."

"I'm sorry," I said quietly. He'd said *was*.

"So am I," he agreed. "But we've done all right, me and Rosemary."

My stomach twisted, and I glanced toward where I could hear the water running deeper in the house. How long did it take for my mate to shower? The longer she was gone, the more uncomfortable it became.

"She'll be out in a minute," he said sympathetically as he cut the sandwich in half and started packing up the supplies again. "I'm guessin' your skin's crawlin' already."

He shook his head as he backed up from the table.

He knew about the physical symptoms of the mating bond. Interesting.

"Were you hurt on a mission?" I asked, changing the subject in an attempt to distract myself. My muscles flexed and tightened as I fought the urge to go find my mate.

"Oh, the chair?" he asked, glancing over his shoulder. "Nah, there wasn't one big event. My discs are fucked from too many of them." He rose to his feet and took a couple of lumbering steps toward the fridge. Bending slightly at the waist, he set the ingredients back inside, then stepped back and lowered himself into the chair again. He met my eyes once he'd spun back around. "I can walk. It just hurts like a motherfucker, especially this time of night."

I nodded in understanding just as the shower shut off.

"So...mates," Gary said, leaning back in his chair as

he pulled off his glasses again and tucked them into his shirt pocket. "How did that come about?"

"I found Rosemary tied up in an abandoned garage when I was looking for my brother-in-law," I replied, watching his expression for any kind of tell. "I knew right away that she was my mate."

"Well, that's how it happens, isn't it?" he asked, reaching up to scratch the scruff on his cheek. "Like a lightnin' bolt, or so I've heard."

"That's as good a description as any." I tilted my head, just a fraction. He hadn't even flinched when I'd described how I'd found Rosemary. "And I can see why you'd understand that with your background, but what I don't understand is why it didn't seem to shock your daughter."

The side of Gary's mouth lifted in a small smile. "Rosemary's godparents are Vampires."

I sat up straighter. "Who?"

"Dalton and Halle Cavendish."

I let out a long breath and stared at him in surprise. I'd known Dalton for longer than Gary had been alive. He'd retired from Vampire Command around twenty-five years before, when he'd met his mate—that was how things worked—and we'd lost touch. I hadn't seen him in years, but I knew my parents had.

"Halle was my wife's best friend," Gary said with a nod. "They met at our wedding."

"What a small world," I replied as a bead of sweat rolled down my back.

Footsteps came down the hall, and I waited impatiently as Rosemary made her way to the kitchen.

"I've been giving Daniel the family history," Gary

told her as he nodded at the sandwich he'd made. "Feel better?"

"Much," she said with a sigh.

"You want to tell me where you've been?" he asked as she strode to the table.

Rosemary shot her father a look before glancing at me. Her gaze moved down my body before jerking away again.

Gods, her hair was longer than I'd realized. The damp strands reached the small of her back. She smelled like something spicy. Cinnamon. Lemongrass.

"Last week the militia picked me up," she started as she reached for her food.

I straightened in my chair at the assurance in her tone. What in the absolute fuck?

"We knew they would at some point," she said with a shrug. "Didn't you get my message?"

"I was givin' it two more days," Gary replied darkly.

"What message?" I asked.

"If I told ya that, I'd have to kill ya," he replied. "Sorry, son."

The irony of a man half my age calling me son was overwhelming.

"Who's we?"

"About that," Rosemary said with a grimace as she took a bite of her sandwich. "Shit, this is good. Thanks, Pop."

He motioned with his hand for her to get to the point.

"I've been working with a team to find out what exactly it is that they're doing—"

"The human militia?" I asked.

"Yeah, I mean, we call them that, but are they really? They seem like a bunch of lowlifes to me."

"Rosemary Halle Whitlock, that vein in your mate's neck is about to explode. Get on with it," Gary ordered.

"So...yeah. I've been working with a team to try to figure out what exactly their objectives are. Uncle Dalton reported that his son had found his mate." She lifted her hands and wiggled her fingers. "The idea was to get some information from the inside, but you saw those losers who took me. They didn't know shit, so it wasn't like they could spill any secrets."

My mind was reeling, and I felt like I was going to come out of my skin. What the fuck had she been thinking? Those humans had *dismembered* my brother, one of the strongest Vampires I'd ever met. She'd thought she was going to infiltrate their organization by posing as a mate? They'd had her for a *week*. She was lucky she hadn't been tortured to death before we'd even gotten there. The thought made bile rise hot in my throat.

I had so many fucking questions I didn't know where to start.

"You reported that you were mated?" I asked, struggling to keep my voice even.

"Well, *I* didn't."

"To one of Dalton's sons," I continued.

A flush rose up my mate's neck until her cheeks and ears were beet red. "Uh, yeah?"

Gary chuckled.

"It's not like it's true," she said, picking at her sandwich as she wrinkled her nose. "But I had to get on their radar somehow."

My heart pounded in my ears as Gary's chuckles

turned into snickers. The idea of another Vampire claiming my mate made a red film flicker at the edges of my vision.

"What's wrong with your eyes?" Rosemary asked in horror, leaning in to get a closer look.

"Which son?" I asked through lips that had gone numb.

Rosemary mumbled something unintelligible and took a huge bite of her sandwich.

"I need you to repeat that," I ordered quietly.

"I don't think that's important right now," she replied nervously, still staring.

Letting my eyes fall shut, I searched in the recesses of my mind for a shred of patience. She hadn't known who I was. She hadn't known we were mates. There was no way she could've anticipated that she actually *had* a mate. She couldn't have realized what she was doing.

"Are you out of your fucking mind?" I asked, my words barely a whisper of sound. I was afraid that if I raised my voice any higher, I'd start yelling.

She was the other half of my soul. I would be by her side until the end of time. I could not start our journey by screaming at her or spanking her ass, no matter how tempting those images were.

"Hey, man," she said with a shrug. "It worked. I mean, sort of. They picked me up, but they left me with their idiotic foot soldiers."

"Thank the Gods they did," I barked, trying to shove down the anger that was boiling up inside me. "Do you have any idea what could've happened to you?"

"I've read the reports," she confirmed, her expression growing serious. "I knew what I was doing."

"You have no clue," I replied. My mouth snapped shut when the sound of a car moving toward us on the gravel driveway filtered in the window.

Fuck. What had I been thinking, bringing her back to the place she'd been abducted? I'd been so concerned with making sure she felt safe that I'd fucked up.

Rising from my chair, I looked at Gary. "Do you have weapons accessible?"

"Of course," he replied.

"Daniel—" Rosemary interrupted, jumping to her feet.

"Get them," I ordered, glancing toward the window. "We're about to have company."

"No, wait," Rosemary said, following me as I headed toward the front door.

Their old bulldog was snoring loudly on a bed in front of the fire. He didn't even lift his head. Clearly, he wasn't a watchdog.

"Stay inside," I ordered her. "I'll let you know when to come out."

"Okay, first of all—"

"Do I need to tie your ass up?" I snapped. Shit, it felt like I couldn't concentrate. Between the car getting closer on the driveway, the scent of Rosemary's shampoo wafting toward me, and the fact that she clearly wasn't wearing a bra under her loose T-shirt, my brain seemed to be misfiring.

"You could try," she said with a laugh, shaking her head.

"Flower?" her dad called from the kitchen. Why the hell hadn't he done what I'd asked?

"I can't fucking think with you standing here," I ground out. "Go."

"Well, lucky for you, I can think for both of us."

She moved faster than I was prepared for and threw the front door open, stalking outside as I spun and wrapped an arm around her waist. Her feet left the porch just as the car outside rolled to a stop.

"Put me down, you pain in the ass," she griped, pulling her knees to her chest as she shoved at my arm.

"Quiet," I breathed in her ear as I watched the car.

My arm loosened as the driver climbed out, and I let out a breath of relief.

"It's about time you showed up," Rosemary called, pushing my arm away as she moved to the top of the steps. "Daniel's practically frothing at the mouth."

"Daniel Boucher," Dalton Cavendish drawled, striding toward us. "It's been a while."

Just then, the passenger door opened and another tall man stepped out of the car.

"Good to see you in one piece, Oregano," he called out teasingly.

I reached out to shake Dalton's hand as Rosemary bounded down the steps toward the stranger.

Sidestepping Dalton, I monitored the interaction closely. My mate shoved at the newcomer with a laugh and then stepped in for a hug. Was that the fictional mate?

Every muscle in my body tensed until she jerked away with a curse. I blinked hard, trying to clear my vision.

"Shit, I forgot," the man said with a grimace, glancing at me as he raised his arms out at his sides. "You okay?"

"Oh, ew," Rosemary exclaimed. "I forgot about that bullshit."

Dalton chuckled beside me. "They grew up together," he informed me. "Nothing to be worried about."

I scoffed. "I'm aware." Even if Rosemary and this pup had anything going on before, it was over now. The mating bond would make it physically painful for them to fuck around.

"Come meet my mate," Rosemary said with a frown, stomping back toward the house. She was barefoot and didn't seem to even notice the rocks beneath her feet.

"This is my son Ian," Dalton said, nodding toward him. On closer inspection, the young Vampire was barely an adult. His face hadn't lost the innocence of youth yet. "Ian, this is Rosemary's mate, Daniel Boucher."

"Boucher?" Ian asked, reaching out to shake my hand.

"Yes, one of those Bouchers," Dalton murmured with a smile. His expression dropped as he looked at me. "I was very sorry to hear about Zeke. You have my condolences."

"Thank you," I replied, finally relaxing a little as Rosemary grudgingly sidled up to me.

"Is Gary inside?"

"Where the hell else would I be?" Rosemary's dad called.

Dalton chuckled as he moved toward the door.

"We can't stay here," I said, stopping him. "Rosemary can't stay here."

"Why the hell not?" she interrupted.

"You were abducted here," I replied slowly. She was

clearly intelligent, but if I were guessing, her sense of self-preservation was completely absent. "You're no longer where they put you. Where do you think they'll look for you first?"

"Oh." Her eyes widened a little. "About that..."

"Have you told him nothing?" Dalton asked incredulously.

"I didn't have time before you and Sunflower here showed up."

"Stop calling me that," Ian hissed in embarrassment.

"Inside," Dalton ordered, gesturing toward the door. "Everyone inside."

If it had been any other Vampire ordering me around, I would've balked, but Dalton had been one of my first team leaders when I joined Vampire Command. I trusted him with my life and, more importantly, with my mate's.

Setting my hand on Rosemary's back, I let her hair tangle around my fingers for a moment as I led her inside. As we moved through the door, she leaned slightly into the touch. Well, that was comforting. At least she felt the pull too. I was beginning to wonder.

Mates were hardwired to be drawn to their other half, even when they didn't want to be. I'd seen it time and again. Even if mates were fighting, even if they couldn't stand each other, even if it was inconvenient and frustrating, they still gravitated toward each other, pulled by an invisible and nearly unbreakable thread.

Rosemary seemed to be able to ignore that thread for the most part, but the longer I was near her, the tighter I felt that thread pulling. I wanted to get my arms around her. I wanted to pull her onto my lap. I wanted those long legs wrapped around my back. I wanted her hair in my face and trailing down my chest.

"Good to see ya," Gary announced, snapping me out of my fantasy as he performed some strange handshake with Dalton.

Ian immediately dropped down on the floor, and the dog scrambled onto his lap, panting like he'd just run a mile.

I took a seat next to Rosemary on the sofa. She leaned against the opposite arm and pulled her legs up beside her, tucking her feet under my thigh. Maybe she wasn't as immune as she was letting on.

Dalton dropped onto one of the chairs. "So what have you told him?"

"Just that you reported that I'd mated one of your sons and they'd picked me up like we'd hoped."

"You put her in this?" I asked Dalton incredulously. "What the fuck were you thinking?"

"I was thinking that my very human goddaughter didn't *have* a mate, and when they figured that out, they'd let her go."

I laughed humorlessly. "You thought they'd let her go?"

"From all accounts—"

"What accounts?" I asked, cutting him off. "From what we've seen, no one has made it out of their little labs. And who the fuck are you working for? Because I'd really like to speak to whoever decided that it was a good idea to send a human woman to those fucking monsters. Are you out of your godsdamn minds?"

The minute my legs tensed so I could rise to my feet, Rosemary moved, crossing the couch to tuck her shoulder into my armpit and her arm around my waist.

I wasn't sure who had taught her the move, but she succeeded in instantly calming me. I nearly let my eyes fall shut as my heart stopped thudding in my ears.

"Why don't I start at the beginning?" Dalton said.

"Calm down," Rosemary whispered in my ear. "Flying off the handle isn't going to get you answers any faster."

I turned my head until we were nose to nose. "I'm going to tear the head off anyone who thought putting you in danger was an acceptable choice."

"I was safer than you're thinking," she replied, her breath whispering across my lips. "Now, shhh."

"We started getting reports that Vampires and their mates were disappearing three years ago—"

"Four," Gary corrected. "Sam came to us four years ago."

"Right," Dalton agreed. "We've known Sam for years. He works at the local tractor store..." He paused when he caught my dubious expression. "Gary and I own a lot of land. We're in there more than you'd expect."

"He said he hadn't heard from his sister in a few weeks, and he was getting worried. She'd never gone more than a few days without checkin' in and shootin' the shit with Sam's wife," Gary explained. "His sister's mated to a Vampire, if you hadn't figured that out already."

"We looked into things for him, but there was no trace of the sister or her mate," Dalton added grimly. "Their house was untouched, cars parked in the driveway. They had no children yet, no pets. It looked as if they'd just left."

"But they didn't come back," Gary said.

"No, they didn't." Dalton shook his head. "And then it happened again about six months later. Someone else mentioned that a Vampire they knew had vanished. There one day and gone the next. They'd assumed that their acquaintance had gone on a trip, but they never returned. The stories kept happening. Vampires and their mates disappearing into thin air. All newly mated, all quietly living their lives, suddenly gone."

"How many?" I asked, my voice rough. My brother Ambrose had found a handful of small tokens hidden in the room where our brother Zeke had been held, so we knew there were others, but this sounded much bigger than any of us had imagined.

"Fifty-four," Dalton replied quietly.

It felt like I'd been punched in the chest. That was far more than we'd heard of. More than I'd ever thought possible.

"Couples," Rosemary clarified. "Fifty-four couples. One hundred eight, total."

"One hundred nine," Gary said. "When we add your brother. He was mated?"

"My brother's mate is safe," I replied, sick.

Gary's nod seemed relieved.

"We didn't put it together," Dalton said apologetically. "As far as I knew, Zeke hadn't been mated, so his death didn't fit the pattern."

My baby brother had known better than to report his mate to our government. There was no record of Charles. Unfortunately, the militia had discovered him anyway. I doubted Zeke had been able to hide his mating heat symptoms for long.

"Tell me the rest of it," I ordered, pulling Rosemary

tighter against me. Her heart beat steady and strong beneath my palm.

"We've kept things quiet," Dalton said. "I didn't want to get caught up in the bureaucratic bullshit that you know would come up. Between the treaties and the political posturing, we'd never get to the bottom of things. Even so, we've hit a wall. That's why Rosemary was sent in. We've managed to track some of the soldiers, but we haven't figured out who's giving them orders."

"Yet," Ian said quietly, still petting the bulldog. "We haven't found them *yet*."

"Nowhere in this story have any of you convinced me why you thought it was acceptable to send my mate into the fucking lion's den," I reminded them. "Or why we're still sitting here waiting for the militia to show up."

"No one knows where we are," Gary assured me with a quick shake of his head.

"Forgive me if I don't take your word for it."

Gary looked pointedly at his daughter.

"I can explain all that," Rosemary said with a sigh, unfolding her legs so she could climb off the couch. "Come on, let's go outside."

CHAPTER 3
ROSEMARY

It was a good thing that I knew what to expect when it came to mates, because I was having a hard time keeping my hands off Daniel. I should've been freaking out that I felt such a strong pull toward him. I didn't even know him.

However, I'd seen the mating bond in action before.

No hesitation on my part would change the outcome. No second-guessing would make things any easier on either of us. When I had a few more moments to myself, I could panic and scream into the void about how unprepared I was to meet the person I'd spend the rest of my life with. I could shake my head in wonder that, out of all the human women in the world, I was one of the few who was connected to a Vampire for all eternity. I could fist pump a little that my mate looked like *that.*

But those moments would have to come later. We didn't have time for them, and frankly, even spending the fifteen minutes apart while I was showering was painful. I'd seriously considered calling him in to sit on the toilet until I'd finished.

"Shoes," Daniel ordered as I opened the front door.

"What?" I eyed him over my shoulder. God, he was handsome.

"Put some shoes on. You're barefoot."

I looked down at my feet.

"You're going to hurt the bottoms of your feet if you go out running in the gravel again."

"I didn't plan on running in the gravel," I countered.

He just looked at me.

Letting out a long-suffering woosh of air, I slid my feet into my dad's old slippers and continued outside. The air was cold against my overheated skin, and I'd come to the realization on the couch that I wasn't actually sick.

The mating bond was making me feel like garbage. It was the reason for the heat beneath my skin and the cramping in my belly and the pressure in my chest. If I'd been thinking more logically earlier, I would've put it together. To be honest, when Aunt Halle had explained the symptoms to my cousins, I hadn't been paying much attention. It was one of the less fascinating parts of the mating bond, and I hadn't thought it would ever apply to me.

"Why are we outside?" Daniel asked as we stopped at the bottom porch steps.

"Uh, well..." I glanced up at the house and back down at my mate. "I'm the sacrificial lamb."

"You're the what?"

"I think they believe that hearing it from me while we're alone will somehow soothe the wild Vampire beast inside you enough that you won't start taking heads."

"Wild Vampire beast," he repeated flatly.

"The crazy mate beast, yes," I confirmed.

His lips twitched.

"So here's the deal," I said quickly, my words running together because I was speaking so fast. "This isn't my house. I live in town. I knew I couldn't go back there, which is why I had you take me to my dad's house. I'm here most of the time anyway, so it wasn't exactly a lie. I was taken from the driveway outside my townhouse, and they're probably watching it, but I don't plan on going back, so...whatever. And because of my dad's history, no one knows where he lives. Like, *no one*. He doesn't get mail here, it's not in his name, he used an LLC to buy it, you get the picture."

"Okay."

"And I was chosen...Well, I wasn't really chosen to go in. It was more like I volunteered."

I could see the muscles in his neck and shoulders tightening.

"Because," I continued quickly. "I'm trained. I started training when I was eight years old. My dad was adamant that I knew how to take care of myself. The chance of anyone from his old life finding him is minuscule, but he made sure I was prepared anyway. I'm proficient in jujitsu, better at Muay Thai, and I'm stronger than a lot of men. Like, a lot. Probably 60 percent of the population. I'm also very good with any kind of weapon I can get my hands on. I'm best with pistols, but rifles are a close second. I'd rather not fight with knives, but I can. Honestly, I could take most guys in a fight with that beer bottle I was holding when we met."

I'd barely stopped to take a breath when suddenly I was flying toward the ground. My back hit the gravel with a surprising gentleness, and I found myself staring into the dark brown eyes of my mate, his lips flattened into a grim line.

"You were saying?" he asked, his hands tightening around my wrists, where he'd locked them behind my head.

"I can see you're making a point here," I conceded, breathless.

"You think?"

I shifted my leg, and both of us paused for a moment as his hips notched between my thighs.

"The difference is," I said, forcing the words out. "I wasn't on guard because I know you won't hurt me. With anyone else, I would've been more prepared."

"Sure, you would."

"They don't expect a woman can fight. Even a woman who looks like me."

"A woman who looks like you?"

"You know, big, muscular."

His look turned incredulous.

"I'm not saying how I look is bad." I pulled against his fists, but my arms were stuck in his hold. "I look damn good. I'm just saying that I'm not some petite little thing."

"Thank the Gods," he said under his breath.

"Want to repeat that a little louder?" I asked, a smile tugging on the corners of my mouth.

"You'd have to be very lucky to come out on top in any fight with a Vampire."

I relaxed into him, my legs falling wide and my back arching just enough to brush our chests together. Daniel's eyelids lowered as he sucked in a slow breath. The moment I felt his muscles shift as he let his guard down, I used just my legs and hips to flip our positions.

"You were saying?" I joked, throwing his words back at him as I straddled his thighs.

His lips stretched into a smile as he let go of my wrists and slid his hands up my arms.

"I get it," he said, brushing my hair out of my face. "You're impressive."

"About time you noticed—" I let out a squeak of surprise as he swiftly sat up.

Our faces were less than an inch apart.

"That doesn't mean that Dalton should've ever agreed to that idiotic plan. You know why they held you for so long?"

"I figured they were waiting for something," I replied, distracted by the way his hands had wrapped around both sides of my throat.

"They were waiting for you to show signs of heat."

My gut sank.

"*We* noticed it right away. You weren't showing any signs of the heat. No sweat. No pain. No jitters. When Chance wrapped his hand around your ankle, you didn't even flinch."

"Fuck," I breathed.

"They've been doing this for years, and they know what to look for. They knew you weren't a Vampire's mate," he said, tilting my chin up a little with his thumbs. "So they were waiting to see why the fuck someone had reported you were."

"They're on to us."

"They've already researched you down to the hospital where you were born."

"I was born at home," I muttered.

"I'm sure they know that now."

"They spent the week researching me." The implications of that weren't lost on me. I'd never hidden my relationship with the Cavendish family. Pop didn't get out much—he preferred to stay close to home—but his friendship with Dalton had never been a secret either. Dalton reporting that I was Ian's mate had just sealed the connection.

"You're putting it together," Daniel said. "Good."

"I need to—" I braced my hands on his shoulders to climb off his lap, but he held me fast.

"Dalton's already realized," he said easily.

"They know he's the one looking into them."

"I'm sure his family is already on high alert."

My mind raced. I'd done plenty of jobs for Dalton since I'd turned eighteen. Vampires couldn't work for Vampire Command—their military force—after they'd found their mates, which meant that a whole lot of mated Vampires possessing a particular skill set had needed a place to use it. Uncle Dalton had created a company in that vacuum. Outside the hierarchy of the strict military, *Strike* had thrived. There were always people and Vampires who needed help and couldn't go through official channels. I wasn't a Vampire, obviously, but because of my training and background, I'd fit in well with the teams I'd worked with. Sometimes they needed a human liaison to smooth things over, or a woman to do things a man couldn't, or just someone who could spend longer stretches away from home, and that's where I'd come in. Many times, their mates had come along because they weren't able to be separated, but they'd never worked with us. Vampires balked at the idea of their mate walking into sketchy situations.

I'd done security in hard-to-find places around the world, helped a family retrieve their daughter from some creepy-ass religious cult in the south, and helped uncover and prove some corporate espionage. I'd even done threat analysis for a very high-profile Vampire wedding in the South of France.

None of it had ever followed me home.

I'd been a nameless, practically faceless, part of a team. After doing my job, I'd come home with a fat bank account, check in on my pop and Thunder, and go about my regular life.

The physical symptoms of the mating heat had calmed with Daniel in such close proximity, but honestly, I didn't feel any better. The thought of bringing trouble home to my pop's doorstep had never even crossed my mind.

"We'll figure it out," Daniel said quietly, his thumbs gliding down the front of my throat.

"Who the fuck are these guys?" I asked in exasperation.

I couldn't imagine that the morons who'd kidnapped me could remember to pay their bills on time, much less organize such a large-scale attack on the Vampire community. They weren't even close to the head of the snake.

"We don't know yet. It has to go pretty high, though. They're targeting new mates, and the only way they'd have that information—"

"You think they're being informed when it's reported," I finished.

"Yes," Daniel replied grimly. "They targeted my brother Beau and his mate within days of my mother reporting he'd found her. Outside of our family, no one else knew."

I barely held back the noise of despair that worked up the back of my throat.

Vampire mates were sacred. They couldn't just go out and meet someone at a bar and fall in love and live happily ever after. Sure, they could fall in love with someone, and I was sure it had happened, but without the mating bond, that partner would age and eventually die. Not to mention the fact that Vampires knew from birth that their soulmate was out there somewhere in the world, so even committing to someone else was abhorrent to most of them. Finding their human mate was nearly impossible, and Vampires had gone centuries without finding their other half.

I'd always known that my cousins would outlive me. I'd never had the chance to feel sad or worried about it, because it was just a fact, like gravity or the change of seasons. But as I'd gotten older, I had mourned the knowledge that I'd probably never meet my cousins' mates. I'd never get to tease them about how ridiculous they became when they found their other halves. We'd never be able to raise our children together the way we were raised, running through the sprinkler in the summer, curling up on the floor late at night to watch movies while our parents hung out in the kitchen, trying to outdo each other on dirt bikes, going sledding down the big hill out back.

"Where is your head at?" Daniel asked, searching my face for a clue.

"Those motherfuckers."

"That about sums it up," he agreed.

"I'm going to live forever," I said, the gravity of that sinking into my bones.

I'd witness Ian stumble over his words and generally act like an idiot when he found his mate. I'd get to see Grant smooth-talk his mate into accepting the bond and watch as cocky little Seamus fell head over heels. My throat tightened. Holy shit.

Aunt Halle was going to *freak*.

"There she goes again," Daniel whispered in amusement.

I snapped back to the present.

"Hopefully, we like each other," I said pragmatically, staring into his warm brown eyes. "Because if not, this is going to suck."

His laugh was beautiful. It started slowly, like he couldn't quite believe it was happening. Just like his voice, it was deep and slightly rough, and I felt it everywhere.

"Sweetheart, I already like you," he said, his lips still curved up in a smile.

"What's not to like?" I replied. "I'm more worried about you."

He chuckled again, like he was fucking delighted.

It was goddamn magic.

I'd been admired before. That wasn't anything new. I'd had partners when I wanted them. But generally, I found that they couldn't take all of me for long. When I was younger, I'd put on a face, trying to trick them into liking me. I'd kept my mouth shut when I'd wanted to shoot something clever back. I'd downplayed how strong I was, how capable I was, how assured I was.

When I'd stopped doing that, my relationships usually fizzled pretty fast. Men were unsurprisingly emasculated by capable women.

If I had to guess? Daniel liked it.

Which was good, because trying to act more demure or delicate or softer-tongued than I actually was would backfire sooner rather than later, and it wasn't as if either of us could walk away.

Daniel's head turned toward the house, his head cocking to the side just a tiny bit, and I knew he must've heard something inside. Someone would come out to check on us soon.

"Do you have any more questions?" I asked, setting my hands on his belly. The muscles there were rock hard. My mouth watered.

"Who's Dalton taking orders from?" he asked, looking back at me.

"What do you mean?"

"He was contracted. Who hired him?"

I looked at him in confusion. My dad and Uncle Dalton had just explained everything to him. Why did he think we'd been hired by someone?

His head snapped to the side again as Uncle Dalton stepped onto the porch.

"Arthur Carruthers," Uncle Dalton said, crossing his arms over his chest.

"The frigging commandant of Vampire Command?" I yelped, my eyes widening.

Daniel's hands were gentle but firm as they slid down the sides of my body and landed on my hips. He lifted me off him like it was nothing, so he could rise to his feet.

"Arthur," he replied, his face expressionless.

"He noticed a pattern about a year ago," Dalton confirmed. "Came to the same conclusions you did. Someone's using the reports to target new mates. It took him a while to put it together because it's only one in a hundred or so mates reported. Since we were already looking into it, we brought him in."

"He told us they believed Zeke's murder was an isolated event."

"That's the official stance, yes."

"But he knew it wasn't."

Uncle Dalton shook his head. "He believed that was true, initially. Zeke hadn't reported his mate, so as far as Command was aware, he didn't have one yet."

"We've given Command the evidence of more Vampires being held at the compound where my brother died," Daniel snapped. "The prisoners had hidden things in the fucking wall. And *someone* knew Zeke had a mate, considering they came after Charles *more than once*."

"We've been a step behind," Uncle Dalton replied apologetically.

Daniel stood silently next to me, practically thrumming with anger.

They were having a staring contest. On Uncle Dalton's side, he seemed to be observing how my mate would react, his body tight in preparation. From Daniel, all I could see was frustrated rage in his eyes. The longer the silence dragged on, the tighter I was wound, until I felt my body preparing to spring into action. Something was going to happen, and I had a very strong feeling that it wouldn't be good.

"I'm cold," I announced abruptly, adding a dramatic shiver for good measure.

Daniel turned toward me and immediately put his arm around my shoulders, like I'd known he would.

These mates were so predictable.

"Let's get you back inside," he said as Uncle Dalton shot me a give-me-a-break look.

He disappeared inside the house as Daniel led me toward the front door.

"We've been doing what we can to get to the bottom of it," I told him softly.

"You shouldn't be connected to this at all."

"But I am," I reminded him, making his arm tighten. "So we just need to figure out where we go from here."

"You're going nowhere. I'll take care of it."

I froze, my feet digging into the boards of the porch as he tried to urge me inside.

"Try again," I ordered flatly.

"You have no idea what these—"

"You're joking, right?" I asked, glaring. "Was it someone else who followed you through the woods tonight? Because I'm pretty sure it was me."

"That couldn't be helped."

"You could've told me to stay in the car with Charles."

"I *did*," he barked. "You didn't fucking listen."

"But you expect me to *now*?"

"We can discuss this later."

"Right, you don't want the rest of them to hear me tell you to shove it," I said with a huff.

"No," he argued, his voice rising. "I'd like to fucking enjoy the fact that I *found* my mate—which is a gods-damned miracle—for half a second before I have to obsess over the fact that she has no sense of self-preservation."

My dad's bark of laughter filtered through the open doorway.

I rolled my eyes but kept my mouth shut and sailed back into the house.

Everyone was back in the same places we'd left them. I dropped onto the couch and leaned against the arm, and let my dad's slippers fall off my feet so I could tuck them in beside me. When Daniel sat down, he was so close that my feet were wedged between his back and the couch.

I wiggled my toes, just to be annoying. He ignored it.

"If Arthur wouldn't have lied, we could've been working together for months," he announced flatly.

"This is off-book," Uncle Dalton replied, leaning back in his seat. "He came to me personally. If there's someone in Command that's leaking secrets, he can't use anyone connected."

"All of us have been separated from Command since Zeke died," Daniel countered. "Except Ambrose, because he's been following leads with a team."

"And did he find anything useful?"

"You show me yours and I'll show you mine."

Uncle Dalton hesitated, and surprise made me straighten.

Daniel let out a huff of humorless laughter.

"It's a delicate situation," Uncle Dalton hedged.

"Maybe in the beginning," Daniel argued. "At this

point, it's got the finesse of a godsdamn machine gun. They attacked *the property* tonight. Used Billy Finau to lure us out so they could target our mates."

"Fuck," Uncle Dalton breathed.

I waited for Uncle Dalton to say something, anything. He had names of human militia members. He knew where a few of their safe houses were. I'd heard him going over things with my pop, but I hadn't paid much attention. I wasn't in charge of strategy like that —it was above my pay grade. I was a soldier. I went where I was ordered. The larger picture interested me, of course, because I wanted Vampires and their mates to be safe, but I didn't know the people my pop and uncle were discussing. I didn't recognize the streets they mentioned or the connections they thought they might've found.

Uncle Dalton said nothing.

Daniel's arm moved across my lap, his hand wrapping around the thigh furthest from him. I wondered if he was as shocked as I was that my uncle wasn't cooperating.

Out of the corner of my eye, I noticed Ian making a face at me. When I moved my eyes in his direction, he wiggled his eyebrows and stuck his tongue in his cheek, moving it from side to side.

I just barely held back a very inappropriate laugh.

He widened his eyes and then rolled them back and dropped his mouth open. Then, quick as a blink, his face lost all expression, and he looked down at Thunder while his ears flushed a deep red.

I turned to find my mate looking at my cousin in amusement. He glanced at me, and his expression turned serious again.

"Rosemary is out," he announced.

"Fuck off," I said in exasperation, digging my big toes into his back.

"They know who you are now," he said, ignoring my toes. "And if they grabbed you again, they'd find the symptoms they were waiting for."

"She's out," Uncle Dalton confirmed.

"That's bullshit." I smacked the arm of the couch.

"The only reason we agreed to let you is because you weren't mated," Uncle Dalton reminded me. "I knew they'd realize that you weren't what they were looking for. Now? You're exactly who they're looking for."

"No one can know we're mated," Daniel continued. "Not anyone outside of family."

"Agreed."

"Not even Arthur."

Uncle Dalton nodded. "You'll have to be very circumspect about being seen together."

"We won't be seen together," Daniel replied. "I don't plan on even bringing her to the house."

"Wait a minute," I said, yanking my feet out of their warm cocoon so I could set them on the floor. "You two don't get to just decide—"

"Erik and Mattie are going to *love* that," Uncle Dalton replied sarcastically, completely ignoring me.

"They'll understand."

"Stop," I finally yelled, shooting to my feet. "I'm a fully grown adult. Neither of you gets to tell me what to do."

Daniel rose beside me. "You think we should advertise that we've mated?" he asked calmly. "Report it to Command?"

"Of course not."

"You don't think it would raise some flags if I started bringing you around my family?"

"No." I shook my head. "I mean, yes, it would."

"All right, so you don't think, as a newly mated human, you're exactly who they're looking for?"

"Not until we've completed the bond, I'm not," I shot back. I enjoyed his look of surprise. "Did you forget that I'm not some delicate human you can gently help usher into Vampire culture? I've been living there my whole life. If we haven't completed the bond, my physiology hasn't changed. Yes, they could find the symptoms of the heat, but they wouldn't find anything else."

The satisfaction I felt when the room was so silent you could hear a pin drop was unmatched.

"So if we don't complete the bond, I'm good. I don't have to wait at home like the little wifey, doing nothing while you guys are out there figuring this out."

"Rosemary," my dad called, his voice low with warning.

"Do you think for a second that I'd ever let them get their hands on you?" Daniel asked, his hand wrapping gently around the front of my throat.

The movement wasn't frightening in the least, but it sure as hell got my attention. Every nerve in my body seemed to come alive at once.

"No, they wouldn't find anything different in your physiology, but that doesn't mean they wouldn't *look* for it."

"Right," I rasped.

"We'll complete the bond," Daniel told me firmly, his thumb running softly up and down my neck. "Once it snaps into place, you'll be safer."

"Immortality won't make me safe," I reminded him.

"Safer," he repeated. "*I'll* make you safe."

CHAPTER 4
DANIEL

"We should get going," Dalton announced, interrupting the conversation I'd been having with my mate. I let my hand fall.

The moment I'd put my hand on her neck, she'd gone practically liquid. Her eyes had softened, her shoulders dropped. It was ironic, considering that the reason I'd done it was because I was trying to keep my hands off the rest of her body. Her father seemed unbothered by the fact that she'd found her mate, but I was sure he didn't want to witness me groping her.

"Give my love to Halle," Gary said as Dalton and his son rose from their places. "You'll keep me apprised?"

"Always," Dalton agreed, slapping Gary on the shoulder.

Rosemary turned from me reluctantly to say her goodbyes.

"You'll let us know if you need anything," Dalton ordered, leaning in to kiss her forehead. He pulled back before he made contact and gave her a nod instead. My mate let out a breath of annoyance. "Call your aunt. She's dying to hear from you."

"I bet she is," Rosemary joked. She reached her hand toward Ian and did a weird shake where they tapped the backs, then the palms of their hands together, and then wiggled their fingers at each other. "I'll call you."

"I'll be there," Ian agreed. He held out his hand to me. "It was nice to meet you."

"You too," I replied. The more I thought about it, the surer I was that Dalton's other sons were too young to have found mates. Ian must've been the one they'd reported. The only reason why I didn't feel more strongly about the little fucker was that he and Rosemary were clearly not romantic. If I'd been confused about that fact, his facial expressions when he hadn't thought I was looking would've assured me. They were cousins, even if there was no blood relation.

Gary followed Dalton and Ian to the door, locking us in after they'd gone. Beside me, Rosemary yawned so widely that her jaw audibly popped.

"Tired?"

"I've been awake for most of the last week," she replied, stretching her arms above her head. I tried not to stare as her nipples pressed against the thin fabric of her T-shirt. "Not the best idea to pass out when you're surrounded by creeps. I'm exhausted."

"You two should head to bed," Gary said, rising from his wheelchair with a grimace. "I'm going to let Thunder out, and then we'll be headed that way too." He frowned at Rosemary. "I haven't slept all week, either."

"Sorry, Pops," Rosemary replied with a small smile.

He waved her off and slowly made his way toward the kitchen. "Make yourself comfortable, Daniel. I'll see you both in the morning."

I waited patiently as expressions crossed Rosemary's face. I was sure that she could put on a mask if she tried—she'd been wearing one when we met—but she wasn't hiding anything anymore. She cycled through anxiety, indecision, a flash of anticipation, fear, and finally landed on determination.

"Come on. I'll give you the tour," she announced, lacing her fingers through mine. "You've seen the living room and the kitchen." She tugged me down a long hallway. "The house is basically a large square. First door is the bathroom." She pushed open the door, and a tiny room lit by a small nightlight was illuminated. The tub, toilet, and sink were avocado green. "Nothing fancy. My mom liked the green shit, but I've been all over the world, and I'll tell you right now, the water pressure in that shower is the best you'll ever get."

"Good to know."

"I'm not kidding," she said, looking at me over her shoulder as she pulled me further down the hall. "It's perfect." She pointed to a door on the opposite side of the hall. "That's my pop's room." We finally stopped at a mostly closed door near the end of the hall. She pushed it open and led me inside. "And this is my room. Ignore the mess." She paused. "Actually, don't ignore it. I'm not super tidy. You should probably know that upfront."

Letting go of my hand, she walked across the room and lit a lamp on the bedside table.

She was right. It was messy. It was also really warm and inviting. A heavy dresser took up most of one wall.

On top of it was a stack of books, a jewelry box that looked like it had been painted by a toddler, a photo of a woman who looked a lot like Rosemary—probably her mother—a glass canning jar full of coins, and a few random socks. There was an old floral armchair in the corner that was covered with discarded clothes. Her nightstand was completely clear of anything except the lamp. Her bed was made of heavy wood, dark from age, and definitely an antique.

"I was born in it," she said, dropping onto the bed with one leg dangling off the side. "This used to be in my parents' room. Dad said he couldn't bear to sleep in it after my mom died. When he eventually decided that he should stop sleeping on the couch, I commandeered it before he could sell it."

"It's a nice bed."

Rosemary laughed. "Swing the door shut, would you?"

I closed us in just as the sound of her dog's nails on the hardwood reached the hallway.

"It's not very big," she said, leaning against the headboard. "But I never imagined I'd be sharing it."

"Why not?" I asked, moving around the foot of the bed so I could sit with her.

"Well, for one, because it's in my pop's house." She wrinkled her nose in distaste. "I have a bigger bed at the townhouse."

"I've got a king at my parents' place."

"Ah, so you were planning on having overnight guests under your parents' roof," she said jokingly, shaking her head in mock disappointment.

"My parents built so that all of our families could live together," I explained. "Once we'd found mates.

Each of our rooms is more like a one-bedroom apartment."

She smiled. "That makes sense. The Cavendish house is like that too. Well, it will be like that. Ian is the only one who gets to have his own little apartment right now. The other two have to share a room because they aren't adults yet, and Aunt Halle says it forms bonds or something."

So I'd been right about only Ian being old enough to report a mate.

"I'd like to live there for a while, if that's okay with you."

"What? The Cavendish house?" she asked innocently, raising her eyebrows.

"With my parents." I watched her expression for a sign of protest that didn't come. "We wouldn't have to stay there forever, but after Zeke—"

"I don't mind living with your family for a while, as long as they aren't assholes."

"Chance is the worst, and you've already met him," I joked.

"Which one is Chance?"

"The one with the long hair."

"Oh, right," she said, nodding. She waved her hand dismissively. "I can handle that one."

"Three of my brothers have found their mates recently—"

"Really?" she asked in fascination, her eyes widening. "That's unusual."

"It is."

"So now four of you have found mates. There are five of you, right? So only one of you is left? Which one?

It's the asshole, right? I bet it's the asshole. He'd mellow if he'd already found his mate."

I laughed at the accuracy of her statement as I let the words wash over me. It wasn't deliberate, how she'd said it. She obviously knew about my brothers and me—which was a bit of a mindfuck if I was being honest—but she hadn't immediately counted Zeke out when she'd mentioned them. There *were* five of us, even though one of us was gone.

I would always have four brothers.

"You're right about the asshole. Chance hasn't found his mate yet. With the way things are going, I wouldn't be surprised if she showed up at some point soon. For whatever reason, we're falling like dominoes."

"That's wild," she said, pulling her legs up so she could cross them. "I bet your parents are thrilled."

"Not sure if it's sunk in yet, to be honest."

Her expression dropped. "Yeah, I can understand that. I'm really sorry about your brother. He was younger, right?"

"Thanks. How the hell did you know that?"

Rosemary laughed a little in embarrassment. "Well, you're all named in order, right? So, if you're Daniel, then Zeke would've come after you."

I grinned. "Ambrose, Beaumont, Chauncey, Daniel, and Ezekiel."

"So I was right!"

"Yeah, you were."

"I can't imagine losing a sibling," she said with a sympathetic frown. "I mean, I literally can't because I'm an only child, but I don't know what I'd do if we lost one of my cousins."

"You lost your mother," I replied softly.

She smiled halfheartedly. "Yeah, that was bad."

"I bet."

"She was sick for a lot of my childhood, but it was still a shock once she was gone. Like, what do you mean I can't go tell her about my day? What do you mean I broke my arm, and she's not there to cuddle with? Who the hell am I going to talk to when I'm happy or sad or mad or overwhelmed? My dad did his best, but it obviously wasn't the same. She was the frigging sun, you know?"

"Yeah, I know."

"She's been gone for almost half my life now. It's weird."

"How old were you when you lost her?"

"Twelve." She grimaced. "That was a hard year for me. I was taller and bigger than all the boys in my class. Chubby. I hadn't figured out how to wear my hair yet, everyone was experimenting with makeup, and I wasn't really interested, hadn't started my period, the whole shebang. Then on top of that, my mom died, which just made me even more of an outsider and someone to talk about."

"That sounds miserable."

"I *was* miserable. It's pretty hard to articulate all the things that are wrong at that age. I was sad and angry and frustrated with the world. It got better, though. Easier to manage. Aunt Halle helped."

"I'm sorry you went through that."

"Me too," she replied simply. She lowered her voice. "Honestly? I'm not even sure who I would be right now if she'd lived. Life would look so different. It's hard to even imagine. Does that sound bad? I don't mean that

I'm glad she's gone. If I could choose, she would still be here."

I reached out and gave her thigh a squeeze. "Of course you would. I didn't think that's what you meant. If my brother Zeke wouldn't have died, I wouldn't have found you the way I did. The sequence of events that led up to finding you in that garage would've never happened. Doesn't mean I would ever wish for him to be gone."

Rosemary let out a breath of relief. Reaching back, she pulled her long mass of hair over her shoulder and braided it into a loose rope.

I'd seen plenty of women get ready. I'd showered with them. Watched them put on their clothes and makeup. But nothing had ever felt as intimate as sitting in that dim room watching Rosemary in her pajamas braiding her hair.

"This is kind of weird, right?" she announced with a sweet smile. "Like, oh, here's your mate. You just met, but fall into bed anyway and complete the bond."

"Can I be honest?" I asked slowly.

"Always."

"I've wanted to fuck you since the moment I saw you."

"Bullshit," she argued, her eyes twinkling. "My hair was one huge knot, my clothes were filthy, I *stunk,* and I was threatening you with a broken beer bottle."

"Didn't matter," I said, smiling back. "Instant attraction."

"Well, I guess that's comforting." Her lips twitched as she tried to hide her smile. "At least I know you'll still find me attractive when I'm huge, pregnant, and don't feel like showering or getting off the couch."

The last words were nearly indecipherable as she realized what she was saying.

"I don't think it's possible to find you unattractive."

"Thank you, mating bond."

I let out a laugh, and she shushed me, glancing at the door.

"It doesn't have anything to do with the mating bond," I argued, lowering my voice. "You're fucking gorgeous."

"I wasn't then."

"Sure, you were. I knew it was there under the grime."

She widened her eyes at me and shoved my shoulder.

The room was quiet as we looked at each other. She was outspoken and so sure of herself since the moment we'd met, but there was a vulnerability there too. She was showing it to me. It felt like a privilege that not many others received.

"So...you want kids?" she asked softly.

"Yeah." The word came out rough. I cleared my throat. "Yeah, I'd like a couple. You?"

"I've always wanted a big family," she replied. "Growing up as a single child was fine—I had my cousins to play with and stuff—but I always thought if I had kids I'd have at least two so they'd have a built-in best friend."

"I liked growing up in a big family," I replied, leaning down on my elbow so I could prop my head in my hand. "There was always someone around to hang with."

"Yeah, exactly!"

"I can continue taking the pills if you want to wait a while, though."

"You're already taking them?"

"When I realized that my brothers seemed to be finding their mates in rapid succession, I figured it would be smart," I confirmed. I'd felt like an idiot doing it, but now I was relieved I had.

"Oh, and I have an implant—" Her sentence cut off abruptly. "Right, my implant won't work."

"Unfortunately, no. But I'm happy to take care of it."

"It's like, I know all of this stuff, but I keep forgetting that it applies to me now. I didn't think I'd be anyone's mate. The odds of that were like winning the lottery or getting eaten by a shark."

"Human men should be taking care of the birth control too."

Rosemary scoffed. "Yeah, right. Have you *met* human men? I mean, don't get me wrong, the good ones are out there. But counting on the majority of them to prevent pregnancy sounds like a terrible idea."

"I don't think we should take any chances while we're dealing with all of this," I said quietly, running my hand over the soft skin of her thigh. "We have plenty of time to start a family."

"Agreed." She took a deep breath and let it out in a whoosh. "So should we just dive in, then?"

For a moment, just a split second, when she reached for the hem of her shirt, I contemplated letting her take it off. I wanted to see her so badly that my teeth ached. But for that reason, I couldn't let her do it. I wasn't sure I'd be able to keep my hands to myself if I got a glimpse of her bare breasts.

My skin felt like it was on fire. Every muscle in my body ached. The tether between us seemed to pulse.

"I'm not going to complete the bond with your father across the hallway," I said, my hand shooting out to stop her.

"But, I thought you said—"

"When we complete the bond, I'd rather your hands weren't shaking with nerves," I murmured dryly, giving her hand a slight squeeze. "You're not ready yet."

"I'm not a virgin," she argued. "And it's not like I haven't had one-night stands before. I didn't know them either."

I tried and failed to hide my distaste at the idea of her having sex with anyone else. Thankfully, she ignored my expression.

"Finding someone you think is attractive and fucking their brains out isn't the same as committing your body and life to someone you just met," I replied, sitting up.

"I thought you wanted me to be protected," she said, throwing her hands in the air.

"I do." Leaning into her space, I inhaled the spicy scent of her hair. Gods, I wanted her. "But your father has exceptional hearing for a human, and I doubt he wants to hear his daughter getting railed across the hall."

Rosemary's breath caught.

"I'm going to fuck you, and if the Gods are merciful, you're going to fuck me—"

"That can be arranged," she replied hoarsely.

I groaned. "I'm not going to be able to get the fantasy of you riding me out of my head now," I chastised, nipping at her jaw. She tilted her head back to give me more room to work. "But it won't be tonight."

I leaned back, and by the furious look in her eyes, it was a wonder she didn't take my head off. I couldn't really blame her. Yeah, she was nervous, but she clearly had no problem touching me. She'd leaned into the fact that we were mates from the moment I'd confirmed it. No hesitation or disbelief, just immediate acceptance.

That wasn't something that happened often—or ever. Being raised in a Vampire family had given her an understanding that most humans didn't have. She didn't seem scared that she was going to be bound to a Vampire she didn't know. She wasn't worried if we would get along or if she could ever love me. She just assumed correctly that those things would come.

I rounded the bed and locked her bedroom door before pulling off my T-shirt.

"Jesus, Mary, and Joseph," she groaned, watching me from the bed. "Are you serious?"

"I should probably shower," I replied, pausing.

"You are not stripping naked one room away," she snapped, shaking her head. "Come on, dude. Be a pal here."

I chuckled as I tossed the T-shirt on top of the clothes already on her armchair and reached for my trousers.

Rosemary let out a quiet grunt as I unbuttoned my pants, flouncing away from me as she tugged the bedding out from under her ass. She scooted down until the blanket covered her to her chin. Seconds later, she pulled out the little shorts she'd been wearing and tossed them on the floor.

My cock ached as I took off my boots and trousers

and slid into the bedding from the opposite side of the bed.

The sheets were cool against my heated skin as I stretched. My feet hit the footboard before my legs were even fully extended. She hadn't been kidding when she'd mentioned that her bed was small. It reminded me of the beds in hotels a hundred years ago. They'd never been long enough either.

Rosemary sighed loudly and reached out to turn off the lamp.

Seconds later, she sighed again.

I stared at the back of her head, less than a foot separating our bodies.

"Something to say?" I asked, smiling.

When she rolled toward me, our knees knocked together. I didn't think she could fully stretch out in the bed either. I wondered how she ever got any comfortable sleep.

"I have a high tolerance for pain," she whispered, the words almost a hiss. "I always have. My dad said that they were terrified all the time when I was little because whenever I fell or hit my head or anything, I didn't cry, so they could never tell how bad it was."

"Okay."

"So just know that, okay?"

"Okay," I repeated.

"But this is fucking miserable," she griped, her voice strained. "My stomach has been in knots for hours. The heat is like living in a sauna with no way to escape. I've been turned on since we came into my room, and my downstairs is starting to ache—and not in a good way. It fucking hurts."

"Ah, baby," I murmured the second I realized that

she wasn't just annoyed that I'd kept my hands to myself.

"I can take it," she grumbled. "But don't expect me to frigging like it."

I smiled into the dark as I reached for her.

"Come here," I whispered, tugging her toward me by the bend in her knee. I didn't stop pulling until her heat was pressed against my bare thigh, the scrap of fabric between us hiding very little.

Her hips gave an involuntary jerk as we made contact.

"Don't fucking tease me, Daniel," she warned.

"Danny," I corrected as I leaned in. "I go by Danny."

"And you thought now was the time to correct me?"

Rosemary's last word was caught in my mouth as I pressed it against hers, running my tongue along the inside of her bottom lip. After that, she didn't bother talking. We kissed like the world was ending, like we couldn't get enough. Desperate. Wet.

She gasped quietly as she came up for air, and I used the moment to press my mouth against her neck, my teeth throbbing as I kept them behind my lips.

I wasn't joking when I said that I refused to complete the bond with her father across the hall. That ritual was sacred, and we wouldn't have an audience, even by chance.

Running my lips down her throat, I pressed my thigh harder against the wet patch of fabric between her legs. She ground down against it and reached up to grip my hair in her fists.

I had to keep my head. I knew that. But we both deserved a little bit more.

Shoving her T-shirt up, I nuzzled between her

breasts before pinching her nipple between my lips. It was small and hard, and my cock jerked as I sucked that little nub before opening my mouth wider to pull in as much as I could get. Gods, she was perfect.

Rosemary gasped as one of my fangs nicked her.

It was an accident. I was trying to be careful and hadn't meant to break the skin, but the moment I got the taste of her blood, my heart thumped so hard it felt like it was going to break out of my chest. My cock was leaking. My balls were pulled up tight against my body.

If I didn't stop, I was going to go too far.

Pulling back, I tongued her nipple as I reached down between us. My fingers slid through her folds easily as I found her clitoris and pinched it between my fingers.

It was then that I realized Rosemary wasn't being quiet. Not even trying. Her moans and mewls were ringing through the room like a beautiful symphony.

I loved it.

I also knew that if she had any idea of the noise she was making, she'd be mortified.

Pulling my hand away, I threw back the blankets.

"What? No," she complained, her hands tightening in my hair. "No, don't stop."

"Shhh," I whispered back, tugging her hands away. "Roll over."

It said something about how close she'd been that she rolled onto her belly without a word of protest. Looking at her shirt tucked up around her neck and the tiny pair of panties she was wearing, I nearly lost all sense of resolve.

"Danny," she whispered, pulling her knees up until her ass was in the air. "Please. *Fuck.*"

Taking a page out of her book, I fisted my hand in her hair and turned her face down.

"Bite the pillow, sweetheart," I ordered as my other hand smoothed down her back and pulled her underwear down to her knees.

As soon as she'd done it, I pressed two fingers inside her. Then three.

The pillow muffled the sounds of her moans, but nothing could hide the wetness that dripped down my hand as I worked her. Using my thumb to manipulate her clitoris, I leaned down to whisper in her ear.

"That's it, Rosie," I praised, practically choking on my words as her pussy clenched around my fingers. "That's it. You're so wet. It's running down my hand, baby. Getting all over me. I can't wait to taste that sweet pussy."

She came with a wail, her face pressed so far into the pillow that I could barely see her. I gentled the movement of my thumb and kept my fingers inside her, enjoying the pulsing of her inner walls. The thought of her doing that once I'd gotten my cock inside her made my eyes nearly roll back in my head.

"You," she gasped as she lifted her head. She jerked her hips away from my hand and pushed me over, her mouth on my chest as I landed on my back. A moment later, her hand had slid into my underwear and wrapped around my shaft. I arched against her without thought, everything in my head growing fuzzy.

"You're leaking," she whispered against my nipple, biting down until the zing of pain made my cock jerk in her hand.

Smoothing her hand over the head of my cock, she gathered up the wet and slid it down my shaft, using it to lubricate as she jerked her hand back and forth. It felt incredible. Too incredible. I wanted to be inside her. I *needed* to be inside her.

Just as I decided that I was an idiot for waiting and began to reach for her hips, her other hand cupped my balls and squeezed.

I came so hard I couldn't even breathe.

Her hand slid carefully out of my shorts, and if Vampires could've died from heart attacks, I would've been a goner as I watched her lick the cum off the palm of her hand with a sigh.

"Gods," I breathed.

Rosemary's eyes closed slowly in relief. Pressing her cheek against my sternum, she smiled. "That's better. Not gone, obviously, but I think I can sleep now."

I was glad she could, but I wasn't sure I'd ever sleep again. The memory of her pussy clenching around my fingers, her hand around my cock, and the way she'd carefully cleaned off her palm with her tongue would never let me rest.

As she rolled off me and reached for the blankets tangled around our feet, I took her in. Moonlight just barely filtered in through the window, but I had excellent night vision and could see the way the muscles in her back and shoulders flexed and shifted as she straightened the bedding. She was sleek and powerful, and it was impossible not to stare.

Muscles like that took a lot of work. I knew the kind of dedication and commitment it required. Even with good genes, no one looked like she did without consistently pushing themselves to the limit.

"You're beautiful," I whispered, reaching out to help guide her panties back up her thighs.

"I do okay," she joked, flopping back down so she could tuck a pillow beneath her head. "I look a lot like my mom, in the face at least."

"Was she tall like you?"

Rosemary shook her head. "Nope. She was a respectable five feet six inches. Pop's not sure why I'm so tall. I caught up to him when I was thirteen. I know you look like your brothers, but do you look like one of your parents, or are you a mixture of both?"

"I'm built like my dad and have his coloring. My mom's blonde, but I have her eyes."

"Blonde hair and brown eyes?" Rosemary said with a grin. She whistled softly. "That's a good combo. When I was little, I always thought that brown eyes and blonde hair were so cool. Or brown hair with blue eyes."

I let out a breath of laughter. "Really?"

"Oh, yeah." She nodded. "Very unique." She snorted.

"Are you fucking with me?"

"I'm not," she wheezed as she laughed. "I really thought that. I was a teenager when I realized that my green eyes were way more unique than Jacy Herbert's brown hair and blue eyes."

"Ah. Jacy Herbert, huh?"

"Mean girl extraordinaire." Rosemary grimaced, pulling the blankets up around her neck. "She wanted all of us to believe she was some special species, but in reality, she was just a little asshole because her mom was an asshole and probably her grandma too. Just passing down the assholery willy-nilly and making the rest of us pay for it."

"What assholes," I replied, trying to keep a straight face.

"I know, right?" she said, widening her eyes at me. "But it all worked out in the end. Last I heard, Jacy's husband is a philandering douche, while *I* have a mate who literally can't touch any other women. I win."

I smiled and found her in the bedding, sliding my hand over the bare skin at her waist where her T-shirt had ridden up.

"Now I sound like an asshole," she complained, blowing a little piece of hair off her face. "But to be fair, I hoped for a redemption arc for Jacy. She just never had one. She's still just as bitchy as the day in third grade that she called me an ogre and made the rest of the class do it too. No one talked to me for a week. Literally. They pretended like I wasn't there."

"Cunt," I replied. "Fuck Jacy Herbert."

"Exactly." She grinned at me, the little dimple in her cheek winking in and out of sight. She yawned, one of her hands sliding out of the blankets to cover her mouth.

"We should get some sleep." I stretched out my legs and remembered too late that there wasn't enough room. My feet hit the footboard with a thump that startled me and made Rosemary giggle. My lips tipped up at the sound, even though I knew I was going to have an epically shitty night of sleep.

"I'll teach you the trick," Rosemary announced. Without warning, she yanked the pillow out from under my head and scooted across the bed. "Come on."

I followed her toward the edge and watched as she carefully set our pillows side-by-side but slightly overlapping to fit in the corner.

"We'll have to sleep close, but if you lie diagonally, there should be more leg room." Lying down, she patted my pillow. "Try it."

Moving in next to her, I lay down on my side and stretched my legs out. The bed still wasn't quite long enough, but by shifting a little—

"Yep, see? Even if it's still a little short, you can at least hang your feet off the edge. Better?"

"Much," I agreed, wrapping my arm around her waist.

Rosemary turned over so her back was to me and scooted until her ass was tucked into my lap. Lifting her top leg, she cocked her knee out, and I immediately filled the space behind it with my own.

"Okay?" I asked, the scent of her hair making my chest clench. The heat had mellowed to a bearable simmer, but I knew it was a temporary reprieve.

"Yep," she replied, her voice already a little groggy.

I lay there thinking about the events that had led us together, and beyond that, the lives that had prepared us for the moment we met. Outside factors meant that the beginning of our life together wouldn't be easy. Always in the back of my mind was the knowledge that somewhere out there were humans searching for my mate—but inside that room? Our relationship was progressing in a way that I'd never have imagined in a hundred lifetimes.

Rosemary wasn't afraid of this thing between us that was completely out of our control. She didn't shy away from it. She didn't question it. She accepted it. Accepted me, just like that. I'd heard the stories, and I'd watched my brothers as they'd struggled to find a way forward with their mates. Beau and Reese had cemented the bond very quickly, but had barely tolerated each other. Ambrose and Lucy had felt the attraction from the beginning, but she'd been pretty reluctant for what felt like a long time about tying her immortal life to a Vampire she'd just met.

Because that's what Rosemary would get from me. Beyond our relationship and the children we made together, she also received immortality. Well, both of us did. As it stood now, I was set to live a very long life—*had* lived a very long life—and it was very hard to kill me. But once we'd cemented the bond? Only beheading would end either of our lives.

We needed to complete the bond, and we needed to do it quickly. I wanted to make it special. Memorable. But with every second that passed—especially in the quiet of the night when Rosemary let out a quiet snuffle and her hand found mine—silent panic seemed to build in my chest.

Because until we completed the bond, my mate was vulnerable.

CHAPTER 5
ROSEMARY

I didn't remember falling asleep the night before, but when I woke up the next day, sunlight was streaming through the blinds, and I was alone in bed. Rolling onto my back, I stared up at the ceiling of my room and replayed the last twenty-four hours.

I had a mate. I had a frigging mate, and he was gorgeous. Tall and built and bearded and tattooed.

I took a moment to mourn that I hadn't yet taken the time to study the tattoos that practically covered his chest and arms.

Beyond his appearance, which I couldn't have improved on if I were imagining him, I actually liked the Vampire. He was protective, but it wasn't suffocating. To be fair, it *was* annoying, but I felt like I could probably push back on that when the time came. He was funny. He clearly loved his family. And holy hell was he good in bed.

I grinned. If he was that good with his hands, I had a strong feeling that he'd be even better with other parts of his body.

I felt like a new person as I climbed out of bed and stretched my arms above me until my fingers brushed the ceiling. It was amazing what an orgasm and a good night's sleep could do for a person.

I hurried to get dressed and made a stop by the bathroom to brush my teeth so I could go search for my mate. I could hear noise coming from out back, and I followed it to find my pop standing by the wood splitter, his wheelchair waiting just a few steps behind him. As I watched, Daniel stepped out from around the shed, carrying a round of wood. He set it on the splitter, my dad pulled the lever, and the piece slowly split in half. As Pop held one half in place, Daniel set the other on the ground beside him and then readjusted the piece on the splitter so they could cut it down into pieces that would fit in our fireplace. They moved methodically, like they'd already gone through the same process a hundred times before. Warmth spread through my chest.

Pop couldn't do much outdoor work anymore. He'd held out as long as he could, pushing himself every day and stumbling into his recliner every night with barely a complaint, even though I'd known he was in agony. He was used to being outdoors, working with his hands and his body. I'd barely held back tears when he'd come home from the doctor one day a few years ago and set his wheelchair just inside the front door. We hadn't discussed it, and it had taken months for him to even use it.

Ian and I tried to keep up with the property. We split and stacked wood when we saw that it was getting low, mowed the grass and blackberries when they got out of hand, and last summer we'd even rebuilt the chicken coop when a summer storm had knocked a tree branch onto the roof—but it was nearly impossible to stay on top of things. There was always so much to do. I didn't know how my pop had maintained it by himself for so many years, and I knew it killed him to see us struggling to manage while he was stuck watching.

My throat tightened.

I should've thought to let my dad control the splitter while I did the heavy work. In less than a day, Daniel had pinpointed exactly where he needed help and given my pop enough room to contribute.

I cleared my throat and crossed my arms.

"Excuse me," I called, striding toward them. "When exactly did you two become best friends?"

"About the time he stumbled into the kitchen asking for coffee," my dad replied over the sound of the splitter, his smile making his eyes crinkle at the corners. "And asked if there was anything he could help out with while you were sleepin' the day away."

"First of all, I needed that rest," I countered, pointing at him. I couldn't hide my own smile. "And second of all, splitting wood is the only fun job on this property, and you stole it like a couple of thieves."

"Sorry, baby," Daniel said with a laugh, heaving another round onto the splitter. "You wanna stack?"

"That's literally the worst part of the whole thing," I grumbled good-naturedly.

Heading into the barn, I grabbed my gloves off the workbench inside. I pulled them on as I went back to help. Thankfully, the weather was cool but not freezing, just nice enough to get away with not wearing a coat. Physical labor while wearing a coat absolutely sucked.

It got so hot while you were working, but if you took the coat off, when the cold air hit your sweaty shirt beneath, you were instantly freezing.

"All of them are already stacked," I complained loudly the moment I'd reached the woodshed. Twice as many pieces were in there than I'd noticed last week, and I knew my pop hadn't split them on his own.

"Danny's been stackin' 'em as we go," my pop called back.

"Well, what the hell am I going to do?" I asked, spinning back toward them.

"You can take the new ones," Daniel replied, tossing them by his feet. "We'll move a hell of a lot faster if I'm not stacking."

"Yeah, it seems like you guys have really been slowed down," I joked, walking over to pick up the pieces.

Daniel cocked his head to the side as he watched me.

"Thank you," I mouthed silently.

I stumbled over my own feet when he winked back.

We worked out there until Danny noticed that my pop was flagging, which was only about five minutes after I'd noticed.

"You ready to take a break?" he asked nonchalantly. "I'm starving."

Pop made a face that was the old man equivalent of rolling his eyes, but he still reached over to turn off the machine.

"Thank God," I gasped dramatically as I carried the most recent firewood toward the shed. "I'm wasting away."

After I'd set the pieces in their stack, I let out a yelp when I turned to find Daniel standing behind me.

"Crap!" I smacked myself in the chest like I could get my heart beating again. "You startled me."

"I wasn't being quiet," he replied, reaching out to pick a piece of wood off the chest of my hoodie. "How'd you sleep?"

"Like the dead," I replied dryly as I pulled off my gloves. "I don't know the last time I slept so late."

"You needed it."

"I thought you were tired," I countered, smacking him lightly with my gloves. "But apparently you were awake with the sun."

"You're not far off," he said as we turned to walk toward the house. My pop had already disappeared inside. "Once the sun came through your window, it was impossible to fall back asleep."

"I'm going to tell you a trade secret," I replied, stopping to turn toward him. "You ready?"

"Hit me."

"You know when the sun comes through the window and it's shining in your face?"

"Yes."

I paused for effect. "Roll over."

Daniel chuckled and started walking again.

"I'm serious," I said, hurrying to match his pace. "It works!"

"Uh-huh."

I smiled, letting the scent of home wash over me.

"Hey, Daniel, um...Danny?"

"Yeah?" He reached for my hand and slid his fingers between mine.

"Thank you for what you did this morning." We

were nearing the house, and I needed to get it out before we got within hearing distance.

"I figured you would thank me for last night," he teased. When his eyes met mine, his expression grew serious.

"I...he—" I stuttered, trying to find the right words. "He's a proud guy, so losing the ability to take care of this place has been, well, it's sucked for him. Big time. And I do what I can, you know, to make sure that it looks okay out here...but it's never as good as it looked before, and I know he hates that. He hates all of it. Ian and I usually process the wood when we see it's getting low, but I've never thought to ask my pop to work the splitter."

Daniel's thumb brushed along mine in a caress.

"I should've thought to do that," I finished.

Lifting my hand, he pressed it to his lips. "I didn't know how to work the splitter, so I asked him to show me," he replied simply. "We've always done it by hand."

I knew what he was doing. He was downplaying it. For whatever reason, he didn't want to acknowledge what he'd done for Pop.

"Still?" I grimaced. "We're in the twenty-first century, bro. Get with the times."

"I might," he said as we continued walking. "We split that wood in less than half the time it would've taken me to do it by hand."

"Modern technology," I agreed, nodding sagely. "What a marvel, am I right?"

It took him a moment to realize I was fucking with him. When he did, I wasn't prepared for the way he reacted. As he yanked me forward, he bent at the waist.

His shoulder hit my gut, and my feet went flying into the air as he threw me over his shoulder.

"What the hell?" I screeched, laughing so hard I could barely breathe. Of course, the broad shoulder pressing against my diaphragm probably didn't help that either.

Then he started spinning.

My hair flew out in a halo around my head as I wheezed and cackled, the world flashing by through my rapidly tangling hair.

"Put me down, you Neanderthal," I yelled, barely able to get the words out as I braced my hands against his back.

"Are you going to keep making jokes about my age?" he asked, his laugh a little breathless as his arms tightened around my thighs.

"I'm not going to lie to you, mate," I choked out, trying to tickle his sides. "I probably will."

His hand hit my ass in a stinging slap as he stopped, and my head swam as he lowered me to the ground again, making me stumble.

"You spanked me," I accused, reaching back to rub away the sting.

"Bet you liked it," he shot back, sauntering toward the house.

My mouth dropped open, and I swayed on my feet as I watched him walk away.

After lunch, we spent the day working on more things around the property. My dad had already fed the chickens and gathered the eggs—that was his responsibility, and it never deviated—but we completed the nasty task of cleaning out the coop. Then we broke down some pallets and stored them in the barn to reuse at some point, trimmed back the rhododendrons my mom had planted that were taking over one side of the house, and cleaned the leaves and debris off the concrete patio out back.

As we worked, the mating heat grew worse and worse. I could hack it. I'd once broken my forearm before having to hike four and a half miles to a rendezvous point, but that didn't mean I enjoyed it. I'd always thought that the mating bond symptoms were bullshit. God or the universe or fate or whatever could've manifested a pull between two mates without making them feel like garbage. It felt a little counter-productive, if I was being honest. How the hell were you supposed to get to know your partner if you had horrendous flu symptoms? If I had to guess, that was probably the point of the whole thing. *Who cares if you know them? Bang them! Bang them now! Complete the bond, and then it won't matter if they're a sociopath because you'll already be tied to them for all eternity!*

I was glad that Aunt Halle had explained the cum trick to me when I was a teenager, though at the time I'd been supremely grossed out. The science of it was a little fascinating, but when Vampires completed the mating bond with their mates, it took three things to really do it. First, he had to actually finish inside her. No condoms allowed. Second, he had to take her blood. And third, she had to ingest some of his too. If any of those things were missing, it would soothe the heat for a while, but the bond didn't take, and you'd have to do it again. According to Aunt Halle—who'd been correct—if you *swallowed* your mate's semen, it had the same effect, soothing the heat for a while at least. You just needed that semen inside you somehow, I guess.

I thought I was hiding the discomfort pretty well, all things considered, but I couldn't hide the sweat. Some of it could've been attributed to working outside, but when Daniel dropped his rake and followed me into the barn, I knew I hadn't fooled him.

"Good Gods, woman," he chastised, stalking toward me. "I've been waiting for you to say something for over an hour."

"About what?" I asked innocently.

Daniel laughed as he got closer. "If I feel this bad, you must feel ten times worse," he replied. "But you're good."

He reached for me, and he hissed as his hands slid beneath my hoodie and gripped my waist. "You're skin's so hot."

"I'm good?" I asked, reveling in the feel of his cool hands against my overheated skin.

"Good at hiding it," he clarified, brushing his lips against mine.

I barely held myself back from tackling him to the dirt floor.

"It would bother me," he continued, his lips gliding along my jaw. "If I didn't know how impossible it is for you to hide anything when I'm touching you."

I groaned as his lips reached my ear and then my neck.

Do it. Do it. Do it pounded in my head like a drum. It wasn't a conscious thought. It was instinct.

"All those noises you make," he whispered against my neck as his hands dropped to the front of my pants, unbuttoning and unzipping them so slowly I nearly screamed at him to get on with it. "You're so loud, mate. So responsive."

"You're talking an awful lot," I replied as he tugged my pants and underwear down to my knees. The rush of cold air felt like nirvana for only a moment before the heat slammed into me even harder.

"Because when I talk to you," he said, leaning back to look into my eyes as his fingers pressed between my legs, the calloused tips gliding easily over the slick skin. "It makes you wet." His fingers curled up, and I rose to my toes, a gasp bursting out of me as his fingers thrust inside. "And I like it when you're wet."

He held me there with just that one point of contact, his gaze never leaving mine, as he used his fingers and whispered words to drive me to the edge, and then over it. By the time we were done, I'd come so hard that tears ran unheeded down my cheeks.

"Gorgeous," he whispered, using his free hand to wipe them away. "Do you feel any better?"

"Not much," I confessed, my voice hoarse.

His expression fell.

Reaching down, I ran my hand over the front of his pants and squeezed my fist around his arousal.

"You're not feeling any better either," I pointed out.

"I'm all right," he choked out, his fingers thrusting one more time inside me before he reluctantly pulled them away. He kept his eyes on mine and lifted his fingers to his lips, sucking them inside as I traced a finger over the end of his cock. His eyes fell closed as he shuddered.

They popped back open when I shoved him back a couple of feet and dropped to my knees.

"Rosie," he murmured, his hands finding my hair. "Baby, don't kneel in the dirt."

I let out a ghost of laughter at his weak attempt to

dissuade me. Unbuttoning his pants, I tugged them down his thighs. He must've taken off his boxers at some point, because he was bare beneath them, and my mouth watered at the sight of him. Apparently, every inch of his body really *was* perfect.

I took my time discovering what made him tick. He loved it when I cupped his balls, squeezing them just enough for him to feel the threat there. He made a little noise in the back of his throat when I laved the tip of him with my tongue. When I sucked him into my mouth and focused on the head of his shaft, he brushed the hair away from my face gently. When I took him back into my throat, his hands tightened into fists.

My pants were still around my knees, and I reveled in the cool air drifting over my swollen, wet, and still supremely sensitive skin. Arching my back, I widened my legs to intensify the sensation.

"Fuck," Daniel barked as his cock throbbed. He tugged a little at my hair and then loosened his grip so that I could pull away.

Instead, I took him as deep as I could, my hand on his balls tightening just a bit as I hummed in pleasure.

He came so hard down my throat that I barely even tasted it until I pulled away, letting my tongue drag along the bottom of the shaft and up over the hole at the tip.

"Come here," he said softly, raising me off the ground before he'd even pulled his pants back up.

"Better," I replied, feeling a little drunk as my thighs brushed against his.

"Mine," he said, kissing me like his life depended on it. His hands found my ass, and his fingers dug in so hard they probably left bruises. By the time he lifted his head again, my lips felt swollen, and my head swam.

I stood there with what I imagine was a very dreamy look on my face as he pulled my clothing back into place before fixing his own.

"Earth to Rosie," Daniel joked, laying his hand on my cheek. "You good?"

"Don't bother me," I replied. "I'm basking in the aftermath."

He burst out laughing, and I couldn't help but smile at the sound. He had an excellent laugh. Deep and rough, like it came from his belly.

"Come on, baby. Let's be done for the day."

He held my hand as he walked me back to the house, pausing only to brush the dirt off my knees when we reached the back door. He shouldn't have even bothered, because my pop paid no attention to us as we moved through the kitchen. The house smelled like freshly baked bread and some kind of stew, and I drew it deep into my lungs as we headed for my room.

Daniel closed the door behind us as I pulled off my hoodie and tossed it toward the hamper.

"Rosemary," he called, his voice more serious than it had been before.

When I turned to look at him, he was thoughtfully scratching at the beard on his cheek.

"What's up?"

"I need to go back to my parents' place."

It hit me with the force of an anvil, like one of the cartoons I'd watched as a kid. We'd had such a good day that for a moment I'd forgotten the rest of the outside world. I hadn't worried about the people who were kidnapping mates or the carnage we'd left behind at his house. I hadn't remembered the awful week I'd spent tied to a chair or the way I'd had to beat back the panic, reminding myself that I *wanted* those idiots to take me.

Instead, I'd been too wrapped up in the mating bond. Wondering what our life would look like. Staring at him as his muscles strained against his shirt. Trying to ignore the heat that built. Reveling in the hands that could do insane things to my body.

"Even if I had clothes here, which I don't, I still need to go home and check in with them. My brother's mate, Lucy, was pretty messed up, and so were my parents." He paused when I jerked in horror. "They're fine. Mated, remember? But I'd still like to see them with my own eyes."

"Of course you do," I replied, reaching for my pants. "Just let me get dressed real quick and I can—"

"You can't go with me," he reminded me gently. "You need to stay here with Gary."

"What? No." The thought of him driving an hour away made my chest squeeze and my guts twist. No, mates weren't supposed to be far from each other. That was what the heat was all about. It forced proximity.

"It's not safe for you to be seen."

"We'll just go straight there," I argued. "We won't get out of the car until we're in your parents' driveway. No one will see me."

"I'm not taking the risk."

"Well, then I'll just lie down in the back seat," I countered feebly. "I could use a nap anyway."

"You need to stay here," he reiterated firmly. "Don't leave the property."

"That's crazy," I shot back incredulously.

"I'll be back as soon as I can. A few hours."

"No. No, that's—" I shook my head, anxiety beating like a drum inside my skull. "What if something happens on the road? No one will have your back. You need me to—"

"That's exactly why you're not going." He shook his head. "I won't risk it."

"It's not your decision."

"Yes, it is."

I didn't understand how he could be so calm when I was ready to tear the room apart.

"I'll be back in a few hours."

He'd been so tender with me all day that it was almost as if I were staring at a stranger. This was a different Daniel from the one who'd gently redressed me in the barn. He was harder somehow, colder.

All at once, I realized this was his game face. This unyielding Vampire was who I would've met if I weren't his mate, and we'd met on assignment. Not unfriendly, not unkind, but unyielding.

I bristled.

"I'm going with you," I snapped, stepping out of my pants. "You don't get to make unilateral decisions for both of us." I turned toward my dresser and yanked out a drawer. "If you think that's how this is going to go, you're in for a rude awakening."

When I turned back around, a pair of jeans in my hand, he was gone.

By the time I'd pulled them on and raced out of the room trying to catch him, he was already driving back down the driveway.

My hands shook as I braced them against the porch

railing. Already, nausea was making bile rise in the back of my throat.

"He'll be back, Flower," my dad called.

"Fuck him," I whispered to myself as cramps joined the nausea. Panting, I tightened my hands around the railing, trying to ignore the panic that thrummed through every inch of my body.

How dare he leave me? He knew what would happen. Anyone knew what would happen.

We weren't supposed to be separated. Not for any reason.

Silently, I took back every kind thought I'd ever had about Daniel Boucher.

I'd somehow ended up with the worst mate in history.

CHAPTER 6
DANIEL

By the time I pulled onto the familiar driveway, my chest felt like it was going to cave in. The pressure there was nearly unbearable.

I'd nearly turned around more times than I could count. The further I got from Rosemary, the more my entire body screamed at me to go back. Instincts were a real bitch when you were ignoring them.

My parents' house was pretty quiet when I parked out front. The bodies that had littered the property were gone, but proof of the assault was still noticeable as I moved toward the front door. Bloodstains marred my mother's pristine white porch, the front window was covered with a piece of plywood, and when close enough, you could still see holes in the siding where stray bullets had hit.

"Hey, fucker," my brother Chance said in surprise, jerking to a stop as I walked inside. He looked behind me. "Missing something?"

"Funny," I replied flatly. "What are you doing?"

"Mom's rug is toast." He kicked the rolled-up rug

on the floor. "I'm going to dump it. Seriously, where's your mate?"

"She's safe."

"But not here?" he asked slowly.

I shook my head. I knew they were curious about her, the same way I'd been curious about my brothers' mates. We'd all been waiting for so long, and it was such a miracle when we found them that it was impossible to even fake nonchalance.

But somewhere deep in my head was the relentless thought that if they knew nothing about Rosemary—if they couldn't tell anyone where she was, or who she was, or anything about her—she'd be safe. I'd never believe that someone in my family would knowingly put her in danger, but there were plenty of ways that they could accidentally slip up.

Ambrose and Beau, along with their mates, were also still targets. If, Gods forbid, they were taken somehow... well, it was just better if they didn't have any information. Not yet.

"How are you still on your feet?" he asked with a huff of laughter.

"It's a close thing," I admitted. The entire back of my T-shirt was soaked in sweat. My skin was so hot that anytime my clothes brushed against me, it felt as if I were being burned. "I need a shower."

"Yeah, you do."

"Where are Mom and Dad?"

"Lower bedroom. I don't think Mom's awake, but Dad is. Don't leave without seeing them."

I nodded and turned toward the back of the house. "I'll go now."

"Hey, Danny boy?" Chance called, grunting as he lifted the rug from the floor.

"Yeah?"

"Uh, is she great?" he asked awkwardly.

I smiled as the memory of Rosemary screeching with laughter as I tossed her over my shoulder came to mind. "Yeah, brother. She's perfect."

"Good," he said. He hefted the rug over his shoulder and carried it out of the house.

I found my parents right where Chance had said they'd be. Poking my head through the door, I locked eyes with my father, waiting until he'd given me a nod to step inside.

My mom was lying on her back beneath the blankets, pale, but breathing steadily in her sleep. "How's she doing?"

"She woke up a few hours ago," he replied quietly, reaching out to brush her hair away from her cheek. "Just long enough to curse me, the house, Alice, humans, and the sheets on the bed, before falling back asleep."

"She's never been a good patient." I grinned softly, perching on the end of the bed. I wrapped my hand around my mother's foot through the blankets.

"True." He looked me over carefully. "You've found her?"

I nodded, my throat going tight as I held back everything I wished I could say. I wanted to tell him about Rosemary's laugh. Marvel with him that she'd grown up around Vampires and had accepted that we were mates from the very beginning. I wanted to mention that she smelled spicy, like herbs, which was so appropriate considering she was named after one. I wanted to tell him about Gary, how he'd dedicated his life and sacrificed his mobility working with Command. Explain how I'd seen Dalton Cavendish and his son, because he was Rosemary's godfather.

Instead, I said nothing.

"Your mother will be pleased," Dad said carefully, his eyes shining. "What's she like?"

That I could tell him.

"Strong," I replied. I cleared my throat. "Gorgeous. Sarcastic as hell. Quick. Funny."

"All good things."

I nodded again.

"She's not here?"

"I..." I paused, unsure how to explain why I'd left her behind without hurting him. "No."

"Things are going well, though?"

"Better than I could've imagined," I confirmed.

"But you didn't bring her with you?" He watched me for a moment and let out a sigh. "Ah. I understand."

"It's only for now," I said quickly. "Just until we've figured this out."

"I don't like it," he said simply. "But I do understand. Before, I would've told you to bring her here. That there was nowhere safer...but that obviously isn't the case."

"She's safe where she is," I assured him. I hoped I was right. "How is everyone?"

Dad ran a hand down the center of his face. His eyes were bruised, and he looked more tired than I'd ever seen him.

"Reese is fine. Not a scratch on her. Lucy'll be okay. She's still sleeping—"

"Best thing for her," I commented. He nodded.

"Sven's still out too."

"Really?"

"He hasn't even twitched. Alice has been by his side since last night. She's hiding it well, but she's scared out of her mind."

"He had a partial, right?"

"Yes. They didn't take his head, thank the Gods, but it was a close thing. Alice was able to repair it. He just hasn't woken up."

"Shit."

"I've been fighting beside him for most of my life," my dad said quietly. "I've never seen him sleep this long without waking at least once."

"He'll pull out of it. If nothing else, just so he can stop Aunt Alice from bitching."

Dad chuckled.

"All things considered, they did well," I said softly.

"They did," Dad replied roughly. "I'd forgotten how fierce your mother is in a fight. The last time she was this hurt was on the way west."

I hummed in acknowledgment. My brothers and I had been fully grown when we made the move to Oregon, but that hadn't changed how terrified we'd been when my parents were attacked. My father had still been on his feet when we'd found them, but my mother had looked dead on the side of the deserted country road.

"Have you spoken to Arthur?" I asked, almost dreading the answer. Arthur Carruthers and I were going to have it out eventually. The only thing I had to do was wait for my moment.

"We let him know we'd been attacked," Dad

confirmed. “He sent out a cleanup team early this morning.”

“No problems?”

“Not one. This is our home. Defending ourselves is our right.”

Straightening, I tried to alleviate the ache in my muscles. Everything hurt, from my scalp to the bottoms of my feet.

“Go,” my dad ordered kindly. “We’re fine here.”

“I may not be around much,” I warned, rising to my feet.

“As it should be,” Dad replied. “You belong with your mate. When it’s safe, bring her home.”

“I will,” I agreed. I hesitated for a moment, then walked toward the door. “Is there anything I can do while I’m here?”

“You can take a shower. You smell like a goat.”

I let out a choked laugh.

“Go. Go,” he insisted, his gaze softening as he looked me over. “We know how to contact you if we need you. Some of us are down at the moment, but Beau and Chance are vigilant, and that’s no small thing.”

“How are *you* feeling?” I asked, my hand on the doorknob. When I’d seen him sitting up in bed, I’d somehow forgotten that he’d been injured almost as bad as my mother.

“I’ve a strong constitution,” he replied gruffly, his old accent barely noticeable in the words. “Go now. Back to your mate, *Arne*.”

I nodded. “Love you.”

“Love you too.”

"You'll let her know I stopped in?" I nodded to my mother.

"Of course."

I didn't bother checking in on anyone else before heading to my room. Beau and Reese were fine—probably in bed, which was where they were half the time—and Ambrose had his hands full dealing with Lucy.

I was startled by Charles sitting halfway up the stairs to my room.

"I thought I heard your voice," he said, shooting me a lopsided grin. He looked beyond me. "She's not here?"

"No." My brother's mate looked like he hadn't slept. His normally tidy hair was sticking out at all angles, and his face looked like shit after the beating he'd received the night before.

"Oh," he said softly. "Well, I just wanted to come say hi."

"It's good to see you," I replied gently. Charles always looked like a stiff breeze could knock him over, but after the last twenty-four hours, he appeared even more fragile. "Lucy's going to be fine, right?"

"Yeah, she is," he said, rising to his feet. "Ambrose told me to be patient, but—" He shrugged. "Not my strong suit. I'm going crazy waiting around."

"Chance is downstairs cleaning up. I'm sure he could use the help," I offered. I could hear him cursing a mop bucket in the living room. "Keep you busy, at least."

"Good idea." He smiled and started down the stairs.

"Hey, Charlie?"

He turned to look at me and lifted his eyebrows in question.

"You did good last night."

Charles scoffed. "It's pretty easy to get kidnapped."

"It isn't easy to put yourself in danger. Don't sell yourself short. You came through when we needed you."

He shrugged.

"If you hadn't done what you did, I wouldn't have found her," I reminded him quietly.

His lips pulled up in a small smile. "Tell Rosemary I said hello."

I jerked in surprise. "You know her name?"

He frowned. "She introduced herself last night."

Shit.

"Keep it to yourself, all right?" I asked, trying to keep my voice level.

"Okay," he replied, the word drawn out.

"The less people know about her, the safer she is."

"Even family?" He was looking at me like I'd lost my mind. Maybe I had.

"Everyone," I confirmed.

He nodded. "Not a word."

"Thanks."

Once he'd disappeared at the bottom of the stairs, I jogged the rest of the way to my room. I'd already burned most of the time I'd allotted myself, and I still needed to pack some things and take a shower. I didn't want to be gone for more than three hours if I could help it, and with Gary's place almost an hour away, it didn't give me much wiggle room.

Thankfully, I'd been packing in a hurry for longer than I could remember. Grabbing what I'd need was practically muscle memory, and a few minutes later, my duffel of clothes and a small cooler of blood were sitting by the door. After taking a cold shower, I didn't even take the time to dry my hair, leaving it loose to dry instead. I hated the feeling of wet hair on my back, but it couldn't be helped.

I probably should've cut it.

At some point, I would.

As I made my way back out to the car, waving goodbye to Chance and Charlie, who were failing to get the bloodstains out of the hardwood, I thought about the bet I'd made with my little brother.

He'd been convinced that I'd never be able to go longer than two months without a haircut. He'd given me so much shit about it that we'd wagered on it. Then I'd deliberately gone even longer. Two months had turned into six. Then a year. Each time we'd been in the same place, the moment he'd seen me, he'd burst out laughing.

I could still see the delight on his face the first time I'd shown up with an actual ponytail. He'd thought it was so fucking hilarious that I refused to cut it. Called me stubborn. Called me Rapunzel.

I thought about Zeke the entire drive back to Gary's, my eyes constantly on my mirrors, being sure I wasn't followed. I couldn't remember when Zeke was born—I'd been too little—but I had a thousand memories of him starting when I was about six years old. He'd always been so anxious to keep up with us, so adamant that he could do whatever we were doing.

He'd driven me crazy.

He was also my best friend.

We'd done stupid shit, whored around, taken risks, helped people when we could, spent late nights talking and sparring and generally raising hell. It was still hard to believe I was in the world without him. I wasn't sure how many times I'd reached for my phone to call him before realizing that I couldn't.

The shower I'd taken was a lost cause. Fifteen minutes into the drive, and I realized I'd already sweated through my shirt again. The heat was getting worse. I'd been able to power through the body aches and the nausea and the tightness in my chest, but the headache that was thrumming between my temples made me glad that I wouldn't be away from Rosemary much longer.

Thank the Gods her pain had been manageable so far. I knew that putting distance between us wouldn't be pleasant for her, maybe even painful, which is why I'd been so conscious of how long I was gone. I hated it, but the necessity of going back to my parents' place was almost as important as keeping her safe.

I'd rather she were miserable for a few hours than dead, at least that's what I told myself as guilt lay heavy on my shoulders for leaving her.

It took everything I had to drive slowly up the long gravel lane, avoiding the potholes when I could while scanning my surroundings. The Whitlock house really was in the middle of nowhere. If you weren't looking, it would be easy to drive right past their driveway, assuming it was an old forest road. Leaving the road in disrepair had probably been a deliberate decision on Gary's part, and even as it made my muscles throb with every jerk, I had to give him credit. The man knew what he was doing.

When I reached the house, Dalton's car was parked out front again. I should've known that he wouldn't stay gone for long. Our conversation the night before had been vague to the point of infuriating, so much so that I hadn't known how or what to pass on when I'd gone home. Between that and not wanting my family to connect Rosemary to the Cavendish family, I'd kept my mouth shut.

We didn't lie to each other, and not telling them that Dalton had been looking into the Vampire disappearances long before we'd even known about them felt a lot like lying. I wondered if I'd done the right thing as I tied my hair back out of my face and strode toward the house.

I knocked on the front door before pushing it open, surprised that Rosemary hadn't come out to greet me. If I felt like I'd been run over by a truck, she must've felt the same, but I didn't see her as I stepped inside the house.

"Kitchen," Gary called.

I followed his voice and stepped into a room filled with Cavendishes. Dalton and Halle sat at the table with Gary while Ian lounged on the counter, his long legs nearly reaching the floor. Two younger boys in jackets and boots looked like they'd just come in the back door.

"Your family all right?" Gary asked as he turned to look at me.

Where was my mate?

"As well as expected," I replied, shifting on my feet. If Rosemary wasn't in the kitchen, maybe she was in her room. I didn't want to be rude, but I had no interest in visiting with the Cavendish family when I'd already been separated from my mate for hours.

"Go on," Gary said, easily noticing my impatience. "There's dinner on the stove when you're ready."

As I hurried toward the hallway, Dalton's mate Halle let out a tinkling laugh. "I remember those days."

"What, yesterday?" Dalton teased her.

I was moving so fast toward the bedroom that I nearly collided with my mate as she stepped out of the bathroom. Stumbling back a step, I reached for her arms to steady us both.

She was wearing nothing but a towel, her hair pulled up in a knot at the top of her head. Little droplets of water beaded on the tops of her shoulders. I was mesmerized as one of them rolled down over her collarbone and got lost in the towel.

"Oh, you're back," she said. "How'd it go?"

It wasn't what she'd said, and it wasn't even how she'd said it...but something wasn't right. I looked up to meet her gaze, but I couldn't find anything there. She didn't look pissed. She didn't really have any expression at all.

"It went well," I replied, following her as she turned away and walked to her room. "My mother was sleeping, but my father said she's healing well."

"And your sister-in-law?" Rosemary asked, her back to me as she started pulling out dresser drawers.

"They're both doing well."

"That's good news."

I opened and closed my mouth a few times, trying to think of something to say. There wasn't any tension in the room. She hadn't come out swinging when she'd realized I was back. On the surface, everything appeared fine. But something was off. There was a stiltedness to our conversation that hadn't been there before, not from the moment we'd met.

"I think Uncle Dalton wants to bring you in on what

he's been doing," Rosemary said as she pulled a sports bra over her head, still keeping the towel in place. "They've been waiting for you to get back."

"He's pulled Halle into it too?" I joked sarcastically, knowing the answer before I'd even voiced it.

"She came to see me," Rosemary replied. She pulled on a pair of underwear, still hiding beneath the towel. When they were on, she finally let it go, and I was treated to the sight of her nearly bare back and thighs. I barely kept myself from moving toward her as she tugged a tank top over her head.

"The boys were curious, so they tagged along. She said normally she would've given us some time, but since we were staying with Pop anyway, she figured that they probably wouldn't walk in on something they didn't want to see." There was no joke in her comment, no lightness in her voice.

"It's a good thing they didn't show up when we were in the barn earlier," I teased as she pulled on a pair of brown canvas overalls. She turned back around as she pulled the straps over her shoulders.

She let out a huff of air. "Yeah, good thing."

"I told you I'd be back in a few hours," I reminded her, moving closer.

"You did," she confirmed with a small nod. She reached out to pat me on the chest before moving around me.

"Hey, where you going?" I asked, turning to catch her.

She paused before the door as I wrapped my arms around her waist and bent my head to kiss the back of her neck.

She had a tattoo there that I hadn't noticed

before. Pulling back a little, I studied it. One small circle about six millimeters in diameter and three dots the size of the end of a ballpoint pen lined up beneath it. I traced it lightly with my tongue, making her shiver.

"It's me and the boys," she said softly. "Ian has the same one, but his circle is the second one, because he's the second oldest. When Grant and Seamus are old enough, they'll get theirs."

"They're more like brothers than cousins," I replied in understanding.

"Yes." She stayed in my arms a moment longer before pulling away. "I tried to get Ian to make his circle the head of a sunflower, but he wouldn't do it."

"Why a sunflower?" I asked as she pulled open the door and started back out of the room.

"You've seen him," she said easily. "When he was little, he was shaped the same way—all skinny arms and legs, but his head was huge."

"It was not," Ian yelled from the kitchen.

"It was," Rosemary confirmed. "But thankfully, he eventually grew into it."

"You were perfect," Halle consoled her son as we entered the room, her voice shaking with suppressed laughter. "Your head was just the right size."

"Yeah, like a bowling ball," Rosemary added.

"It's all right, Ian," the youngest boy said with a grin. "Not all of us can be perfect from birth."

"You were cross-eyed until you were five!" Ian shot back.

"Boys," Halle said, her voice ringing with warning. She looked over her shoulder at Rosemary and lifted her eyebrows.

"Daniel, this is my family. The shortest one over there is Grant, and the other one is Seamus."

"The pretty one," Seamus added.

"And this is my Aunt Halle."

"It's nice to meet you," I said with a nod. The boys were on the far side of the table, still standing near the back door. Halle was closer, but I knew better than to try to shake her hand. Not only was it...impolite to touch another Vampire's mate that wasn't family, but it would also most likely be uncomfortable for the woman.

Halle nodded back while the boys offered hellos.

"Strange that the two of you never met before," Dalton said, leaning back in his chair.

"I think the last time we spoke, you'd just met," I offered, while Halle sat silently.

"Makes sense," Dalton replied. "Boys, go outside and make yourselves useful."

Grant and Seamus deflated, but neither of them said a word as they turned back toward the door.

"There's an old dirt bike under the tarp in the barn," Gary said. "Picked it up at an estate sale. You get it workin', you can have it."

"No shit?" Grant asked, grinning.

"No shit. Go see what you can do."

"Damn, Pop," Rosemary said as she walked toward the stove. "Just giving stuff away."

"You've already got one," he replied with a scoff. "And it's in much better condition than the piece of shit in the garage."

Dalton laughed. "At least it'll keep them busy."

"For the next year, probably," Gary agreed.

Rosemary ladled some kind of soup into two bowls and brought me one of them.

"Thanks," I said quietly.

They must've put an extra leaf in the table, because it was much bigger than it had been when I left. Around it were folding chairs that I'd seen earlier in the day stacked against the side of the barn. I sat down in one between Gary and Halle as Rosemary sat down across from me. The empty bowls and glasses littering the table indicated that everyone else had already eaten.

Rosemary had waited for me to eat dinner.

"I doubt those two will stay away from the door for long, so we should probably jump right in," Dalton said as I lifted a bite to my mouth.

It felt like Halle was staring a hole through the side of my face, but when I glanced at her, she was looking at her mate.

"I've brought over a file that has everything we know so far," Dalton said, setting a USB drive down in the center of the table. "It's embarrassingly small. We've been tracking the disappearances and mapping them, but there doesn't seem to be a pattern beyond the fact that every Vampire was newly mated. Some came from large families. Some were loners. Many of them quit administrative roles in Command. Only a few had been on the teams, which we could take one of two ways. Either they didn't think that taking highly trained Vampires was worth the hassle, or, more likely, the pool was just a lot smaller. There've only been fourteen team members who found their mates in the last ten years, and four of them were you and your brothers."

"Add Billy Finau to that list of fourteen if you

haven't already," I replied, setting my spoon down. "He showed up at our place, going on and on about how they'd taken his mate from a gas station and was desperate to get her back. We knew we were on the militia's radar, so we sent Charlie—my brother Zeke's mate—into public, and they took the bait. Nabbed him at the grocery store like we were hoping, and we followed them back to the garage where Rosemary was being held."

"You didn't find Finau's mate?" Dalton asked.

"She wasn't there," I replied. "And Finau disappeared. He took off while we were breaching the perimeter."

"He knew she wasn't there," Gary said in understanding.

I nodded. "He was showing all the signs of the heat, so either they're paying him very well to spend time away from his mate or they have her and they're controlling him that way."

"It's not money," Dalton replied. "I knew Finau well. The only thing that could make him turn on another Vampire would be his mate."

"We would've helped him if he'd asked." I let out a humorless chuckle. "We *did* help him when he asked. If he would've been straight with us, he might even have her back by now."

"I'll put out feelers and see if he'll reach out," Dalton said thoughtfully.

"You do that," I replied, shrugging my shoulders. "But if he does, keep me out of it. I'm grateful that the clusterfuck brought me to Rosemary." I looked up at my mate, but she was staring into her soup. "But while we were putting our asses on the line to save Finau's mate, my home was being overrun by humans. He lured us out so they could get to my brothers' mates. It's a fucking miracle that none of them were taken. Billy Finau can go fuck himself with a bat covered in barbed wire."

"They weren't taking any chances," Rosemary added quietly. "They sent *so* many. You should've seen the piles of bodies. It must've been like a stampede toward the house."

"But they held them off?" Gary asked.

I nodded. "They underestimated my brothers' mates and my mother. By the time we made it back, things were mostly over, and Alice was treating the wounded."

"How is Alice?" Halle asked. "Ian, Alice delivered you."

"She's well. Sven got a partial in the attack—"

Halle gasped.

"What's a partial?" Rosemary asked.

"They nearly decapitated him," Gary replied grimly.

"He hasn't woken up yet," I added. "But he's alive, and he's a tough old fucker. He'll be okay."

"Break it down from the very beginning," Dalton ordered after a moment. "Tell me everything you can remember."

"Do you think they'll come for us next?" Halle asked softly.

"I'd like to be prepared if it comes to that," Dalton replied, setting his hand over hers.

I spent the next two hours giving details that I hadn't even realized I remembered, starting from the moment Billy Finau had come knocking. Rosemary shot me a look when I didn't mention Matthias or Josiah helping us in the woods, but she didn't say a word to contradict me. By the time I was done, Gary was rubbing at the silver scruff on his chin, and Halle had tucked herself against Dalton's side. Even Ian had left his place at the counter and sat down with us at the table.

"They didn't have enough people to send while you were home," Dalton said finally. "That's something."

"There had to have been at least fifty bodies," Rosemary countered, looking at me for confirmation. "Right?"

"Fifty humans to six Vampires isn't good odds," I reminded her. No one had known that Matthias and Josiah had flown in too, making the humans' odds even worse. "Plus, they had to have known that we had guards on the property. When you add those Vampires—"

"It would've been a bloodbath," Gary mused.

"It *was* a bloodbath," Rosemary said smugly. "I bet they won't underestimate mates in the future."

"They've been doing this a while," Dalton reminded her. "What happened at the Boucher house was an anomaly. Most mates won't have the skill set that the Boucher mates do. This won't slow them down."

"But it might make them pause before going after Rosemary," Halle said hopefully. "Knowing that the others in that family didn't go easily."

"As far as anyone knows, Rosemary is Ian's mate," Dalton replied.

"Shit," she whispered.

I curled my hands into fists against my thighs. Now wasn't the time to tell them to fucking correct their bullshit announcement... or maybe it was.

"Command might have their bond on record, but the militia know—or at least suspect—she's not his mate," I argued. "That's why they kept her for so long. They were watching for signs of the heat. When we got there, my brothers noticed straight off that she wasn't showing any."

"So, best case, they believe the mating notice was a lie," Gary said grimly. "Worst case, they're even more curious about her and searching high and low to get her back."

"And if they get their hands on her again, they'll find all the symptoms she didn't have before. They're not killing newly mated pairs for shits and giggles. They're experimenting on them. To them, Rosemary would be a fucking prize."

Ian's fist hit the top of the table so hard, it reverberated around the room like a gunshot.

"Control it," his father ordered.

"Sunflower, you know I can take care of myself," Rosemary said soothingly. "Don't stress."

"Who the hell are these guys?" Ian spat. "Who the hell is helping them? How could any Vampire *help* them? Mates? They're going after fucking *mates*? We *protect* mates. Always. Whether they're ours or someone else's. This is *insane*."

The silence in the room when he was done speaking was absolute.

All of us felt that way, but especially Dalton and me. Gary, Rosemary, and Halle understood the mating bond and the fact that Vampires waited multiple lifetimes to find their own, but none of the humans could fully comprehend the millennia of instincts to protect them that were bred into our bones.

Mates were sacred. That knowledge was not only taught from the cradle but built into our genetic makeup. When a Vampire could only procreate with the other half of their soul, that other half became absolutely imperative to the survival of our species. We would die for them willingly. Kill for them easily.

Just the thought of another Vampire losing their mate was abhorrent. Losing our own was inconceivable. Physically and mentally debilitating. If someone had asked me before if I'd ever believe that another Vampire would do anything to put mates in jeopardy, I would've answered an unequivocal no.

But *someone* was passing on information. Somehow, the human militia was finding out about newly mated pairs when most humans didn't even know what the mating bond entailed. We had a traitor in our midst.

"That bike is so sick," Seamus exclaimed as the younger boys burst back into the house in a tangle of arms and legs.

"You figure out what's wrong with it?" Gary asked.

As the boys spoke over each other, detailing a long list of things they needed to fix to get the dirt bike running again, I tuned them out and watched my mate. She'd barely made a dent in her soup, even though we'd been sitting there for hours. Her hand moved absentmindedly, stirring in a circle, but I couldn't even remember her taking a bite.

I glanced down at my own bowl, which I'd somehow finished as we'd discussed things.

The symptoms of the heat had become manageable the moment I'd touched her outside the bathroom, and I didn't feel like my head was going to explode anymore, but the fire beneath my skin and the tightness in my chest were still there. I looked her over, trying to see if she was suffering too. Her skin was a little pale and clammy—and I'd bet everything in my wallet that her skin was hot to the touch—but beyond that, she looked fine, if a little distracted.

"We'll see what we've got at home, and you can bring it when we come back," Dalton said, cutting off his youngest sons as he stood from the table. "Thanks for dinner, Gar."

"Thanks for the company," Gary replied with a nod.

The Cavendish family said their goodbyes, with the younger boys going in for hugs before Ian shoved them away from Rosemary in warning. Sheepishly, they nodded their heads with apologetic smiles.

"Oh, that's bullshit," Rosemary barked, yanking Grant against her. She wrapped her arms around his shoulders and loudly kissed the top of his head. "The day you can't hug me is the day I'm dead, and even after that, you can cuddle my urn, all right?"

"Yeah, okay," Grant grumbled as he hugged her back.

He didn't notice the tightness around her eyes as she let him go and reached for Seamus.

"You too, numb-nuts," she said, doing the same thing to the youngest. "Nothing's changed. You're still my best dudes."

"I'm the best," Seamus said as he wrapped his arms carefully around her waist. "Ian and Grant are your worst dudes."

"That's 'cause you're my baby," she crooned, rocking him from side to side for a moment. "Now get out of here before that vein in your dad's forehead starts pulsing."

The boys left the house as noisily as they'd come back in. Halle was the only one left when Rosemary leaned down to hug her.

"They understand, Flower," she chided softly in Rosemary's ear. The words were meant for my mate, but after twenty years with a Vampire, Halle must've known I could hear them. "Don't hurt yourself just to prove you love them. They already know that."

"It's fine," Rosemary brushed her off. "It was nothing."

"It's inconvenient, I know," Halle continued before Rosemary cut her off.

"This stupid bond is not going to stop me from hugging the only little brothers I've ever known," Rosemary hissed, pulling away. "Fuck that."

"Love you," Halle said with a sigh, patting Rosemary's cheek affectionately. "Call me tomorrow."

"I will," Rosemary promised.

"Thanks for dinner, Gar," Halle said, blowing the man a kiss. She turned her head toward me and nodded, then left.

"Brr," Gary joked with a dramatic shiver. "She don't like you."

"You noticed, huh?" I asked dryly.

Rosemary moved to start cleaning up the table, and I followed to help her.

"She takes a minute to warm up," Gary explained.

My mate was noticeably quiet.

"Was she like that with you?" I asked Gary, just to keep the conversation going.

"Hell no," he replied, carefully pushing himself out

of his wheelchair. "By the time we met, she'd already had her best friend talkin' me up for a month at least."

"Ah, so that was the problem," I joked. "Rosemary didn't spend enough time listing my good points."

I expected Rosemary to make a joke or at least acknowledge what I'd said, but she was silent as she loaded the dishwasher.

"Thunder," Gary called. The old dog scrambled up loudly from his place in the living room, then slowly made his way into the kitchen.

"Pop, take your chair," Rosemary scolded as Gary opened the back door for the bulldog.

"You worry about yourself," Gary replied easily. "I've been sitting all day. I can walk out to the porch while Thunder does his business."

He disappeared outside, closing the door behind him.

Rosemary and I finished cleaning the kitchen in silence, carefully moving around each other. By the time she opened the door and called out a good night to her dad, I was completely confused.

I'd known that she wasn't happy I left her behind when I'd gone to see my family. I even understood it. But she wasn't acting angry. If I spoke to her, she responded. She said thank you when I wiped down the table with a dishrag. From the moment I'd gotten back, she hadn't sent me a dirty or dismissive look.

"I'm exhausted," she said, walking back toward me. "Want to go to bed?"

Absolutely nothing sounded better than getting into bed with her.

"Yeah."

I hadn't noticed—for obvious reasons, she'd been

in nothing but a towel—but it looked like Rosemary had spent some time cleaning up while I was gone. The piles of clothes were missing from her chair, and the top of the dresser was neatly organized. She'd even changed the sheets on her bed.

"I don't have any room in my dresser," she said, taking off the straps to her overalls as she walked to the opposite side of the bed. "But you brought some clothes, right?"

"I forgot them in the car," I replied, closing us in for the night. "By the time I got back, I wasn't thinking about anything but you."

She smiled, but it didn't seem to reach her eyes.

"Well, you can use the chair when you bring them in," she said with a shrug, stepping out of the overalls. "It's the best I can do."

"I'm used to living out of my duffel." Pulling off my shirt, I tossed it onto the offered chair.

"Makes sense," she replied, contorting her arms so she could slide the sports bra out from beneath her tank top. She dropped it to the floor and reached out to pull the blankets low enough to slide in.

I'd never been someone who stared when I noticed a beautiful woman. I could remember something in my head just fine without making someone else feel uncomfortable—but I couldn't take my eyes off her breasts. They were small and soft and bounced a little with the movement of her body, her nipples tight and pressed against the thin top.

My mouth watered as I kicked off my boots and shoved my jeans down my thighs. By the time I climbed in beside her, I was hard as a rock, and she was already curled on her side facing me, her knees pulled up nearly to her chest.

"I'm going to stay here tomorrow," I assured her, finding her thigh under the blanket. Her skin was so soft and so hot. Gods, she was like a furnace. "They don't need me at the house."

"Okay," she said easily with a nod. "Everything was okay when you got there?"

"It's going to take some time," I replied, propping my head on my bent elbow. "They're going to have to replace some windows and probably sand the floors. My mom and Lucy will probably sleep for the next couple of days while they heal, but yeah. Everything was okay."

"Do you think they'll attack there again?"

"They'd be idiots to try. My brothers won't leave their mates any time in the near future, and I can't imagine an entire human army succeeding where the others didn't."

"That's good," she breathed. My hand paused where I'd been brushing it against her thigh, and she moved just slightly so that I'd start again. "Why didn't you mention your cousins when you were talking to Dalton?"

I *knew* she'd noticed. "They're incredibly private," I explained. "Paranoid to a fault. They wouldn't want anyone to know that they'd been involved. One of them has a mate that's completely off the radar, and I can't repay them for their help by running my mouth."

"Gotcha," she sighed, her eyes growing heavy. "Well, I won't say anything."

"Appreciate it."

"He trusts you, you know?"

"Who? Dalton?"

"Yeah. He told me before you got back that you were one of the best teammates he'd ever had."

"Aw, he was talking about me?" I joked. "I'm touched."

Her eyes lost the glassy look. "He was reassuring my aunt, who was pissed when she got here and you weren't here."

"Ah, that didn't win me any points, huh?"

"You're lucky she'd calmed down by the time you got back, or there's a good chance you would've been buried in the backyard."

I grimaced.

"It's all right," Rosemary said, patting my chest. For a split second, it felt like I was being burned until a rush of cool swept through my veins. "Once she realized I was fine, she mellowed."

"Were you?" I asked quietly, smoothing my hand up her side. "I wasn't. I was sweating so much my dad said I smelled like a goat."

Rosemary let out a choked laugh.

"I nearly puked all over my lap while I was driving," I continued. "Knowing that I'd be the one who would have to clean it up was the only way I kept that shit down."

"Sounds terrible."

"It wasn't pleasant," I conceded, wrapping my hand around the side of her neck. Her pulse beat comfortingly against my palm, and my mouth watered. "How bad was it for you?"

Something flashed in her eyes, but she just shrugged. "Nothing I couldn't handle."

"Did the shower help?" I asked, remembering the beads of water on her shoulders.

"Not really," she replied. "It felt pretty similar to getting the tattoo on my neck. Lots of little needles hitting everywhere."

I flinched at the thought.

"A bath would probably be better," she mused. "Not as violent."

"Well, I'm here now," I murmured, leaning forward to brush my lips over hers. "No bath needed."

"Convenient," she whispered back, leaning into the touch.

Her hands slid out from beneath the pillows, and I sighed in relief as they smoothed over my bare chest and down my stomach. They'd cooled a little since we'd been lying there, and each touch felt like a mixture of floating on my back in the middle of a lake and the first seconds of the downward slide of a rollercoaster. Every molecule in my body stood at attention while my heart seemed to slow its angry pounding.

It didn't take long before both of us were naked. We'd kept a small barrier of clothing between us until then, as if it somehow made a difference, and maybe it had. Because the moment she pressed her bare body against mine, my willpower was toast. Spending those few hours apart had only intensified the instinct to get as close as possible. We were too hungry for the feel of skin on skin, too impatient. I moved with her as Rosemary rolled to her back, then froze as my hips settled between her thighs, the underside of my cock pressed against hot, wet skin.

"We're not leaving here anytime soon," Rosemary reminded me, her legs wrapping around the backs of my thighs. "Unless you want to ask my pop to leave his own home to give us privacy, we'll have to do it here."

I was paying attention to the best of my ability, but it felt like my brain was short-circuiting. She was right there. We were so godsdamned close. My hips moved without conscious thought, and Rosemary let out a little whimper of need.

"It's supposed to be special," I replied, focusing on her eyes. The pupils were huge with arousal, and around the edges, her irises had darkened into a thick line of darker green. "It's the beginning of everything."

Rosemary lifted her hands to frame my cheeks in her palms. "If you haven't realized that our beginning started already, you haven't been paying attention."

I groaned and pressed our foreheads together as her hips rolled languidly.

"What are you waiting for?" she whispered.

Every euphemism and cliché I'd ever heard felt absolutely correct as I pressed inside her, both of us barely breathing. We fit perfectly, like a lock and key, a pair of puzzle pieces, a glove. She shuddered as I paused, fully inside her.

It was a miracle. The culmination of my entire life. There would never be anything better than that moment, with the light from the lamp illuminating her beautiful face, her nails pressed into my shoulders, and her body welcoming mine.

"Please tell me you've done this before," she said nervously after a moment.

I choked on a laugh. I must've been lost in my head for too long. She looked so concerned.

"I've done this before," I confirmed against her lips.

Catching her hands in mine, I tugged them up

above her head and braced myself on my elbows. Then, I finally began to move.

It was nearly impossible to keep Rosemary quiet, but I did my best. I caught every sound in my mouth as I memorized what made her gasp or moan or curse. While I held her hands captive, she used the rest of her body to drive me out of my mind. Her hips rolled in counterpoint, her knees bent and fell wide, her back arched, and her legs wrapped around my back, holding me to her like a vice.

When it all felt like too much, my skin so sensitive it felt like I might go out of my mind, I found myself suddenly pressing my mouth against the pulse point on her neck.

Rosemary tipped her head back further, urging me on as she whimpered.

I'm not sure what I expected to happen. I'd thought about it a lot during my life—the moment when I would complete the bond with the other half of my soul—but nothing had prepared me for when it actually happened. As the first taste of her blood hit the back of my throat, I came so hard that the world around me went silent.

It was *everything*.

Somehow, I had the presence of mind to pull away before I hurt her, and when sound began to make sense again, I realized that Rosemary was making these little gasping noises as she pulled at the hold I had on her hands.

"What?" I asked frantically, letting go of her. "Baby, what?"

"You have to do it," she said, turning her head to savagely bite my arm. When she pulled away, little lines indented where her teeth had been, but the skin was intact. "I can't do it. You have to do it."

"Shhh," I murmured, understanding the problem. Lifting my hand to my mouth, I quickly bit down to break the skin and offered it to her.

As she pulled the fleshy part of my thumb into her mouth and took a long pull, her body tightened around my cock. The two sensations were so powerful that another orgasm rolled over me, and by the time her mouth grew slack and her head dropped back to the bed, we were both shaking with exhaustion and maybe a little bit of shock.

CHAPTER 7
ROSEMARY

Carefully lifting the heavy arm off my waist, I scooted off the side of the bed. The floor was freezing against the soles of my feet, and if I could feel the discomfort of it, that meant my body temperature must be somewhere close to normal.

The heat had dissipated.

I'd known that it could happen, and I also knew that it wouldn't last long.

I tiptoed across the floor and grabbed some clothes out of my dresser, inwardly cursing at every sound. Daniel never stirred, and I barely breathed until I was out of my room and making my way down the hallway in my socks.

It wasn't as if I was sneaking away, not really. I just needed a little time to myself. After the upheaval of the day before, culminating with the completion of the mating bond, I needed a breather. I needed a moment when everyone wasn't looking at me.

Their looks had run the gamut the day before. The eyes on me had ranged from shock to love to sympathy to possession. And while I didn't normally pay attention to the opinions of other people, it was hard to ignore those opinions when they matched your own.

Confirmation bias or whatever.

Aunt Halle was confused? Felt bad for me? Was pissed for me? Yeah, I knew exactly how she felt.

The fact that Daniel had taken off without even looking back had been like getting a bucket of cold water thrown in my face.

Mates weren't supposed to do that. Mates weren't supposed to leave each other's sides. In all honesty, he shouldn't have been able to leave me. It should've been so painful for him that he rethought his actions. The knowledge that I would be in pain should've had his instincts screaming to go back and fix it.

But he'd still left.

I knew I sounded like some whiny codependent teenager. I *knew* that. But if a Vampire could leave their mate like that, without a single glance backward, then everything that had ever felt true and real and constant in my life seemed suspect. Uncle Dalton and Aunt Halle's bond was the center of their family. It was the North Star, and by necessity, it had become mine after my mom died.

Knowing that they would never leave, and I would always have them *because* of that mating bond? Well, it had given the whole thing an almost mythical level of importance in my head, and I hadn't even realized it.

So when Daniel left, and I felt that tether in my chest pull so tight that I thought it might snap?

I may have lost it a little.

I'd followed him. Barefoot. In the gravel. Sobbing.

It had felt like something was being torn from me. I

couldn't breathe. I'd vomited twice. My muscles had flexed so tight that it felt like they were going to tear away from my bones.

And while I logically knew that he was coming back, I hadn't been able to stop myself. It didn't matter that he'd be back in a few hours. In that moment, I'd been inconsolable. Out of my mind with grief and panic.

Thankfully, I'd eventually gotten a handle on it enough that I'd turned around before I reached the main road. When I got back to the house, Pop had been waiting on the porch with a joint to share.

I was high as a kite when Uncle Dalton and Aunt Halle showed up.

I was pretty sure Pop had called them. He would've noticed when I took off down the driveway. I don't think I was quiet about the whole thing.

Pulling on my gloves, I looked at the huge tractor tire that I hadn't touched since last summer. Dad had brought it home when I was a kid, and I loved to climb. It had been many different things over the years. A mountain I shoved Ian off. A makeshift tent when we convinced our parents we were old enough to sleep outside by ourselves. A small refuge where I could read in peace. The perfect hiding spot. A pirate ship. Thunder's pen when he was a baby, and we were afraid he'd get lost in the woods. The place I'd gone, tucking myself safely inside, with Ian at my head and Grant at my feet on the night they'd burned my mother's body in Vampire tradition.

Now that I was grown, I made use of it in a different way. My massive emotional support tire.

Bracing my feet carefully, I crouched and tucked my fingertips under the edge of the tire.

Nearly every muscle burned as I raised it, first an inch, then six, then a foot off the ground. By the time I'd reached my waist, I was trembling. Then, it was standing straight up. I shoved it over with a small grunt.

Then I did it again.

My breath seesawed in and out of my lungs. My fingers ached.

The sweat that beaded on my forehead felt natural for the first time in days. Clean. Straightforward. I was pushing my body to do hard things, and that's why I was hot. It wasn't out of my control. I could stop at any time.

I flipped it again. And again.

Eventually, I ran out of room and had to flip it in the opposite direction.

I'd just gotten it back to the place I'd started when I noticed Daniel standing on the back patio, watching me.

Straightening, I put my hands on my hips and squinted at him. I'd been so focused on what I was doing that I hadn't even realized when he'd come outside. At some point, the sun had come up, and the way it filtered through the trees made him look like he was illuminated.

"Holy fuck, Rosie," he said, starting toward me. "How long have you been out here?"

"Um." I looked around me. I wasn't sure when I'd climbed out of bed, unable to sleep. Had it been late enough that I could potentially act like I was just an early riser? "Not sure."

"I woke up, and you were gone," he said softly, reaching out to brush a stray hair away from my cheek when he reached me. "I nearly tore the house apart before I realized I could hear you out here."

Oh, he'd been worried that I'd left? Well, wasn't that just too bad. I held every what's-good-for-the-goose-is-good-for-the-gander comment tightly behind my teeth.

"I've been sitting on my ass for too long," I replied instead of what I really wanted to say. "I needed to use my muscles a little."

"You used them pretty well last night," he joked, sliding his arms around my waist.

"Maybe if I were on top, I could use sex as cardio," I mused, tilting my head. "But missionary? Nah."

Daniel laughed and let me go as I moved around him.

"Your dad's making breakfast."

I nodded. "He likes to cook."

"Are all those cookbooks his?" He fell in step beside me as we headed for the house.

"Some were my mom's," I replied. I knew exactly which ones. "The rest are his. I started buying them as birthday and Christmas gifts, but now that I can afford better presents, I usually try to grab him a local one when I'm traveling. The trick is finding them in English. They're a pain in the ass to translate."

"Do you travel a lot?" he asked curiously.

"Once I started working with Uncle Dalton, yeah. People contact us from all over. We go where we're needed."

"Morning," Pop greeted as we let ourselves inside. "Made a scramble. It's on the table."

"Thanks, Gary," Daniel replied as he sat down.

"Mm-hmm," Pop replied, pouring himself a cup of coffee. "Dig in."

I glanced at Daniel before bumping Pop out of the way with my hip and pouring my own mug. Did my mate realize how furious Pop was?

My father had spent more years than I'd been alive controlling every micro-expression on his face. His life and the lives of his teammates had depended upon it. Most of the Vampires I'd met were like bulls in a china shop. They didn't need to hide their feelings or opinions—that's what came from being born at the top of the food chain. Their human counterparts were different. I didn't know most of what Pop had done while he was working with Vampire Command—I'd never know—but I'd picked up enough over the years to know that he'd spent a lot of time undercover. He'd infiltrated places that would give me nightmares. Cozied up to madmen so well that when they were finally taken down, they'd looked to him for help. He'd listened in on conversations that would still, to this day, get him killed if anyone ever found out.

So when he'd greeted Daniel the day before like everything was just fine, I hadn't even been surprised. Pop watched and he waited and he *listened,* and if there ever came a time when he needed the information that he'd burrowed away like a squirrel getting ready for winter, he'd use it. His body may be failing him, he might not move like he used to, but my father was the most wily and intelligent person I'd ever known—human or Vampire.

"Coffee?" I asked Daniel.

"Please," he said, half rising from his seat. "I'm sorry, I should've gotten it."

I waved him off. "No worries. You're the guest."

The words stung, even though I hadn't meant them to. I could see it in the small way he'd flinched as soon as they were out of my mouth.

What did he expect? He didn't live here. Hell, I didn't even live here. I'd built my own home in a little townhouse fifteen minutes away. Sure, I kept plenty of things at Pop's house, because when I wasn't traveling, I liked spending most of my time up here. But I had my own place. It was girly and feminine and smelled like spiced apples year-round because I stocked up on the candles in the fall and carefully burned them through the other seasons.

God, I missed my house.

After handing him his coffee, I sat down and unzipped my sweatshirt, peeling it down my clammy arms. I nearly lifted my arm to check my pits, which I would've done if my mate wasn't watching me across the table. Instead, I just pressed my arms unobtrusively to my sides and hoped that I didn't reek. As soon as I could escape, I was taking a long shower.

"Saw you out with the tire," Pop said with a little grin. "Get all your feelings out?"

"Just needed some exercise," I countered, loading my plate. He'd made some kind of hash with ham, eggs, potatoes, and peppers. I wanted to bury my face in it. "I don't think I've gone this long without working out since I was like thirteen."

I missed the gym I'd set up in my spare bedroom.

"I think I've got some equipment out in the loft somewhere," Pop offered. "If you want to go looking."

"It's fine, Pop," I replied. "The tire works just fine."

We fell into silence as we ate, but it wasn't comfortable. Daniel and my pop seemed totally fine, but I wasn't. I was having a very difficult time wavering between wanting to drag Daniel into the woods to have my way with him or, alternately, dive across the table to pummel him.

He was so calm. Happy, even. To Daniel, the world outside might be on fire, but in our little house in the woods, all was well.

For me? The fire was coming from inside the house.

"I was thinking I could fix that lattice on the front porch today," Daniel told Pop between bites of food. "I saw you had some replacement pieces leaning up against the little shop next to the coop."

"You don't have to do that," Pop replied gruffly.

"I don't mind," Daniel said easily. "I'm not used to sitting around. You've opened your home to me. It's the least I can do to take care of the projects you haven't had time for."

"About that," I said, interrupting them. "Did you ever really say that Daniel could stay here?" I propped my chin on my palm. "Because, as I recall, the rule was no boys in my room, and you've already let him stay two nights. Getting soft in your old age?"

Pop looked at me in amusement. "Nice try."

"I'm just saying—"

"If this is the safest place for you, then you're staying here."

"Of course," I gasped dramatically. "But Daniel, on the other hand, seems to have free rein to go wherever he wants, so—"

"Are you trying to kick me out?" Daniel asked dubiously. He looked at Pop. "Is that what she's doing?"

"Seems so," Pop confirmed.

"What the fuck, Rosemary?"

Leaning back in my chair, I shrugged my shoulders. "Just saying, the hypocrisy is *thick* around here."

"He's your mate," Pop said dryly. "Not some little boy you decided you were in love with because he got his hands on your boobs one time."

"Gary Maurice Whitlock," I hissed, my eyes widening. "First of all, how dare you? Second of all, he got his hand down my pants, for your information."

"Rosemary!" Pop barked, throwing the salt shaker at me. "The hell is the matter with you?"

I caught the salt as I laughed. "You started it!"

"And you took it and ran so far across the damn line I can't even see the line anymore."

"Don't dish it if you can't take it," I replied primly, setting the salt carefully back in its place.

"I've lost my appetite," he grumbled, shoving his plate away.

"Not me." I shoved a huge pile of food into my mouth. When I looked up at Daniel, his expression was a mix of puzzlement and laughter. Like he couldn't quite understand what had just happened, but he was here for it.

I looked away.

I'd known before I said anything that it wasn't as if my pop would suddenly decide that Daniel couldn't stay at our house anymore, therefore backing my mate into a corner so he was forced to let me leave the property. With the way things had been going, he probably would've just agreed and left me behind *for my own good*. The idiot.

It wasn't as if I couldn't just leave on my own. I wasn't being held captive, for god's sake. My pop left his keys in his truck most of the time, and even if that wasn't available, I could've dragged my dirt bike out of the garage if I was desperate.

I could leave. Hell, I could fucking disappear if I wanted to. I had the skill and enough cash to get by for a very long time without anyone knowing where I was. If I thought that would help the situation I was in, I would've used it in a heartbeat. But it wouldn't.

Leaving the property when Daniel was so adamant that I stay there for my safety was more trouble than I was willing to deal with, especially since I didn't *need* to be somewhere else. Even if I wanted to slap him, and curse him, and beg him not to leave me behind again, I wouldn't, because we were linked forever now.

Daniel and I would spend the rest of our very long lives together. There was no way around it and no way out of it—not that I'd ever try to get out of it. Even if he seemed to be confused about how a mating bond should look, I wasn't.

I was his, and he was mine. The end.

"I'm going to take a shower," I said with a sigh as the now familiar tightening in my chest made another appearance. I'd known relief wouldn't last long, but I could've been happy with a few more hours of minimal symptoms. "Don't do the dishes, Pop. I'll clean up when I get back up."

"Gonna run the dishwasher while you're in there," he said, staring into his coffee.

"Joke's on you," I replied as I walked away. "I'm taking a cold shower."

Ten minutes later, Daniel had the audacity to slide back the curtain and climb into the shower behind me. I couldn't even pretend I was annoyed.

"I thought you were taking a cold shower," he said teasingly, sliding his hands from my ribs to my hips.

"Does my father know you just snuck in the shower with me?" I asked as his hands traveled slowly back up my belly to my breasts.

"He went to the grocery store," Daniel replied, pressing his lips against my shoulder. "We have the house to ourselves."

"Well, that was kind of him." My breath hitched as he pinched my nipples between his fingers.

"That's what I thought. Put your hands on the wall."

Reaching out blindly, I bent slightly and pressed the palms of my hands against the cool tile as Daniel nudged my feet apart with his own.

His lips disappeared from my shoulder, and his hands left my breasts, but before I could turn, I felt those same hands gripping my ass, pulling my cheeks apart.

I nearly lost my balance as he nudged my feet even wider and licked from my clit to my ass in one slow, luxurious motion.

"Fuck," I whimpered, arching my back to give him better access.

He ate like he was starving. Like he'd never had anything better. Like he didn't care about my pleasure at all because he was too caught up in his own. His beard rubbed at my thighs and brushed against my over-sensitized clit as he shoved his tongue inside me. His fingers dug into my ass cheeks, using them to position me exactly how he wanted.

I came, but he didn't let up. Groaning with pleasure, he continued, shoving his shoulder under me until I was practically sitting on his face so he could suck my clit into his mouth and worry it with his teeth.

My second orgasm wasn't even over before he rose to his feet behind me and thrust inside, one of his hands on my hip and the other wrapped around the front of my throat to hold me steady. My hands slipped on the tile, and I dug my fingertips into any crevice I could find.

I had never had anything like it before.

Completing the mating bond had been life-changing. It was overwhelming and exhilarating and wonderful.

This wasn't that.

As he fucked me in the shower, I felt transformed. Stronger than I'd ever been in my life. More powerful. Like I could do anything.

"Trying to get me kicked out of the house," Daniel whispered in my ear with a light laugh, his voice dark and raspy. "Good fucking luck with that, mate."

I let out a gasp as his hand tightened briefly on my throat and then fell away as he pulled back and then slammed inside me again. His hand shoved between my thighs, pinching my clit between his fingers as he continued thrusting. The wail that left my throat hurt like it had torn something loose inside me.

I barely noticed as he let go. I was trying so hard to keep my balance as my hands lost purchase on the tile and then found it again.

Seconds later, he was shuffling me out of the tub, carefully helping me step over the ledge while still locked inside me. At that point, I was beyond caring. As long as he was still inside me, we could go wherever he wanted.

Turned out, we weren't going far.

Gently, he lowered me to my knees so my hips were braced on the edge of the tub.

"Better, baby?" he asked softly, brushing my wet hair over one shoulder.

I nodded, letting my head fall forward. The shower was still on, and tiny droplets of water sprinkled against my face and neck as I braced my hands on the floor of the tub.

He kissed my jaw in acknowledgment, then leaned back. Cool air rushed over my skin as he slowly pulled out and then thrust back inside, his balls slapping against my clit. I widened my knees so it would happen again.

"That's it," he praised, running a hand down my spine.

I was gasping for air, desperate to pull it into my lungs.

Then his hand was between us, sliding along my lips that were stretched wide around him. I shivered as his thrusts slowed, my focus narrowed on that light touch that was so at odds with what he'd been doing. He dragged his fingers back and forth, back and forth, and then he was rimming my ass with them.

"Keep them wide," he ordered softly as my thighs tightened.

One finger pushed inside my ass, and every muscle in my body locked tight.

I thought it would hurt.

It didn't.

Moving slowly, he pulled his finger back out as he thrust his cock inside.

I was past the point of embarrassment or shame. The nerves in my body screamed with pleasure as he pulled his cock back and thrust his finger back in.

His cock slid back in, and his finger back out.

Then there were two fingers. Pushing, pushing, pushing. So slow and yet so overwhelming. The pressure was so intense that I could feel my jaw aching from clenching it so hard.

My arms trembled.

His fingers and cock rubbed against each other through my walls for just a moment as he moved in counterpoint, and I jerked at the sensation. By the third time it happened, I was waiting for it. Leaning into it. Quietly begging for it.

I was pretty sure I was sobbing.

And then he really started to move, and I screamed, the orgasm hitting so hard that my vision went dark.

I was still coming when his fingers pulled out of me completely, and his hand slapped down beside mine as he curled his body over me. His other arm pressed against my mouth, and I opened, sucking the small wound into my mouth as the taste of him intensified every single sensation.

The feeling of his teeth biting into my neck was almost secondary. I was swimming in such a sea of sensation.

By the time I came down, I was draped over the edge of the tub, my forehead resting on my bent arm.

"So fucking beautiful," Daniel murmured against

the skin on my back as he kissed his way down my spine.

I felt so empty when he pulled out that I nearly whimpered. Moving slowly, I let him help me back into the shower, which had grown cold, so he could quickly rinse us off. I wasn't much help. Every limb felt like it weighed a thousand pounds as Daniel helped me back out of the shower and dried us off. Without a word, he looped my arms around his neck and once I'd latched on, grabbed the backs of my thighs so I'd wrap my legs around his waist.

He carried me naked to my room and tucked me firmly beneath the sheets with a kiss to my forehead. As I let my eyes drift closed, he left the room, came back to get dressed, and then left again. Seconds later, I could hear him just a wall away, cleaning up the bathroom floor where we'd left a huge puddle of water.

Then, nothing.

When I woke up alone, I panicked.

Jumping out of bed, I hurriedly threw on whatever clothes I could find, not even bothering with a bra. He wasn't in bed with me. Why wasn't he in bed with me?

I'd fallen asleep thinking that he was just cleaning up the evidence of our debauchery before climbing in with me. Instead, Daniel had left me naked and alone.

My heartbeat thundered in my ears as I lunged for the door to my room, throwing it open so hard that it banged loudly against the wall. The house was so quiet that I knew no one was inside. Not even Thunder's snores broke the silence.

Holding back a sob, I raced through the kitchen and out the back door, searching for him. The barn was dark. The yard was empty. The door to the smaller shop was closed and locked, and the chickens weren't making the noises they made when someone was near their coop. Ignoring the wet ground, I jogged around the house, searching everywhere.

I came to a stumbling stop when I reached the edge of the front porch.

Pop was sitting in his wheelchair, Thunder lying beside him, and Daniel was on his knees in the flower bed, painting the new lattice he'd installed beneath the porch.

"Hey, sleepyhead," Pop called. "You get dressed in the dark?"

My cheeks burned as Daniel's gaze met mine, and I quickly looked away and down at what I was wearing.

The pajama pants I'd thrown on were zigzagging stripes of lime green and neon orange. The socks—purple. And my shirt was a button-down that Aunt Halle had bought me that I'd never worn before, because I generally didn't have any reason to wear blouses, and it reminded me of the color of baby poop.

"I, uh..." I stuttered. "How long have I been asleep?"

"A couple of hours," Daniel replied, pushing to his feet. "Gary came back about half an hour after you fell asleep, so we decided to get this done after we'd put the groceries away."

"Well, aren't you helpful?" I asked snarkily.

I wasn't sure why I'd said it or even why I'd used that tone. I wasn't mad at him.

"You're grouchy when you wake up," he said, his lips twitching like he was trying not to laugh. "Good to know."

"I am not," I argued as the panic in my chest started to calm.

I was stiff as a board when he reached for me, his thumb gently tracing the curve of my cheek. "I wouldn't leave without letting you know first."

I nodded, though I found that hard to believe. Daniel seemed to think he knew what was best for both of us, and if he thought that leaving without telling me was best, he'd do it.

"You want to help me finish this up?" he asked, jerking his head toward the porch.

"It looks so much better," I replied grudgingly as I walked over to inspect his work. The lattice under the porch had been broken for months. It had begun slowly rotting and was just soft enough that when Thunder had been chasing some animal that ran through the holes but hadn't been agile enough to stop in time, he'd crashed right through it and gotten stuck. We'd then had to widen the hole just to get him free.

I looked up at him. "This is all your fault, you know."

"Leave poor Thunder alone," Pop ordered, leaning down to pet his head. "He doesn't get around like he used to."

"He was moving fast enough to break through the dang lattice," I countered, picking up one of the paintbrushes. "I think he's playing you."

Thunder lifted his head off the porch, his sad eyes looking me over, then dropped it back down.

"You're such a con artist," I accused, laughing.

He just slowly closed his eyes like he couldn't be bothered.

"If I would've known you'd be doin' projects around the property," my pop said as he watched Daniel and me paint, "I would've let you start havin' boys over a whole lot sooner."

I glanced at Daniel, who was studiously staring at the lattice. He had to be thinking the same thing I was —if my father had any idea what we'd done in the bathroom, he would've shot Daniel in the ass as he chased him off the property.

"I fix stuff all the time," I argued, trying to ignore the heat in my cheeks. "Ian and I mowed and cleared all the brush at the end of summer. Plus, I've swept off this porch and the patio out back like fourteen times since then, *and* I pressure-washed them too."

"But you didn't fix my lattice," Pop pointed out with a small chuckle.

I grinned at him. "Ass."

"Brat," he shot back, still smiling.

I glanced at Daniel. "Is it strange when he calls you a boy?" I joked with a snicker.

"Just a bit," Daniel replied dryly, shooting a look at my dad.

"To be fair," my dad said. "The boys she brought over before were *boys*."

"Well, this one isn't," I reminded him. "He's older than dirt."

"Offensive," Daniel sputtered, pushing just hard enough on my shoulder that I almost lost my balance.

"Sorry, not dirt. Just older than telephones and cars and airplanes and Jell-O and sneakers and—"

"No, I'm not," he argued, flicking paint at me. "All of those were invented before I was born."

"Seriously?" I asked in surprise.

"Okay, a couple of them were."

I giggled and then made the mistake of looking at his disgruntled expression and laughed even harder.

His eyes widened, and before I could dodge him, he'd reached out and drew a wide line of white paint down the front of my chest.

"Hey," I complained, lunging for him. I barely made contact with the sleeve of his shirt, but his biceps and elbow got the same treatment as my chest.

"Actin' like a couple of teenagers," my dad announced as he turned his wheelchair and went back into the house.

I scrambled to my feet as Daniel stared at the paint on his arm. He dodged quicker than I expected when I swiped at his face.

"I don't think you want to do this," he warned as he rose.

"You started it."

"That seems to be your go-to response, huh?" he said as he stalked me through the yard.

"I don't know what you mean," I replied loftily, lowering my center of gravity a little as I moved around his car.

"That was your excuse when you were talking at the breakfast table about some kid who got his hand down your pants," he reminded me.

"Jealous?" I taunted.

The grin on his face could only be described as wicked.

"Baby, I doubt he had his fingers in your ass."

My mouth dropped open in shock.

"And he sure as fuck didn't taste your blood. So, no, I'm not jealous."

"You sound jealous," I wheedled, still carefully backing away.

"There's nothing to be jealous of," he said easily, his arm shooting out to put a matching stripe of paint down my arm. "You're mine."

"Maybe he was better with his hands," I countered, swinging my brush so little droplets splattered the front of his shirt. "Did you think of that?"

His laugh was deep and throaty and delicious.

"There's no fucking way," he replied. "But keep it up, mate. I don't mind proving you wrong."

I saw the change in the way he was distributing his weight a second before he lunged, and I was already spinning out of his reach. Using the car as a barrier, I ran like hell around the back of it and toward the backyard. I could hear him behind me, laughing under his breath, and I screeched when I felt his fingers or the brush against the small of my back.

"You'll never outrun me," he warned as I jumped over a pile of rocks that Seamus had built for his RC cars.

"I don't have to outrun you," I panted, twisting toward the barn. "I just have to outthink you."

I cut the corner into the barn door and grinned when I heard him bang his shoulder into the doorway, and then I was climbing like my life depended on it. There was a series of moves that Ian and I had developed over the years. Hopping onto the workbench along the wall, I ran across it, praying that I didn't step on anything sharp, and then leaped for the top of an old metal cabinet. It swayed under my weight, but I didn't stop to steady it. I just kept going, tossing the paintbrush ahead of me before jumping just high enough that my gut slammed into the floor of the loft. As soon as I caught the board that was a little less than an arm's length from the edge with my fingertips, I pulled my lower half to safety.

When I'd recovered the paintbrush—that was now absolutely filthy—and spun around, Daniel was standing just inside the doors, staring.

"What the fuck was that?"

"What?" I asked breathlessly, unable to keep the huge grin off my face.

"You're like a fucking cat."

"You could try to follow me," I told him, crossing my legs and bracing my elbows on them. "But the cabinet would never hold your weight. Or, you know, you could use the ladder." I nodded toward it. "But I'd probably jump down before you made it up here."

He moved further into the barn, his head tipping back to keep me in sight.

"I'm done," he announced, dropping the paintbrush. "Come back down."

"Truce?"

"Truce," he confirmed.

Leaning forward, I dropped my own paintbrush over the ledge. It landed with a smack in the hard-packed dirt.

Climbing to my feet, I grimaced. "I'm not cleaning those."

"I'll buy new ones," he replied. "Wait, don't—"

But I was already falling through the air. My feet hit the dirt, and I dug my toes in, knees bent to soften the landing, and my arms outstretched in case I'd overcompensated on the trajectory. It hadn't happened since I was fourteen, but there was always a risk, and I didn't feel like getting a face full of dirt.

CHAPTER 8
DANIEL

My heart was in my throat as my mate jumped barefoot off the loft in the barn, her tangled hair flowing like a ribbon behind her. The moment her feet touched the ground, I moved forward on instinct, pulling her against me.

She knew what she was doing—she'd made that clear by the way she'd easily used the different pieces of furniture like a staircase—but it only took one small miscalculation to land wrong when jumping off something so high. Humans were so fucking fragile.

"You're barefoot," I reminded her, breathing in the scent of her hair.

"You're wearing a gray shirt," she replied.

I pulled back to look at her.

"I thought we were stating the obvious. You've got a beard. My shirt is the color of baby poop. You—"

"Very funny," I shot back as she pulled away.

"I've been running barefoot over this property since I could walk," she informed me, leading me out of the barn. "We should clean up the paint."

"I'll grab the brushes." Spinning on my heel, I walked back and grabbed the filthy brushes off the dirt floor. I'd wash them so we wouldn't have to throw them away.

When I made my way back to her, she grabbed my empty hand like she'd done it a million times before and towed me toward the front of the house. I couldn't figure Rosemary Whitlock out.

Half the time, I felt her glaring at me like she was going to stab me, and half the time she treated me like we were an old mated couple. She'd leaned into the mating heat like it was the most natural thing in the world, nothing to be nervous about, but she'd also put up some kind of wall between us. It was like she was giving the appearance of letting me in, but only to a point.

I looked down at her bare toes.

"Anything could be on the ground out here," I chastised her. "Especially in the barn."

Rosemary just shrugged. "I'm up to date on my tetanus vaccine. Stepping on something sharp isn't going to kill me."

"Maybe not, but it'll hurt like hell."

I couldn't read her expression as she glanced at me.

"My brother lost one of his toes by dropping an axe on it," I told her, struggling to push past whatever the weird look was.

"Oh," she breathed, her eyes widening. "Gnarly."

"It wasn't pretty."

"And Vampires don't regrow shit," she pointed out, like I was unaware of that fact.

"Neither do humans."

"Does it affect his balance?" she asked, letting go of

my hand to crouch down so she could put the lid on the paint can.

"Let me do that," I ordered, taking it from her. "No, it didn't affect his balance. Looked pretty weird, though."

"I bet. No sandals for him."

I laughed, rising to my feet. "It didn't seem to bother him much. He lost it when we were kids."

"Multiple lifetimes with a missing toe," she mused as she led me up the porch steps. "It's a cruel world."

"I'm goin' to Dalton's for dinner," Gary announced as we stepped inside the house. "You two are on your own."

"I want to go," Rosemary gasped.

"Too bad. You weren't invited."

"Bullshit!"

"Stay here," her dad ordered dryly. "There's plenty of food in the fridge."

"I'm calling Aunt Halle," Rosemary replied, rolling her eyes as Gary shuffled past us. "Give me that."

She practically tore his folded wheelchair out of his hands and stomped out of the house.

"See you in a bit," Gary nodded to me before leaving, the old bulldog following at his heels.

I could hear them arguing outside, but I stayed just inside the house. I knew Rosemary was getting more frustrated by the hour that she was stuck on the property, but I was glad that her father and I agreed that it was the safest place for her. Even if by some chance the human militia discovered it existed, there were so many defensible positions that we could keep them at bay until reinforcements arrived. Gary had planned his home with purpose.

"Do you cook?" Rosemary asked as she sailed back into the house, swinging the door shut behind her.

"I can," I replied, following her into the kitchen.

"Me too." She stopped in the middle of the kitchen and huffed in annoyance. "At least we'll never starve."

"What do you want?" I asked, moving toward her.

"Grilled cheese," she stated firmly. "And homemade tomato soup."

"Sounds good," I murmured as she stomped to the fridge.

"Wait a second," she said, looking up at me. "Where's your blood?"

I looked down at my body.

"Very funny," she said, rolling her eyes. "Didn't you bring blood back with you? I mean, you weren't planning to complete the bond, right?"

"It's in a cooler in the car," I replied with a grimace. After we'd completed the bond, I'd completely forgotten it was there. Once a Vampire was mated, donor blood was no longer an option. It would keep us alive, barely, but only our mate's blood could keep us healthy.

I hadn't even thought about the blood I'd left in the car. There was a chance it was still cold, but more likely I'd just wasted hundreds of dollars.

"Whoops."

"I forgot about it," I said, taking the items she handed me as she searched through the fridge.

"Easy to do. It's not like you need it now."

She said it so easily that I was reminded again of how lucky I was that my mate understood the ins and outs of the mating bond. There was no tiptoeing or trying to explain the finer points in a way that wouldn't make a human woman run screaming into the night. Rosemary wasn't surprised by any of it.

"My brother Beau went back to donor blood very briefly after he and his mate completed the bond," I told her as I sliced cheese. "She freaked out when she found him gray and passed out on the couch."

"Why the hell would he do that?" Rosemary asked in surprise, her mouth dropping open. "That doesn't work."

"He was trying to respect her wishes." I shrugged my shoulders. "Not sure what was going on with them —I didn't ask—but they clearly weren't sharing blood."

"What a bitch," she replied, shaking her head.

I let out a huff of laughter.

"What?" she asked. "That's a shitty thing to do."

"It's her choice," I reminded my mate. "Her body."

"Okay," she conceded. "That's true. Still, yikes. That must've been hard for both of them. It's not like she was comfortable withholding the exchange."

"When she found him, she cut open her wrist so he'd feed—"

Rosemary shook her head in exasperation.

"She meant well," I said with a smile. "But my father had to stitch her up. She just expected it to close on its own if Beau licked it or something."

She laughed. "Not quite."

I smiled back. Gods, she was lovely.

"I can't imagine getting saddled with a mate—"

"Hey, thanks," I cut in.

Rosemary laughed. "*Getting saddled with a mate* who was completely clueless. Like everything must seem so overwhelming and strange."

"I imagine so," I agreed.

"Like the biting," Rosemary continued, glancing my way. "What if I didn't know that I needed your blood too? I'd just be in a suspended state of animation for God knew how long? Sounds like hell."

"A Vampire would have to be raised by humans or something not to know that," I pointed out.

"Fair enough," she agreed. "But *still.* The heat and the forever and all of it? What a mindfuck for a human expecting to live like eighty years."

"It's an adjustment," I agreed. "Both my sisters-in-law struggled for a while."

"With good reason," she said, swiping the cheese I'd cut so she could assemble the sandwiches on the stove. "Even I was shocked, and I know what it's all about."

"You seemed to accept it pretty quickly," I replied, leaning against the counter to watch her.

"Well, yeah." She kept her eyes on the stove as she answered. "Once we met, I knew it was inevitable. Fighting it would just suck for both of us. What's the point?"

I hummed in agreement.

"It's different for me anyway," she said softly.

"How so?"

"I never thought I'd live long enough to see my cousins mated or meet their children or any of that," she said, staring at the grilled cheese. Her voice grew husky. "Most of the people I love are immortal or *will* be."

"But not your pop," I replied quietly.

"But not my pop," she confirmed, finally looking at me. "But I always knew I'd outlive him." She let out a huff of pained laughter. "I mean, I hope we're both really old when it happens, but yeah. He was fifteen years older than my mom when they met, so he was over forty when I came along. You've seen him. He's not exactly aging gracefully."

"You've still got a lot of time," I assured her.

"I know." She swallowed hard. "Plus, he'll be with my mom when he goes, and I know he's looking forward to that." She wrinkled her nose. "Okay, that sounded morbid, but you know what I mean. It's not like he'll be alone."

"Yeah." Reaching out, I let my hand slide down her back. I couldn't imagine knowing that I would live forever, Gods willing, but I'd only have another twenty years with my parents if I were lucky. Rosemary would live most of her life without her parents. The first forty years would eventually be just a blip.

Grief hit me suddenly. I'd had Zeke for over a hundred years, and that still hadn't felt like enough. And I hadn't had to watch him grow old, his body slowly failing, his memory not quite what it used to be.

I'd never really taken the time to think about the sacrifice that human mates made when they tied their lives to ours. The benefits were too large to fully explain, but the expense was almost inconceivable. They had to watch as all the people they knew in their previous life died one by one.

Moving to her back, I wrapped my arms around Rosemary's waist and pressed my lips to the side of her neck.

"I'm good," she said with assurance, patting my hand. "Really. I'm fine."

"We can live here if you want," I said, watching as

she flipped the grilled cheese and stirred the soup. "Instead of my parents' property."

"You're sweet," she said, turning her head to brush her lips over mine. "But this house isn't big enough. Once we start having kids, it would feel like a clown car."

My stomach swooped at the thought of having children.

"Then we'll add on. Or build another house," I pressed. "There's plenty of land."

"Maybe," she said, like she was actually imagining it. "We'd have to clear some trees."

"I think we could manage that."

"Dinner's done," she announced, pulling away from me. "It's not fancy, but wait until you taste the soup. It's my mom's recipe."

"Smells good."

The couple of feet separating us felt like too much, especially after talking about the future that still wasn't promised. Rosemary let out a woof of surprise when I reached under her chair and scooted it closer.

I needed to figure out who was responsible for the attacks of Vampires so my mate would be safe. Every moment I stayed with Rosemary, making dinner and chasing her around, was another moment when they were making plans, regrouping, and potentially tracking her down. It put me in a terrible position, because I knew where I wanted to be—with her—but I *needed* to be with my brothers investigating the threat.

I couldn't just ignore that it was out there. The knowledge that they could find Rosemary at any time was like a constant drum beating in the back of my head, impossible to ignore for long.

"This was always a comfort food when I was little," Rosemary said, taking a bite of her sandwich. She closed her eyes as she chewed. "My mom made it on my first day of school, after doctor appointments, you know, that kind of thing."

"For good reason," I replied. I hadn't paid close attention to how she'd made the soup beyond noticing a home-canned jar of tomatoes, but it was excellent.

"I know, right?" she said with a small laugh. "It hits the spot every time."

"Did you spend most of your time with your mom?" I asked, watching as she dunked the corner of her sandwich into the steaming soup.

"Yeah, my dad didn't retire until she was pretty sick," she replied. "He was only home sporadically before that. Just long enough to get used to him again, really."

"It must've been an adjustment when he was suddenly home all the time."

"I loved it," she said, grinning. "Having both of them home all the time was my dream. I hated going to school. I begged them to homeschool me."

"They told you no, huh?"

She nodded. "Their excuse was that neither of them was qualified to teach me, but I think they just wanted the alone time."

I laughed.

"I don't blame them. They never really went on dates or anything," she said with a smile. "If I wasn't in school, it was always the three of us. I can probably count on one hand the number of times I had a babysitter, and that was usually just Aunt Halle."

"It was the same with us," I replied, remembering

those times when my brothers and I were young. "But worse because we lived in a one-room house."

"Nooo," Rosemary moaned with a laugh.

"We were sent outside to play a lot," I replied ruefully. "But my parents didn't really let us go to other houses. It was different back then."

"Well, no one knew what you were," she said reasonably. "Imagine if you fell and should've been hurt but weren't. People would've lost their minds."

"Exactly."

"What was it like?" she asked, bracing her elbow on the table so she could rest her cheek on her palm. "When you guys went public."

"Mayhem," I answered honestly. "Humans were suspicious of anyone, usually other humans. It wasn't as if they'd noticed us before, so I was never sure why they thought they'd pick us out of a crowd once they knew we existed."

"People are idiots."

"They were afraid of what they didn't understand."

"So...assholes?"

"Some of them," I agreed. "And then you had the usual suspects. The ones who acted like they'd known all along that we were out there. The ones who pretended like they didn't care, even though they clearly did. The groupies. The protestors."

"But it eventually calmed down," she said as if asking for confirmation.

"When we didn't jump out of the woodwork and start kidnapping virgins, yes. It took a while, though."

"That myth always cracked me up," Rosemary said, sitting back up. "Why would anyone want a virgin? Like, why is the ideal someone who hasn't done something before? Logically—and for literally anything else—everyone would prefer a partner who had experience."

"Purity," I replied.

She made a gagging noise.

"I'm not saying I agree with it," I said, taking another bite. "But that was the culture when I was young. A hymen was very prized by human men."

"But not Vampires?"

"I think Vampires have always been a bit more pragmatic, at least the ones I've known. A virgin's first time is always a little shocking. Add in the mating bond and exchanging blood? That seems like a lot to deal with in one go."

Rosemary chuckled. "Fair point."

"My first time was with a widow," I mentioned, enjoying the way her head jerked in my direction.

"Do tell," she said dryly.

"She was pretty."

She moved her hand in a circle, gesturing for me to keep going.

"She had blonde hair."

"A pretty blonde widow," Rosemary murmured. "That's all you remember?"

"Of course not."

"Well?"

"She had two sons. One was around six and the other was four. They were napping inside, and we did it against the outside of the house."

She grinned.

"She was very concerned about pregnancy," I said dryly, making her cackle.

"All good there," Rosemary commented. Vampires could only procreate with their mates.

"It was over far more quickly than either of us anticipated," I joked, my cheeks flushing at the memory. "Which was a good thing since her younger son started hollering out the front door before I'd even buttoned my trousers back up."

"I'm sure she didn't think it was a good thing," Rosemary countered.

"She did not," I agreed. "But I made it up to her later."

"I bet you did."

It was the first time I'd thought of Ella in more years than I could count. She'd been quiet and petite, and I'd been more than surprised when she'd let me into her bed. Years after we parted ways, I'd seen her at a distance, her grown son helping her down the street. She'd never remarried. She hadn't needed to. Her dead husband had left her enough to get by on, and from what I remembered of the man, I knew why she hadn't married a second time.

"Did you love her?" Rosemary asked quietly.

"No." The answer was instant and firm. "But I liked her. She was a sweet woman."

"I'd tell you about my first time," Rosemary said dryly. "But I think you'd have a different reaction."

"Oh, yeah? Why's that?"

"Because mine is still alive," she joked, raising her eyebrows. "It's much easier to feel glad that you had a good experience knowing that the other woman is dead now."

"How do you know she's dead?" I asked innocently.

Rosemary froze.

"I'm fucking with you," I assured her, smiling. "She was dead before your grandparents were born."

"Well, mine isn't," she said primly, rising from her seat. "I saw him at the store last year."

"Oh, yeah?" I asked, playing along as I leaned back in my chair. "Did you have the burning desire for another round?"

"I didn't have a burning desire the first time," she replied, rinsing her dishes. "I just wanted to know what all the fuss was about."

"I'm sure that went well."

"Two teenagers with no clue what they're doing but a basic understanding of anatomy went pretty much as you'd imagine," she replied, turning to face me. "But I figured out what worked eventually."

"With the same boy?"

"Oh, hell no. He sucked. I found someone who knew what they were doing." She pointed to my dishes. "Are you done?"

"I can clean them," I assured her as I rose and took them to the sink. "So there's no boyfriend I have to worry about showing up here, right?"

She scoffed, leaning against the counter beside me. "It's a little late for that question, isn't it?"

"I didn't really think about it before," I confessed. It was only the mention of her seeing an old boyfriend at the market that had reminded me that she had an entire life before we met, and that life included sexual partners.

"No boyfriend," she replied. "I mean, I've *had* boyfriends, but no one current. With my job, I'm never in one place very long."

"We can travel," I told her as I washed my dishes

and then hers. "If you want to. We don't have to stay in one place if you'd rather—"

"I liked my *job*," she corrected. "I don't mind staying in one place, assuming I can *leave my house*."

"This won't last forever," I reminded her. "Just until we know you're safe."

"It could be years before we stop them," she countered in frustration. "Do you really think that I'm going to stay on this property for *years*?"

"It won't be years."

"It's already *been* years."

"It's been less than a year since we lost Zeke," I argued, grabbing a towel. "Give us a minute to—"

"Oh, because the Bouchers are going to sweep in and fix everything, right?" she said, throwing her hands in the air. "Uncle Dalton and my pop have been searching for these guys for a lot longer than you, and they still barely have anything."

"I realize that."

"What makes you think that you're going to find things out so much faster?"

"Well, for one, we won't be using mortal humans as *bait*," I bit out, my hackles rising.

"Then what was Charlie?" she snapped back.

"Charlie is immortal." I tossed the towel back onto the counter.

Rosemary's mouth snapped shut, and her head jerked back in shock. "What?"

"He's mated. He's no longer mortal."

"But Zeke—"

"Is dead," I said flatly. "They completed the bond before he was killed."

Rosemary stared at me, her eyes growing glassy. "Oh, man. Poor Charlie."

I nodded. "Lucy tethers him here. For now, at least."

"Lucy is his sister, right? Ambrose's mate?"

"Yes. When we went searching for Charlie after we lost Zeke, we found Lucy."

"I can't believe he's..." She paused. "He seemed okay. He—I talked to him. He introduced himself."

"He struggles," I replied. "Obviously."

"I've never met someone who'd lost their mate before."

"They usually don't live long afterward."

"I know. But Charlie, he's choosing to stay?"

"Yes."

"Incredible." She shook her head. "How fucking sad. I can't even imagine it. I mean, I don't even like you that much, but I don't know if—"

"Hey," I protested, yanking her toward me. I didn't want to hear the end of her sentence.

"Fine, I like you a little," she conceded, smiling. "So don't die, okay?"

"I'm not going anywhere," I promised.

She continued to smile, but her gaze shifted away from mine. "Let's finish cleaning up."

I washed, and she dried the pans, and then we made our way outside and sat down on the sofa on the back patio. The night was clear enough that the stars were easily visible between the clouds, and I felt my body relaxing against the cushions. It was cold outside, but Rosemary seemed comfortable enough pressed up against me, and I liked being able to hear everything going on around us.

The walls of the house muffled a lot of the sound, and I found myself listening more intently than I usually needed to, trying to be sure that there wasn't anyone getting close to the house. There wasn't anyone around for a pretty good distance, and being there reminded me of home. The closer you got to town and neighbors, the harder it was to filter out the noises that were normal and those you had to be aware of. I'd spent my entire life doing it, and it was second nature, but that didn't mean I didn't notice and enjoy when I didn't have to do it.

"I didn't expect to start a family so soon," Rosemary said after she'd been quiet for a long time.

"We can wait." I kissed the top of her head.

"Once we cemented the bond, we only have ten years," she countered softly. "If we don't want to have babies one after the other, we'll have to start soon."

"We don't have to think about it yet."

"But if we wait until all of this is over," she argued. "We might miss our chance."

"We'll figure it out before it becomes an issue."

"You don't know that."

Instead of arguing with her anymore, I held my tongue. I didn't want to waste one of the only times we'd been alone going back and forth about it.

I wanted to hold my mate in my arms and stare at the stars. I'd been waiting my whole life for that moment.

"I should probably go back to school," she said after a little while.

"Why's that?"

"Well, I know that Uncle Dalton won't let me work for him in the field anymore," she replied tiredly. "And since I don't want to work for another security company, I should probably learn a new skill."

"What do you think you'd like to do?" I asked, wondering what I would do now that I could no longer work for Vampire Command. It didn't really matter. I was wealthy enough that neither of us ever had to work again if we didn't want to.

Rosemary sighed. She wasn't going to be content without a purpose, and I understood the feeling.

"Probably something with computers," she said finally. "I'd like to continue working for Strike if possible. Filing and answering phones isn't really my jam, and I don't want to work with money. But I could do IT shit."

"Is that a formal position?" I asked.

"IT shitter," she replied, nodding. "Very lucrative."

"We'll figure it out, baby," I assured her. "We have time."

"You keep saying that."

"Because it's true."

I *felt* the moment that the reality of just how much time stretched out before her finally sank in. Her body seemed to sink into mine, going boneless against me.

"Shit," she whispered.

CHAPTER 9
ROSEMARY

I liked a plan. I liked executing that plan well. I liked making new plans once I'd completed the old ones. I liked structure. Predictability. I liked knowing where I'd be, when I'd be there, how I'd get there, and what steps I needed to take.

So waiting around my pop's place for something to happen was basically torture.

When Daniel had reminded me that I had *time* to figure out what I wanted to do with my life, it had taken a moment for his words to sink in fully. It wasn't just a platitude or a way to keep me from worrying. He'd meant it. The amount that stretched out before me was almost hard to comprehend.

I'd lived my entire life with an end in sight. Sure, I'd assumed that I wouldn't die until I was old, barring any missions that went bad, but I'd always known, as everyone does, that there was an end date planned for me. Logically, I'd always understood that Uncle Dalton and Aunt Halle were different, but I'd never let myself imagine what that felt like.

It wasn't for me, so I'd pushed it out of my head.

Now, it seemed to be the only thing I could think about.

Daniel left again. And again. And again.

I would've thought that it would get easier because he came back every time, but it didn't. The panic and sorrow and pain seemed to be getting worse, not better, when he drove away.

I'd been reassuring myself since I was a child that I could get through anything, because nothing lasted forever. Dinner was gross? It only took fifteen minutes to eat, and then I was done. I couldn't go out to play until my parents woke up? I only had to wait an hour, and then the whole day stretched out before me. I didn't like my teacher? I only had her for one year. My arm needed to be set? It would only be a couple of minutes before the doctor was done. The mission I was on was miserable? A month, tops, and then I could leave the shithole behind.

I was tied up in some nasty-ass garage? I just needed to stay put until I heard something I could take back to Dalton.

It became a habit to break the tough times into bite-sized, accomplishable goals.

But when you had no idea how long something would last, it was harder to trick yourself into believing you could stick it out.

And the knowledge that Daniel could continue to leave me whenever he decided to, with no end in sight, made me feel like I was coming out of my skin.

For the rest of my very long life, assuming my immortality had come to fruition, I was tied to a mate that didn't behave like one.

I knew he was going to check on his family. I knew he would make it back in less than three hours. I knew that he was conscious of every minute we spent apart because the moment he got back, he found me and held me and stripped me bare as he whispered how much he hated being away from me.

But he kept doing it. Over and over until I thought I might lose my mind.

It became all I could think about.

He'd brought back a laptop after one of his trips home, and he spent hours on it, searching for something that he never quite explained. He didn't hide what he was doing, and he loved when I curled up next to him to read or watch TV while he worked, but the names he was researching meant nothing to me. I didn't know if they were Vampires or humans, potential victims or villains—and Daniel was so adept at giving roundabout answers that I usually didn't even realize that he hadn't actually answered me until later.

When he wasn't glued to the computer screen, Daniel teased and played and treated me like a queen. He was quick and funny, and he rarely took the bait when I was giving him shit. He had the filthiest mouth I'd ever heard. He knew exactly how to touch me. When we were together, there was nothing better, and as the days passed, I understood more and more how well we'd been made for each other.

But even when we were together, during what should've been the happiest period of my life, I was waiting for the moment he said he had to go again.

I couldn't shake it. Couldn't ignore it.

He timed his visits home randomly out of an abundance of caution, so I never knew when the bomb would drop. Some days it was before the sun rose. Other days, it was before dinner or right before bed. There was no way to know in advance, and I refused to ask because I wasn't sure if knowing would even help. Then, instead of being braced for it, I'd be counting the minutes until I knew he had to go.

No. He didn't *have* to go. He *chose* to.

It would be different if he didn't have a choice.

If he didn't have a choice, then it would've felt like we were in it together.

He was *choosing* to leave me, and I was in it alone.

I lay in bed, my hands clenched at my sides, staring at the ceiling as he moved around the room, getting dressed.

It had been more than two weeks since we'd found each other, and nothing had changed. I hadn't left the property once, and still, Daniel's family's investigation had turned up no more information than my uncle's. We were spinning our wheels.

"You should try to sleep in," he whispered, sitting down on the edge of the bed. "Then maybe by the time you wake up again, I'll be back."

"Yeah, maybe," I replied, keeping my expression neutral.

I wanted to scream at him. I wanted to ask why the separation was so easy for him. Why he had to go back every day, sometimes twice. I wanted to tell him that if he left, I was leaving too. That I couldn't stand being stuck in the house for one more stupid day. I wanted to remind him that he hadn't seen a single sign of the militia on his trips back and forth, and there was no reason for him to leave me behind. I wanted to ask if he was hiding me for some other reason, like maybe he just didn't want me to meet his family. Did I embarrass him somehow? Did he think they wouldn't like me?

The words caught in my throat until it felt like I was choking on them.

"I'll be back in a few hours, yeah?" he said, leaning down to brush his lips over mine. "Stay just like this." His hand slid under the blanket, smoothing over my bare belly and thigh. "I like imagining you curled up in bed, warm and naked."

"I'll see you soon," I replied.

He brushed his lips across mine one more time before getting to his feet. Then he left, closing the door quietly behind him. I listened as his footsteps faded away down the hall and flinched at the sound of the front door opening and closing.

Scrambling up from the bed, I threw on a T-shirt and a pair of shorts. The routine had become almost second nature, and I knew I only had about two minutes before his car disappeared. By that time, I'd locked myself in the bathroom and was on my knees, heaving into the toilet.

It was always worse when he left in the mornings, because there was nothing to throw up. It was just fifteen minutes of dry heaving until my stomach settled. Then, I had approximately eight minutes to take a quick shower before the body aches kicked in. After that, it was a crapshoot. Those two symptoms of the mating heat were easy to predict, but the panic and paranoia and sweating and racing heart were a little more choose-your-own-adventure. I was never sure which way things would go, or in which order.

My pop was waiting outside the bathroom when I finished. He handed me two gummies that I immediately swallowed, then took my hand gently as he walked us into the kitchen. On the days when luck was on my side, I was high before the body aches set in.

That day wasn't a lucky one.

"You need protein," he said as my jaw clenched, and I gripped the edge of the table. "Carbs and fats, too, but protein is most important."

"I'm not hungry," I countered through my teeth, staring at the salt and pepper shaker.

"I'm not askin'," he replied firmly, setting down a plate of eggs and bacon in front of me.

"I'm just going to throw them up."

"Maybe not."

I let out a huff of disbelieving laughter and stuffed a piece of bacon into my mouth.

"Finish that entire plate," he ordered. "Thunder! Let's go outside, boy."

I struggled to choke down the food once they were outside. I knew he was right—I needed the calories—but the food tasted like ash in my mouth.

I was losing weight. Not a lot, and it wasn't super noticeable, unless you knew me very well. My shirts hung a little looser, my jeans had a gap in the waist that wasn't there before, and my collarbone was just a little more prominent. I was losing muscle mass that I'd worked for years to gain.

I was throwing up too much, and even when my stomach settled, I had very little appetite.

Pop had noticed. Daniel hadn't.

I couldn't fault him for it. He had intimate knowledge of my body, but it had only been weeks since we met. There was no way that he could've known that the only time my weight fluctuated normally was when I'd put on more muscle or I was sick. He didn't realize that my cheekbones shouldn't have hollows beneath them.

Pop noticed everything—that was what came from a career in intelligence and then years of watching the love of his life waste away. He clocked the changes instantly, and they were impossible for him to ignore.

My phone began ringing where I'd put it on the counter and forgotten about it, and I nearly jumped out of my skin in surprise. I looked at it for a long moment, wondering if it was worth getting up for, but when it continued ringing, I got to my feet with a groan. Everything hurt.

Aunt Halle called every day, always when Daniel was gone, always when Pop was out of the room.

Like I wouldn't realize that he was telling her when to reach out.

"I'm fine," I answered, walking toward the living room. "Getting ready to watch a movie."

"You sound like crap," she argued. "Did Gary give you—"

"Yes, I'm high. No, it's not touching it."

"Maybe you need more."

"If I have any more, I'm going to feel like shit *while* I'm drooling like a baby."

"It should be taking the edge off," she fretted. "It always does for me when Dalton has to go away for a day."

"Maybe it is," I replied. What a scary thought. How much worse would it be if my pop wasn't dosing me? "Why is it still this bad? I thought once we completed the bond, the symptoms would get better."

"They should be," Aunt Halle replied. "Have you noticed any difference?"

"It's worse," I complained as I curled up like a shrimp on the couch.

"That doesn't make any sense."

"Reassuring," I grumbled, pulling a crocheted blanket off the back of the couch so it would stop digging into my hip.

"Everyone is different," she reminded me quickly. "And it's not all sunshine and rainbows right now. Your body is probably reacting to that. Your mind and your emotions and your body all work together, you know. If you're anxious, of course you'd feel worse."

"Right."

"Do you want me to come over?" she asked.

"What, so you could watch me lie on the couch all day? No, I'm fine."

"You really don't sound fine."

"This is the best I'll sound for the next few hours," I told her.

I wasn't joking. The panic hadn't set in yet, but I knew it would. It always did.

"How long has he been gone?" she asked sympathetically.

"About twenty minutes."

"So three more hours?"

"Maybe a little less."

"I don't like this," she said sharply. "I don't like this at all."

"I can handle anything for three hours."

"You shouldn't have to," she argued. "I'm going to talk to Dalton about this—"

"Don't you dare," I snapped in horror, lifting my head from the couch.

"Daniel should know better than this," she continued. "How did no one teach him his responsibilities to his mate? I know his parents, and it just doesn't make sense. Maybe if Dalton spoke to him."

"Don't, Aunt Halle," I warned. "Leave it alone."

"He must be in pain too," she retorted. "And the human mate's symptoms are even worse than the Vampire's, so how is he just—"

"Maybe he's not in pain," I countered, voicing the thought that had been whirling through my mind for days.

"That's not possible."

"He's leaving every day, and it doesn't seem to have any adverse effects," I told her quietly. "He comes back completely fine. So maybe he doesn't think that it hurts me because it doesn't hurt him."

"I doubt that's true."

"Either way," I replied, willing to let it go. "He's gone for the next few hours, so I'm going to lie here in my misery. Want me to call you later?"

"Yeah, do," she said with a sigh.

I lay there for a while, staring into the empty fireplace. Intellectually, I knew the house was cool. Outside, it was sprinkling rain, and the wind was making branches from the willow tree on the side of the house clack against the siding, but it felt like the hottest day of summer beneath my skin.

Rising, I went to find my pop and Thunder. Misery loves company and all that.

I was so sick of everything. Sick of the panic and the pain and Daniel and the house and my own weakness.

"How ya doing?" Pop asked as I joined him on the patio.

"Why are you sitting out here in the rain?" I asked,

raising my arms to catch the droplets. I was surprised they didn't sizzle when they made contact.

"This ain't rain," he said with a scoff.

"You should have a coat on."

"Worry about yourself," he retorted.

"Oh, I'm doing that too," I said, shaking my head. "If I'd known mating heat was like this, I probably would've hesitated at least a little."

Pop chuckled. "No, you wouldn't."

"I thought it would be easier," I blurted out. "Uncle Dalton and Aunt Halle—"

"Dalton and Halle fought their own battles before you knew your letters," Pop interrupted. "Just because you've always known them settled doesn't mean they didn't fight to get to that point."

"Really?" From the stories Aunt Halle had told me, their bond had been rainbows and butterflies from the beginning.

"Of course," Pop said in surprise. "No relationship is perfect, Flower. Mating bonds are more difficult because you're not getting to know someone in order to decide whether you want to spend your life with them. That decision has been made for you already. It's all backward."

"You like Daniel, right?"

"Sure, I do." He looked at me closely. "Seems to worship the ground you walk on. Protective. Polite. Loves his family. Why?"

"Just asking."

"The more important question is if *you* like him."

"I..." I paused, trying to find the words. "Yes. I *adore* him. He's just so..."

Pop watched me expectantly.

"I don't know if it's the same for him," I sputtered out finally.

Pop scoffed. "That Vampire would happily die for you, Rosemary."

"He keeps leaving," I argued. "He leaves and—" I gagged and had to take a deep breath, in through my nose and out through my mouth. Great, the nausea was back. "He makes me feel like this. He won't take me with him, but he insists on going every day. What am I supposed to think?"

"Have you told him?" he asked reasonably.

"He should know," I yelled in frustration. Turning, I took two steps and threw up the breakfast Pop had insisted I eat. Tears rolled down my cheeks as I swiped at my mouth with the back of my hand.

God, I was miserable. The rain no longer felt cooling against my skin, just wet. All of my clothes were damp and sticking to my skin, the friction like tiny razor blades all over.

"He should know," I repeated, turning back to Pop. "He's well aware of what the mating heat entails. It should be hurting him too."

"I'm sure it is."

"Then why does he keep leaving? Huh? Why would he keep putting us through this? Why would he keep putting *me* through this?"

"You know, some days—most days—I wish your mother were here. I never know what to say to you. Didn't know how to comfort you in high school when you got that terrible haircut that made you look like a mushroom. Had absolutely no clue how to use tampons and had to read the directions before I talked to you about them. Hell, I forgot to put sunblock on you more times than I could count." He rose to his feet and braced a hand on the back of the chair. "But this? This I know. This I can set you straight on."

"Enlighten me," I ordered, throwing my arm out.

"Daniel is so terrified that you'll be hurt and he won't be able to save you that he's willingly making you both miserable for a few hours a day because he knows you're safe here. That's his goal, Flower. Keepin' you safe."

"That's bullshit."

"He's gotta go home to his family to check in. Lost one brother already, house was attacked, his family is healin' in more ways than one."

"I know that."

"Don't you think he'd rather have you with him?" Pop asked curiously.

"I don't know what to think!"

He just shook his head. "When you're done havin' a pity party and want to talk logically, we'll talk."

"Oh, that's real nice," I grumbled. "Seriously. Thanks for being on my side."

"I am on your side," he said, waving me off before letting out a short, sharp whistle for Thunder. "But you can't see the forest for the trees."

I was too pissed to follow them inside, so instead I stomped over to the barn. The inside was a mess of random shit that we didn't have room for anywhere else. I swore under my breath as I grabbed a pair of gloves out of the cabinet and got to work.

Random tools littered the room where Grant and Seamus had left them, and I took my time—mostly because everything hurt and I wasn't moving very fast—as I rolled up the cords and put them away in the bottom of the cabinet. I stacked short two-by-fours and pieces of plywood against the wall. Pop's portable air conditioner was on wheels, so I covered it with its little bag and shoved it into the corner, looping the air tube over the top of it. I searched the ground and found four pairs of pliers, two Allen wrenches, and various-sized sockets and bits that the boys had left out. I needed to remind them to put shit away where it belonged, so if Pop came outside, he didn't have to go searching for the tools he needed.

After a while, I had to sit down on a crate to catch my breath.

I hated feeling so weak.

After an hour of sitting there, watching the rain and urging myself unsuccessfully to get up and do something, I finally made my way back into the house.

I paused inside the doorway.

The kitchen table was covered with newspaper, a pile of rags, solvent, oil, and various firearms.

"Grab a rag," Pop offered, nodding at the pile.

"Is there a reason we're cleaning our weapons?" I asked.

"Needs to be done," he replied, reaching for a rifle barrel.

"And you chose today." I shook my head and moved around him. "Let me change my clothes first."

My shirt was still damp with a mix of sweat and rainwater when I took it off. The shorts were better, but not much. I kicked them into the corner of my bedroom and pulled a new set out of my drawers. I needed to do laundry, but it was hard to find the resolve to do it. I wasn't going anywhere. No one saw me except Pop—

who didn't care—and Daniel, who was more interested in taking off whatever I was wearing.

I sometimes wished I were one of those people who were productive when they had extra time on their hands, but I wasn't. Too much time just made me bored out of my mind.

As soon as I was dressed, I lost all sense of time as I crawled onto the bed on my knees and curled into a ball, my feet tucked under my ass and my arms sandwiched between my torso and the bedding. I didn't even bother pulling a pillow under my head as my chest tightened, aching like it was being squeezed in a vice. It was time for the panic, and although I always thought I was ready for it, I never was.

Thoughts raced through my mind like lightning, the last one barely fading away before another one took its place. Daniel getting into a horrific car accident, being ambushed on the drive to his parents' house, stopping for gas and getting ambushed there, fighting off the militia on the front porch I remembered from the night we met, stepping in front of a faceless woman that I knew was his sister-in-law and being taken down in the process—the scenarios felt endless and devastatingly specific.

They weren't premonitions. I didn't have some magical connection with him that would tell me he was in danger. No, these were my own worst fears slapping me in the face. And while I knew that they weren't real, and I was terrified for no reason, my body didn't get the memo. I was frozen on the bed, shaking and gasping for breath as I struggled to snap myself out of it.

Eventually, my body was so exhausted from the

tense muscles and irregular breathing that I fell asleep. It was the best possible scenario.

When I woke up hours later, expecting the symptoms to be lighter, even manageable, they weren't.

I was still on fire. My stomach still roiled with nausea. My ribcage still felt too small for my lungs. My muscles still ached from prolonged contractions.

I scrambled out of bed and stumbled into the living room in shock as I realized that the sun was going down.

"Where is he?" I asked, finding only Pop in the living room.

I hurried to the front door and swung it open.

Daniel's car wasn't there.

"Still not back," Pop replied, his tone grim.

"What?" I looked at the clock on the wall, even though I knew it hadn't worked since my mom died. "What time is it? Why isn't he back?"

"It's five o'clock."

The urge to scream burned at the back of my throat. We'd passed the three-hour mark hours ago. I'd been asleep all day.

Where was he?

Where was he?

Where was he?

"He's not answerin' his phone," Pop said as he pushed himself carefully out of his seat and took a shuffling step toward his wheelchair. "So I called Dalton, and he was going to get a hold of Daniel's parents, see if he could get in touch with him that way."

"He wouldn't stay longer than three hours, Pop," I said, my voice rising with hysteria. "It's always three hours or less. He always says he'll be back in three hours, but it's always a few minutes less than that."

"I know that, Flower," Pop soothed, wheeling toward me. "But he must've gotten held up. There's no need to panic when we don't know anything."

"Call Uncle Dalton back," I ordered. "Give me your phone. I'll call him."

"He said he'd call me back, and he will."

Visions of Daniel's brother-in-law Charlie flashed through my mind. He'd seemed so normal. Sure, kind of twitchy, but anyone would be after they were kidnapped. He hadn't seemed like a mate without their Vampire, at least not the way Aunt Halle had always described them—people who were so mired in grief that they wasted away or made the decision to end their lives.

Was Daniel dead?

My heartbeat pounded like a drum in my brain, the pressure so intense that, for a minute, I was afraid I was going to black out.

Would I be one of those mates that lie in bed all day, wasting away because I'd lost the other half of my soul?

Just the idea of Daniel being dead made my skin burn like fire rippling across the surface.

I looked down at my arm dumbly, expecting to see that I'd actually been set alight.

"I need you to calm down," Pop said, moving closer. "Calm down, Rosemary."

"I can't." I looked to the door again.

My mate was out there somewhere. He should've been home already. He should've climbed into bed with me so I'd woken up to strong arms wrapped around my waist and the pleasant heat of his body instead of this horrific burning sensation.

He could be hurt. He could be in danger. He could be dead.

Without conscious thought, I was out the door and jogging down the front steps. When I hit the gravel, I picked up speed, ignoring the sound of my father yelling for me to get back in the house. Rocks dug into the soles of my feet, but I found the pain to be a welcome distraction to the way the rest of my body burned.

It took less than a minute before the house disappeared behind me.

It took ten minutes to get to the road.

It would've taken nine, but I'd had to stop because I was dry heaving so hard that I'd begun to stumble.

I wasn't sure where I was going. The route we'd taken when Daniel brought me home that first night was a bit of a blur, but I had to assume that I was at least moving in the right direction. I was ten minutes closer to the highway when a familiar truck came into view and swerved into the opposite lane, stopping on the side of the road less than a foot from where I was.

"Going for a run?" Uncle Dalton asked calmly as he climbed out of the truck.

"Did you get ahold of Daniel's parents?" I demanded, shaking my arms out at my sides.

It felt like I had bugs crawling all over me.

"I did. They weren't sure where he was, but said that he and Chance had gone somewhere together."

I wouldn't have been more surprised if Uncle Dalton had slapped me across the face.

"What?" I asked hoarsely, swaying on my feet.

"I called Chance because I knew you'd want to know," Uncle Dalton said, taking a few steps toward me. "He said things are all good. They're just getting a few things done, and he'd fill me in later."

"No, he wouldn't do that," I argued. "He said he'd be back in three hours. He wouldn't just *not* come back. He wouldn't do that."

"I didn't speak to Danny," Uncle Dalton replied quietly. "But I've known Chance a long time. I don't think he'd lie to me."

"But he—" I gagged and shook my head. No, that wasn't right. Daniel didn't like leaving me behind. He was just in a tight spot. Even my pop said so. He was being pulled in two different directions, so he was doing the best he could. That was all. He wouldn't leave me longer than was necessary. Three hours. That was the limit *he'd* set.

"Why don't you climb in, and I'll drive you home," Uncle Dalton said soothingly. "You made it a hell of a lot further than I thought you would before I got here."

"No," I replied, shaking my head as I sidestepped closer to the road. "No, something is wrong. I know something's wrong."

"It's the bond," Uncle Dalton argued. "I know it's confusing, Flower, but you need to trust me on this. Your body doesn't like the separation, and it's making the situation feel like life and death. It isn't. Danny is fine."

"No, he's not," I barked, lifting my hands to my hair. I wrapped it around my fingers and clenched my hands into fists, trying to make the sting in my scalp focus my thoughts.

"I'll call him," Uncle Dalton said, lifting the phone to his ear. "How about that?"

I nodded silently, watching the phone like a hawk.

"Chance," Uncle Dalton greeted. "Any way I can talk to Danny?" He paused. "I've got a very concerned mate on my hands, and I'm not sure she'll listen to anything I say unless she speaks to him first." He waited for a moment and then nodded, extending the phone to me.

I felt like my body wasn't my own as I put the phone to my ear.

"Rosemary?" Daniel called. "What's going on, baby?"

I felt like I was being strangled.

"You there? I'm sorry it's taking longer than I thought, but I'll be back within the hour, okay?" He waited for me to respond. "Rosie? Where are you?"

A car pulled up slowly beside us, but Uncle Dalton waved them on, assuring them we were fine.

"Did you leave the house?" Daniel asked, his voice rougher than before. "Please tell me you didn't fucking leave the house."

My hand felt numb as I dropped it back down to my side, the phone dangling precariously from my fingertips.

What had I become? Who was this person? Because I no longer felt like me.

I felt like a shell of myself. The strong, independent, capable woman I'd always been had been replaced by this whimpering mess, my body too weak to do anything of note, my mind no longer logical but filled with anxiety and fear.

I was standing on the side of the road—on the

verge of collapse—and I'd run there myself, with bare feet and no bra, because I'd been in so much relentless pain and in such a panic that my mate was in trouble that I hadn't even taken the time to realize I could've driven my pop's truck.

And the whole time, my mate had been perfectly fine.

He'd just lost track of time.

Something inside me splintered.

"I'm sorry," Uncle Dalton said, catching me as my legs buckled. "I'm sorry. I'll hurry."

I knew he was worried that the touch hurt, but honestly? I couldn't feel it beyond everything else.

I already felt like I'd been run over.

It took only a few minutes to drive me back to Pop's. It would've been funny, considering how long it had taken to run there, if it hadn't been so fucking sad. As soon as he put the truck in park, I tiredly opened my door and slid out.

Pop was waiting for me on the porch.

"You scared the shit outta me," he chastised as I made my way toward him. "What the hell were you thinking?"

"She wasn't," Uncle Dalton answered for me. "It was instinct. You remember what it's like at the beginning of a bond—"

The last of his words were cut off as I walked inside. They could talk about me all they wanted. I didn't really care.

Oh, I looked crazy?

Funny thing. I felt crazy.

I didn't know who I was anymore.

CHAPTER 10
DANIEL

Chance insisted on coming with me back to Gary's house, and I relented because after the morning we had, I was feeling pretty raw, and I also didn't want to take the time to drop him off somewhere.

"Damn, Danny boy," Chance said, leaning forward to get a better look out the windshield. "Where's your banjo? Feels like we need some banjo music."

"Rosemary's father is really fucking smart," I replied distractedly. "Lives completely off-grid. If Rosemary hadn't told me where to go, I never would've found the place."

"And you said he's ex-Command?" Chance asked with a hum. "Weird coincidence."

I nodded. "He didn't want to bring work home with him."

"Can't blame him for that," Chance said, leaning back in his seat. "Bad enough for us, but a human? Fucking forget it." He paused as the small house came into view. "Looks like Dalton's here."

"Good," I murmured with relief. From the moment Rosemary had called me and I'd heard a car in the background, I'd had to beat back the panic that threatened to choke me. We'd agreed that she wouldn't show her face in public. She *knew* that it was for her own safety.

What the hell had she been doing out on the road?

"Time to bring him in on things?" Chance asked.

He'd been pressuring me about it since the moment we'd found the USB drive my brother Zeke had hidden before his death. It was filled with account information and names and dates and photos, but the hundreds of files weren't labeled, and nowhere in Zeke's information did he explain how they all fit together.

My baby brother must've been gathering intelligence for a long time before his death, and he hadn't said a word to any of us about it. We'd been scrambling for the past couple of weeks to make sense of the information he'd left, and it wasn't until that morning we'd finally been able to piece most of it together. We'd gathered to look at photos from when Zeke and Charlie met, and unbeknownst to Charlie or his sister, Zeke had filmed a goodbye video to his mate on Lucy's camera.

He'd left a cryptic message for us on the video.

The fucking asshole.

If we hadn't found the files he'd stashed and looked over them until we couldn't see straight, we never would've known what the message meant.

The dipshit couldn't have just explained what he found. Instead, it was like some kind of fucked-up scavenger hunt, as if we weren't in the middle of a godsdamn war and didn't even know who the enemy was.

"We'll tell Dalton everything," I confirmed as I parked.

At least he was already at the house, and I wouldn't need to track him down. After the day I'd had, that seemed like a boon.

I wanted to get our little meeting over with as fast as possible so I could get my mate alone and just breathe her in. Seeing Zeke's face on that video, the pain in his eyes as he said goodbye to the other half of his soul, had felt like someone was reaching inside my chest and twisting my insides into a knot. Witnessing Charlie's reaction to the goodbye had almost been worse.

My skin was on fire. My head pounded. I'd vomited more in the last month than I had in my entire life. My muscles were knotted and painful. Being away from Rosemary was awful. It was the worst thing I'd ever forced myself to do. I ached for her.

But if I had to make the same choices again, I would, because nothing mattered more than keeping her safe. She was safe with Gary on that piece of land that no one knew how to find.

"You're back," Gary greeted as he wheeled onto the porch to meet us.

"It took longer than I thought," I replied.

"You didn't tell me he was in a wheelchair," Chance muttered, coming up beside me. "How is he supposed to protect your mate?"

I clenched my teeth together in frustration.

"My hearing's not so bad," Gary replied, looking Chance over. "At least she'll have a little warning before men start repelling onto the roof."

"Sorry, my brother's a jackass," I told Gary, walking toward him. "Chance, this is Gary Whitlock."

"Nice to meet you," Chance said easily, as if he hadn't just been completely offensive.

"You too," Gary replied flatly, rising to his feet to shake Chance's hand.

"Aw, shit." Chance nodded. "Hiding in plain sight."

"You're a fucking idiot," I snapped.

Gary just shook his head.

"Is she inside?" I moved to pass him, but jerked to a stop when his hand landed heavily on my arm.

"A little warning," Gary said, his voice low. "She's been giving you a long leash. You no longer have one."

I wasn't sure what he meant until I entered the house. Immediately, the sound of pacing steps was audible, thudding over the hardwood.

Dalton nodded at me from the couch and jerked his head toward Rosemary's bedroom.

When I found her, my breath left me in a whoosh, and I couldn't seem to drag any back in.

Rosemary was a mess. Her hair was wet and tangled so badly that it looked half as long as it actually was. She was wearing a pair of shorts and a shirt that were too big for her and didn't match. There were little scratches all over her forearms and the lower halves of her legs.

Her face was haggard, her eyes hollow.

And her feet were leaving bloody footprints all over the floor.

She jerked to a stop, her eyes on me. "You're back."

"What the fuck happened?" I asked, my heart thundering in my throat.

I wasn't prepared for the way she flew at me, but I would've caught her anyway.

I didn't get the chance.

Her nails raked across my face so quickly that I didn't even dodge them.

I was too shocked to defend myself as she shoved at my chest, her fists pounding against my sternum.

"Three hours!" she screamed, her voice breaking. "You said three hours."

"I got held up," I countered, finally catching her wrists. She tried to rip them away, and I struggled to hold her captive without hurting her.

"Held up?" Her eyes widened in disbelief, and her face jutted toward mine. "Fuck you!"

"What the hell is wrong with you?" I asked in confusion.

In the next moment, I was flat on my back, my top half in the hallway, and my bottom half still in her bedroom. My head bounced off the floor.

Rosemary was straddling me, her eyes filled with a level of anger that I'd only seen a few times before and never from her.

"You left me here," she raged, leaning down into my face. "You left, and you didn't come back!"

"I'm here," I shouted back, mostly because I didn't think she would actually hear me if I spoke normally.

"You said three hours."

"Things took longer than I thought they would," I said, trying to soothe her. I ran my thumbs over the delicate tendons in her wrists. "I lost track of time."

Rosemary stared at me like she'd never seen me before.

"What kind of mate are you?" she whispered scathingly.

"Yours," I replied instantly.

"You—I—" she shook her head. Her body lost the

tension she'd been holding, and her shoulders slumped. "There's something *wrong* with you."

"What the hell is going on?" Sitting up, I ignored the sore spot on the back of my head and gripped her hips before she could climb off me. "You're bleeding."

"I'm fine," Rosemary replied tiredly.

"You're not fine."

"No," she let out a humorless laugh, the sound bordering on hysteria. "No, you're right. I'm not. *Let go of me.*" She shoved at my wrists.

Letting my hands fall away, I stared as she rose slowly to her feet and stepped over me. A second later, the bathroom closed almost silently behind her.

"So I see things are going well," Chance noted sardonically from the end of the hallway. "That's good."

"Shut up, Chance," I spat, getting to my feet.

"Nice face."

Lifting my hand to my cheek, I pressed it against the stinging there. The tips of my fingers came away with blood on them.

"Shit."

"I mean, it could be worse," Chance said, following me to the kitchen. "She could've kicked you in the balls. Did she kick you in the balls?"

"Shut the fuck up, Chance," I repeated.

"You seem to be walking fine, at least."

Dalton and Gary seemed to have moved to the kitchen table, probably to give Rosemary and me a bit of privacy, not that we really had any in a house that small. Vampire hearing was very acute. We could hear anything happening inside the house, no matter which room we were in.

Grabbing a paper towel, I wet it and set it against the scratches on my cheek. When I turned, Dalton was staring.

"Deserved that and worse," he announced, his tone grim.

"What the fuck is going on, Gary?" I asked, rounding the table so I could see his face. I had a feeling that the man had been deliberately ignoring me when I entered the room.

"I've stayed out of it," he said, meeting my eyes. "I understand the mating bond, and I'd never get between that. I also understand the drive to protect the people you care about. There's not a thing on this earth that I wouldn't do for Rosemary or for her mother when she was alive."

I could hear a *but* coming.

"But if you don't pull your head out of your ass, I'm going to do it for you." He glanced at Chance. "And I might be in a wheelchair, but I've tussled with quite a few Vampires in the past, and I think I'd surprise you."

"Lay it out like I'm five years old," I ground out, still completely fucking confused.

When I'd left that morning, everything was *fine*. Rosemary had been lying in bed, sleepy and satisfied. How the hell had she gone from that to a complete hellcat in the hours I'd been gone?

"How in the fuck do you keep leaving your mate?" Dalton asked, his head tilted a little to the side.

"She's safe here—"

He slashed his hand through the air. "No, I understand why you're doing it. I'm asking *how*."

"What do you mean?" I glanced between Dalton and Gary.

"How is it physically possible?" Dalton asked flatly.

"Are you asking if it hurts?"

"I *know* it hurts."

I just looked at him.

"How in the hell are you leaving her every day for hours at a time?"

"It's not fucking comfortable," I snapped, becoming frustrated with the questions. "Obviously."

"You're not in pain?"

"Yeah, it's painful. I feel like shit."

"But it's manageable," he mused, his brows drawing together in thought.

"He's got a high pain tolerance," Chance said conversationally, leaning against the kitchen counter. "Doesn't really feel things like the rest of us."

"No, I don't," I argued, waving him off.

"Yes, you do." He crossed his arms over his chest. "You fell and broke your collarbone when we were kids and didn't say anything. Walked around with it for a week before anyone noticed. Mom finally saw you with your shirt off and lost her mind."

"It wasn't a bad break."

"You were deformed."

"Would you shut up for a minute?" I turned back to Dalton.

"You also pulled a bullet out of your own leg, what..." Chance paused, counting off on his fingers. "Eight years ago."

"It wasn't deep," I shot back.

"It was in your thigh," Chance said with a chuckle. "You're lucky you didn't lose your balls."

"Shut—"

"Didn't mention that one either," Chance drawled.

"Gods dammit," I muttered under my breath.

"Oh, and you've torn off every fingernail you have at least twice."

"On a scale of one to ten," Dalton said, cutting in before I lunged for Chance. "What would you rate the pain when you're separated from Rosemary?"

"Six," I replied, lying through my teeth.

Did it hurt to leave her? Fuck yes. It felt like I was coming out of my skin. I loathed it when we were apart.

But I'd made a decision when Zeke died that I'd take care of my family. I'd hold them together however I could. I'd help find my brothers' mates, and I'd protect them once they were found. Leaving Rosemary where she was safe while I did so was the only option open to me.

I refused to put my mate in danger for any reason.

The consequences would be catastrophic.

"That's fucking fantastic," Rosemary said from behind me. I spun to face her.

She'd showered. Her hair was in a sleek fall down her back. She'd changed into a matching set of pajamas, and her feet were covered in a pair of thick hiking socks.

"Ask me," she ordered Dalton.

"On a scale of one to ten, what would you rate—"

"Seventy-five," Rosemary said before he'd finished. Her gaze moved slowly to me.

"Rosie," I whispered, the knowledge knocking the wind out of me.

"I'd rate it a seventy-five," she repeated, her eyes on mine.

She looked away. "Now ask me about that time in Grenada."

Dalton cleared his throat. "On a scale of one to ten, what would you rate your pain when you were stabbed in Grenada?"

"Fourteen," she said quietly.

"You were stabbed?" I asked in disbelief. I hadn't noticed any scars, and I'd seen every inch of her body. She shifted uncomfortably on her feet, and I remembered the blood on the floor of her room. "Why are your feet bleeding?"

"They aren't anymore," she replied, moving past me to sit at the table.

I ground my teeth together in frustration.

"She went for a little run when she woke up and realized you hadn't come back," Gary answered for her.

"Pop," she hissed in warning.

"Oh, are we just going to ignore this shit some more?" he chastised. "Tell your mate what happened."

Rosemary stared at him mutinously, her lips pressed tightly closed.

Gary turned to me. "She lost it. Took off running before I could stop her. She made it to the road before Dalton got there."

"Where the hell were you going?" I asked in disbelief.

"To find you," Gary told me, looking at his daughter. "Didn't even stop to put shoes on."

"Quiet, Pop," Rosemary ordered. He looked away from her.

"She's handled the separation. Pukin' her guts out, the shakes, the fever, the muscle aches. Losin' weight because she can't hardly keep anythin' down. But apparently, you not showin' up when you're supposed to was too much."

Guilt was my constant companion. We were old friends. I'd learned to live with its voice in my ear, whispering about all the shit I should've done and all the things I shouldn't have. I was used to it.

This was something different.

This felt more like shame.

"Why didn't you say anything?" I asked Rosemary, taking a step toward her.

"What was there to say?" she asked simply. "You knew before you left that there would be physical repercussions."

I opened my mouth to argue, but stopped when her head gave a little jerk.

"Every Vampire knows that," she said dryly. "It's common knowledge that any separation between mates causes the symptoms to intensify. You also know that a human mate's symptoms are worse than the Vampire's, but I guess if your pain level was only a *six*..." She let out a little laugh. "You get the benefit of the doubt. Maybe you didn't think my symptoms would be very bad if yours were so *manageable*."

"You should've said something," I argued.

I thought back to every time I found Rosemary after I'd been at my parents' house. Always freshly showered. A little subdued, but glad to see me. Not once had she made any reference to having a rough time while I was gone. Not once had she complained or mentioned the mating heat being too much.

"What is there to say?" she asked dully. "You made up your mind. You were going without me, whether I wanted you to or not."

I opened my mouth to reply, but nothing came out.

"Weed helps," she said with a shrug. "Edibles work

the best, but they take a while to take effect. A blunt will do in a pinch."

"I won't—" the words caught in my throat.

I couldn't promise not to leave her again. Chance and I were about to tell Dalton that we'd narrowed down our list of Vampires to three that were involved in the human militia's war on Vampires and their mates. Things were going to start moving very quickly, and my brothers would need me.

"You're going to keep going," she said in understanding.

The worst part is she wasn't even surprised.

That small burst of anger when I'd arrived had been the extent of her fight. By the look in her eyes, she'd already moved on to acceptance.

"You said you had a high pain threshold," I reminded her, my voice rough. It was no excuse, but it was the only explanation I had. "You didn't ever say how bad it was, so I thought—"

"Complaining about things doesn't change them," Rosemary said, pulling her knees up to her chest. "It just makes you a whiny little bitch."

"I'm sorry today took longer than it should've," I said, moving closer. "This morning, we found a video of my brother Zeke."

"You don't need to explain," she replied. "It is what it is."

"I should've called."

"Yeah, you should've."

"Zeke had been gathering information before he died," I explained, gutted at the lack of emotion in her voice. "It's what I've been going through on my laptop, and none of it made any sense until we found that video this morning. We have names, baby. We're getting closer to ending it."

"Good news," she replied with an unconvincing smile.

"Zeke left you information?" Dalton asked. "Why haven't you said anything?"

"We weren't sure what we had—"

"You ever think that I could've helped with that?" he asked, glaring.

"I think we didn't know what we were dealing with," Chance cut in. "And until we did, we weren't sharing the information that our brother died for."

Dalton looked at him in surprise. "You know me."

"We know a lot of Vampires," Chance replied with a shrug. "What does that have to do with anything?"

"Knock it off," I shot at Chance over my shoulder.

He made a zipping motion over his lips.

"It's almost over, baby," I whispered, reaching out to wrap my hands around Rosemary's thighs. "All right? We won't have to do this much longer."

She just nodded.

"Breaking it down, we've got three names of Vampires who have money coming in and out of the human militia's war chest." I looked at Dalton from my place crouched in front of Rosemary. "Multiple transactions. They were trying to hide it, the payments were filtered through dummy corporations and overseas banks, but the proof is there."

"Who is it?"

"Guess," Chance said. "Try to guess."

I was going to kill my brother.

"Keihley, Morren, and Adamson."

"No way in hell," Dalton replied.

"The numbers don't lie, Cavendish," Chance practically sang.

"I know Adamson," Dalton said in disbelief.

"Like we know you?" Chance wheedled.

"He wouldn't do this. The Vampire is loyal to a fault."

"He's dirty," I replied. "The evidence is extensive."

Dalton was silent for a long moment. "Can I see what you have?"

"Chance?" I asked.

"I'll get my laptop, since yours is shit," he grumbled as he stomped away.

I stared at my mate. Even with the remote look in her eyes and her face void of expression, she was still so beautiful that it made me ache. I didn't understand how I'd missed how much pain she was in—pain that I was causing. She always looked so ready to take on the world when I saw her.

Realization hit without warning. She hadn't just been keeping the effects of the mating heat to herself.

She'd been actively hiding it.

The showers she'd barely finished when I walked through the door. The light conversation that didn't really touch on anything she'd done while I was gone.

"Come with me," I ordered, rising to my feet.

Chance could answer any questions that Gary and Dalton had.

Without a word, Rosemary rose and followed me out of the room. I paused long enough for her to slip on a pair of boots before leading her out the back door. The rain had stopped, but the air was thick with moisture as I led her to the barn.

"Did a little cleaning today?" I asked as I looked around the space.

"I had some time on my hands."

"Why?" I asked, turning to face her. "Why didn't you say anything?"

"What would it have changed?" she shot back, pulling her hand from mine. "Would you have stopped going? No. Would you have taken me with you? Also, no. So why would I say anything?"

"Because I'm your mate," I argued. "Because I have a right to know if something is hurting you!"

"You knew it was hurting me," she countered. "You knew, but you thought I could handle it, so you just kept doing it."

"That's not it—"

"Isn't it?" she asked. "I told you I had a high pain tolerance, so you thought that gave you permission to do something that you knew would hurt me."

"I know it's uncomfortable," I replied.

"Uncomfortable for you," she spat. "Not for me. Uncomfortable is the flu. Uncomfortable is being tied to a chair for a week. Uncomfortable is spraining your ankle. When you leave, it isn't *uncomfortable.* I can't *think* straight. My entire body seems to be working toward one goal—driving me insane."

"I'm so sorry," I said, reaching for her. "I didn't know—"

"I ran our entire driveway barefoot today," she said, jerking away. "I didn't even have a bra on."

"I was fine. I just—"

"I *know* that," she said, throwing her hands in the air. "And if the paranoia hadn't gotten so bad, I would've known that then. But I didn't. I was convinced that you were in trouble or dead somewhere. I was practically fucking feral!"

"I was a couple of hours late," I yelled back.

"More than a couple of hours!"

"You're safe here." Gods, I felt like a broken record. "But I cannot make sure that you're safe *everywhere* if I don't find the head of the fucking snake."

"So...go," she screamed, shooing me away. "Go find the head of the snake, or watch videos of your dead brother, or whatever hell else you want to do. Don't mind me. I'll be *fine*. Just like I was fine today and fine yesterday and fine the day before that. I'm dealing with it. I tied myself to you, and I'm fucking dealing with it, okay?"

"You regret the bond?" I asked, jerking back from her.

"What bond?" she hissed. "This isn't a mating bond. This is some cosmic joke."

"Are you fucking serious?"

"You shouldn't *want* to leave me," she screamed, grabbing a wrench off the workbench to throw at me. "If we were mated, it would be agony for you to leave me."

"It *is* agony," I argued, catching it.

"Oh, yeah, a six out of ten. Sounds really terrible."

"I lied," I roared, dropping the wrench.

"Yeah, right."

"I fucking *hate* leaving you," I said, moving toward her. She backed away with each step, and a part of me liked it. I wanted to fucking chase her. This time, she'd never make it into the loft.

My emotions were too close to the surface. The small box that I'd stuffed them into on the day we'd seen Zeke's mutilated body was coming apart at the seams.

Anger pounded between my temples. At Zeke. At the people who'd murdered him. At the situation I'd found myself in, torn between my family and my mate. At Rosemary for not understanding that I was trying to do the right thing.

"What's wrong with your eyes?" Rosemary asked. She lifted her chin a bit, but I could hear the tremor in her voice.

"Nothing," I lied.

"That's not nothing," she argued. "It's like they're flickering."

"Stop talking about my eyes."

"I can't—"

"You should've told me how bad it was," I said, catching her around the waist. I ignored the way she strained against my arms. "I had no idea—"

"Well, now you do," she said as she stopped trying to pull away. "Tell me, what difference does it make?"

"I know now."

"So you're going to start taking me with you?"

When I didn't immediately reply, she scoffed.

"That's what I thought."

It wasn't that simple. How in the hell was I supposed to willingly put her in danger? Once she was out in the world again, she'd be seen. Once she was seen, she'd be on their radar again. It wasn't a matter of *if*, but *when*.

But I couldn't stop searching for the Vampires and humans responsible for murdering my brother. I had to be out there, following up on leads and watching my brothers' backs.

Didn't she realize that the only way I could do that was if I knew she was safe here with her pop?

How had I become the fucking bad guy in this scenario for protecting my mate?

"You know what?" she said after a moment, taking a step away. "It's fine. I'm fine. You keep doing what you're doing, and I'll keep doing what I'm doing, and we can meet up once a day to fuck and exchange blood. That works for plenty of mates, and my body will just have to *deal*."

"You know that's not what I want," I argued, following her out of the barn. My frustration grew. "I'm here with you twenty-one hours of the fucking day, Rosemary. Don't act like you're being neglected here."

"Oh, I'm not."

"What the fuck?" I barked, stopping at the edge of the patio. "I understand that it's been hard for you. It's been hard for me too. None of this shit is normal."

Rosemary spun to face me, backlit by the porch light.

"You know, I've never been the woman who follows her partner around begging for scraps. It's just not my personality. It's like, you want to do your own thing? Cool. Me too. But when you told me that I was your mate, I thought we'd be in this shit together." She shook her head. "It is physically painful, to the point of losing all logic, when we're apart. Them's the breaks. I knew it would happen, and I was prepared for it because I know that mating bonds happen for a reason. What I didn't know is that you would ignore the fucking bond unless it suited you."

I opened my mouth to argue, but didn't even get a word out before she continued.

"Yes, that's exactly what you're doing. Your mate is a highly trained operator. Whether or not you acknowledge that fact is *your* issue. It doesn't change the truth. Instead of keeping me with you the way nature fucking intended, you've basically forbidden me from leaving this property while you go out hunting bad guys. Hell, you're not even hunting them at this point. You're trying to figure out who they are."

"You know they're looking for you," I shot back.

"I know that *you're* convinced they're looking for me," Rosemary spat. "That's what I know. I also know that you're so afraid of your own fucking shadow that you're ignoring the fact that you're not the only one in this. Even if we ignored that you've been putting me through excruciating physical symptoms because you *didn't think they'd be that bad*, I was working on discovering who these assholes were before you were, you self-righteous asshole!"

She stormed into the house, letting the door slam before I could catch it. I nearly tore it off the hinges as I followed her inside.

"Afraid of my own fucking shadow?" I yelled, catching up to her before she'd left the kitchen. I ignored the spectators around the table. "Do you have any idea what they did to my baby brother?"

"Danny," Chance said softly, rising from his seat.

"They tore him apart," I barked, ignoring him. "They cut off his arms and legs in pieces before they took his head."

The color drained out of Rosemary's cheeks.

"Yeah, baby. That's who we're dealing with. That's who had you tied up for a week in their little safe house." I took a step forward, then stopped myself. "So if I'm careful with you, I apologize," I said mockingly. "*So* fucking *sorry* that I'm willing to do whatever it takes to make sure that I don't have to identify your mangled body piece by piece."

"Trust me to take care of myself," she replied tentatively, taking a step toward me.

"They managed to take down Zeke," I argued. "A fully grown and fully trained Vampire, and you think you'd have a chance?"

"Your mom and sisters-in-law—"

"Got lucky," I roared. "That's all it was! Pure fucking luck."

"All right, Danny boy," Chance said. I jerked when his palm rested between my shoulder blades. "Time to take a step back."

"I'm a fucking horrible mate, right?" I asked the room. "I'm such a monster for leaving Rosemary behind for a few hours at a time. I better pull my head out of my ass, because I'm really fucking up!" I let out a laugh. "I'm a real motherfucker because I don't want to find my mate in *pieces*."

"And now is when we take a little walk before we say something we can't take back," Chance said, shoving me back toward the door.

"That's rich coming from you," I huffed.

"That's right, take it out on me," he crooned, still shoving at me. "Your brother, who loves you."

"You're such a fucking prick," I replied, jerking my shoulder away from his hand as I stepped back outside.

I walked to the far edge of the barn and let the cool air roll over me. I fucking hated all of it. I hated that Zeke was dead. I hated that Rosemary was pissed at me, and everything was going sideways. I really hated that I'd found my mate in the middle of such a cluster-fuck, and it was ruining the beginning of our story.

I hated that I had to leave her. I hated that she was in pain when I did. I hated that I had no other choice.

Of course I wanted to stay with Rosemary. For fuck's sake, if it were up to me, we'd never leave her bed—no, we wouldn't even be in her bed. If it were up to me, we'd be in *my* bed, where we had some room to move. If it were up to me, we'd be in our own little bubble, talking and fucking and getting to know one another without all the rest of this shit hanging over our heads.

None of this was fair.

"So...she's pissed," Chance said, leaning against the barn.

"You think?" I replied sarcastically.

"Don't blame her. It sounds like the symptoms are pretty bad when you leave."

"It's not like I want to leave her." I shook my head. "I'd rather have my fingernails pulled out."

"Beau, Ambrose, and I could take care of things."

"How would that be any different? Beau and Ambrose have mates too."

"Fine, then I'll take care of it myself." Chance shrugged.

"Not going to happen."

"What? You don't think I'm capable of handling it?"

"I don't think any of us are capable of taking on this group alone."

"Well, we need to figure something out because, by the looks of your face, your mate might just tear your throat out with her fingernails the next time you leave the house," Chance said, his lips twitching.

"You think this is funny?"

"I think it's refreshing seeing little easygoing Danny with his feathers ruffled because his mate isn't a doormat."

"I don't want her to be a doormat."

"No, but you want her to listen to you," he said in amusement. "And I think that ship has sailed."

I turned when the back door opened and waited as Dalton crossed the yard. When he reached us, he stopped, his arms crossed over his chest.

"Looked over the information you've collected."

"You're welcome," Chance said, popping a piece of gum in his mouth. "You got the organized version. We had to search through piles of bullshit to find those gems."

"You've convinced me," Dalton said with a sigh. "Edgar Adamson looks dirty as hell."

"Told ya," Chance replied.

"Is he always this fucking annoying?" Dalton asked me.

"Always," I confirmed.

He nodded, rubbing the back of his neck. "Adamson is at his house on the coast this week," he said, raising his eyebrows. "Arthur mentioned it a few days ago."

Chance perked up like a dog on the scent.

"I'm not sure how long he'll be there," Dalton said grimly. "I know the timing is shit, but we could get out there and back within a few hours."

I looked at my brother.

"I'll head home to the armory and meet you back here," he said, putting his hand out.

I dropped my keys in his palm and watched as he jogged away.

"I need to head home and gear up too," Dalton said as we made our way back to the house. "I'll grab Ian so we've got another set of hands."

"What about Gary?" I asked.

Dalton shook his head. "There's no one I'd rather have with me, but he's not up for this kind of shit anymore. His back's too fucked."

"Shame," I muttered.

"Better to have him home with Flower, anyway," Dalton said as we reached the house. "She shouldn't be here alone."

When we got inside, only Gary was still in the kitchen.

"Rosemary?" I asked.

"She's in the bedroom, I think," he said tiredly.

I moved past him.

"I know you're doin' your best," he said to my back. "But this shit isn't working."

I didn't bother to respond as I went searching for my mate.

Rosemary was in the bedroom, sitting on the chair where my clothes usually got tossed. She'd shoved them all onto the floor.

"Nice of you to join me," she said, her legs thrown over the arm of the chair. "Have a good talk with your brother?"

"I know you're pissed."

She huffed.

"You think I like this any more than you do?" I asked, keeping my voice level.

Arguing about it wasn't going to help. This was the situation we were in. We either found a way to make it work or we were miserable. Those were the two options. Walking away wasn't possible. Ignoring the militia that would all too happily kidnap and kill her wasn't possible either.

"I think that you took off this morning and didn't bother coming back until Dalton called you."

"I was on my way back when you called."

"Sure, you were."

"How do you think I got here so fast?" I asked, crouching down in front of the chair.

"Why the fuck wouldn't you call to tell me you'd be late?" she asked in exasperation. "Seriously, what the hell?"

"Honestly?"

"No, lie to me," she replied sarcastically.

"After we saw that video and Chance asked me to go with him to talk to some contacts he had in the city, I didn't call because I was afraid that I'd have to bail on him if I heard your voice."

She just stared at me.

"I lied when I said it was a six. It's much higher than that. I fucking hate it, okay?" I murmured, running my hand down her thigh. "I don't enjoy being away from you. The physical symptoms are miserable, and I'm constantly fighting the instinct to get back to you in any way possible."

"Then why are you making me stay here?" she whispered.

"Because the only thing worse than that would be taking you with me and taking the chance that one of those militia members gets a glimpse of you." Reaching up, I let my fingers tangle in her hair. "But we're getting close to the head of the snake, baby. Depending on what happens tonight, this could all be over soon."

"What's happening tonight?" she asked suspiciously.

"Chance, Dalton, Ian, and I are going to go see Edgar Adamson."

"One of the names on the list," she said in understanding.

"Not just one of the names on the list. The Vampire is a lieutenant general in Vampire Command. He holds thousands of Vampire lives in his hands every minute of the day, and his name is all over those files Zeke gathered."

"Oh shit," she murmured.

"That about covers it," I confirmed. "But after we speak to him, we may know more about who's controlling all this."

"You have to go." She let out a disappointed sigh.

"I have to go," I confirmed. "But I'll make it as fast as I can, and I won't be alone."

"I'll make sure Pop's got the edibles ready." She swallowed hard, looking a little nervous.

I think I'd been hearing it but not really processing what everyone was saying. Rosemary's mating heat symptoms were bad when I wasn't in close proximity. They seemed to be relatively mild when we were together, but the moment I left, they intensified. She was in pain when we were apart. I was too.

But it wasn't until I watched her throat move with that nervous swallow that it fully sank in just how terrible the symptoms must be. Because if Rosemary was nervous for me to leave, if just the thought of what was coming made her eyes go dark like that, then things were much worse than I'd been imagining.

This was a woman who'd been stabbed. Who'd

deliberately gotten herself kidnapped in an attempt to get information from a bunch of murderers. Who'd been tied to a chair for a week, waiting for them to slip up and reveal something. A woman who had been willing to take on a room full of Vampires with just a broken beer bottle and who had followed me into a pitch-dark forest searching for intruders after seeing our property littered with bodies.

"Come here," I ordered quietly, taking her hand.

I fell to my ass and pulled her into my lap on the floor.

"Where does it hurt when I go?" I asked, brushing her hair away from her face.

Her eyes fell closed. "Everywhere."

"Here?" I asked, kissing her shoulder.

"Yes."

"Here?" I asked, moving to her neck.

"Yes."

"Here?" Her jaw.

"Yes."

As I stripped her shirt and bra off, I kept asking. Her answer was always yes. When I asked about the places that my mouth couldn't reach, I smoothed over them with my hands instead. Eventually, I stopped asking, but I knew if I'd said the words, what her answer would be.

Taking my time, I touched every part of her, apologizing silently for what she'd been through and what I knew she would go through again.

When I finally shoved my trousers down far enough that she could sink down over me, both of us let out a sigh of something between relief and pleasure.

That was where she belonged. It was where we

belonged. Locked together in a quiet room, sharing breath, our scents mixing until they were indistinguishable from each other.

The taste of her blood as I came was like coming home. It was life and death and every sunrise and sunset I'd ever seen.

I'd barely lifted my head when her teeth sank deep into the meat between my shoulder and neck. Jerking in surprise, I held the back of her head as she sobbed silently and came. When she let go, she shuddered and raised her face to mine.

"Let me see," I whispered, using my thumb to gently raise her top lip.

Her canines had elongated. Not enough for the average person to notice, but long enough that she no longer needed me to nick my skin for the blood exchange.

"I think it happened today," she said, kissing the tip of my thumb. "Do you think this means I'm immortal now?"

"Yes," I replied roughly, staring at her mouth.

"I'm still not going with you, am I?"

I stared into her eyes, unable to get the words past my throat. I knew the moment she realized what I wasn't saying.

Her gaze shifted away in disappointment.

CHAPTER 11
ROSEMARY

Running my tongue over my sharp new teeth, I watched from the edge of the bed as Daniel got dressed. He'd dug a pair of black utility pants out of his duffel bag and paired them with an equally dark thermal shirt. As he sat down to pull on a fresh pair of socks and his boots, I tried to find something to say.

I'd known before I asked that he wouldn't let me leave. The most ironic thing about the entire situation is that it wasn't like he was forcing me to stay. He knew that I could leave the property when he wasn't there. I wasn't a hostage. But knowing the way that fear would tear him up inside if I left was enough to hold me where I was. No matter how angry I was with the situation, I wasn't stupid enough to believe that I could leave the safety of the property without repercussions, especially if I wasn't careful.

"What do the tattoos mean?" I asked finally, eager to break the silence between us.

"I don't think we have enough time for that conversation," he replied with a small smile.

His brother Chance was waiting out in the living room, and they expected Uncle Dalton and Ian any time.

"Tell me about one of them, then," I pushed.

"Which one?"

"The bird."

He frowned at me in consternation. "It's an *eagle*."

"Well, excuse me," I joked. "What's the eagle mean?"

"My dad had nicknames for all of us when we were kids. He called me *Arne* because he said I saw everything."

"Arne means eagle?"

He nodded.

"Did all of you have names like that? What did he call your brothers?"

"Ulf, Bjorn, and Happ."

I watched as he laced up his boots and then rose to slide his belt through the loops.

"Who is who? You're missing one."

"Zeke didn't have another nickname," he said, glancing at me. "My mother named the rest of us, but Zeke was named after an old friend of my father's."

"Ah, gotcha."

"He didn't feel the need to improve upon a name he chose," Daniel said with a huff of laughter. His head jerked up. "Dalton's here."

My stomach twisted.

"Walk me out?" Daniel asked softly.

I nodded and stood from the bed, taking the hand that he held out.

"I'll make this as fast as I can," he assured me, wrapping his other hand around the side of my throat. "Stay here with Gary. Even if it takes longer than we think, remember that if anything happens, someone will call you."

"I know."

"Remember it, baby, so you don't freak out."

"I won't freak out," I promised.

"I won't be back in three hours. It's going to take longer."

"I know."

"I don't want to fucking do this." He leaned closer, our noses brushing. "You know that, right? I want to carry you back to that bed and stay there for a week."

I nodded.

"Soon, Rosie."

"Be careful." I tilted my head so our lips brushed.

"I will."

I was afraid to hope as he led me out to the living room, where everyone was waiting. The Vampires were grim and determined as they greeted each other and me. Even Chance had lost his sardonic smile as he handed Daniel weapon after weapon that my mate stashed all over his body.

"You good?" I asked Ian, stepping in next to him.

"Yeah, I'm good," he replied. "You good?"

"I'm fine."

He shot me a look.

"Better than I was earlier," I said, rolling my eyes. "Not looking forward to this next part, but you guys have the harder job."

"I'm just hoping that he'll have something to tell us," Ian said quietly. "My dad's pretty fucking pissed that this guy is involved. I guess they worked together for years."

"Hopefully, he gives you enough information that we can take them all down," I said, bumping my shoulder against his biceps. "I love the old man, but I'm getting tired of living with him."

"I heard that," my pop said, not even bothering to look at us as he helped Uncle Dalton with something I couldn't see.

Ian had been on missions before, but never something like this. From the conversation that flowed around me as they finished getting dressed, they planned on taking a helicopter to the coast and then traveling to the house on foot. They weren't sure how much security Edgar Adamson had, but they weren't very concerned about neutralizing anyone who got in their way.

Neutralizing, not killing. The Vampires guarding the lieutenant general were part of Command. They wouldn't kill any of them for doing their job unless there was no other choice.

Edgar Adamson, on the other hand, would meet swift justice if they confirmed that he'd been in league with the Vampires and humans responsible for the murders.

Daniel pulled me close and kissed me hard as they filed out of the house.

"Remember, I'm fine unless you hear otherwise."

"I know," I whispered back.

He stared at me for a moment. "I love you."

I didn't even have time to process what he'd said before he was out the door and jogging down the front steps. Seconds later, they were driving away in one of Strike's black SUVs with Uncle Dalton at the wheel.

"Can I shut the door now?" my pop asked dryly. "Or you wanna keep staring at the taillights some more."

I shook my head to clear it and then looked at him.

"Did you hear him?" I asked, not quite sure if I'd heard what I heard.

"He wasn't bein' quiet," my dad replied, swinging the door shut. He locked both the deadbolt and the handle as he chuckled. "Your response left a little to be desired."

"Shut up."

"Like a deer in the headlights," he continued as he wheeled himself toward the kitchen.

"I was not," I argued, following him.

The muscles in my abdomen tightened painfully, and I held back a gasp.

I was fine. Daniel was fine. The symptoms were temporary. He would be back as soon as he could be.

"Well, neither of us is sleepin' tonight, so how about a drink?"

"Whatcha got?" I asked, ignoring the sweat that had broken out on the back of my neck.

My entire body was sore from my little excursion earlier in the evening, and I dropped onto a kitchen chair with a groan.

"Shitty timing for them to fly to the coast," Pop said as he set down two glasses and a bottle of whiskey on the table between us. "Glad I picked up a little something while I was out this week. How're you holdin' up?"

"Everything hurts," I replied dryly. "But I can hack it."

"He needed to know," he told me as he poured the whiskey. "You've always been tough, kid, but hidin' how bad you're feelin' is just plain masochistic."

"I figured he knew that it was bad."

"How the hell would he know that when you weren't tellin' him?" he asked dubiously.

"Because it's common fucking knowledge?"

Pop blew a raspberry and shook his head. "You know that it affects everyone differently. There was no way to know how bad yours had gotten."

"It's not even that bad—"

Pop laughed. "Try pullin' that shit with someone that'll believe you."

"You're right," I huffed. "It sucks. But I wasn't going to try to guilt him for going home, you know? Like, if he was okay with me feeling like I'd been run over by a truck, then what the hell would spelling it out for him do?"

"So you didn't want to tell him about it, but you wanted him to realize it anyway and make changes," he replied drolly. "That's some backward shit."

"No," I argued. I paused, struggling to explain it. "He knows that mating heat symptoms are painful, right? So if I whined to him about it, what difference would it make, really? Like, hey dude, I know you already know that this is painful, but I'm going to reiterate that fact for you."

Pop watched me for a few quiet moments. "I don't think that's it."

"You don't?" I asked flatly.

"Nope." He took a sip of his whiskey. "I think that you didn't say anything because you didn't want to inconvenience him."

I scoffed.

"And you were afraid that even after you'd told him how bad it was, he would keep doin' it anyway. Then where would you be?"

I saluted him with my glass and took a sip. The whiskey burned all the way down my throat.

"Feel like you should know this already," he continued. "But it's all right to be vulnerable once in a while. People might surprise you."

"Are we going to share our feelings now?" I joked, leaning forward on my elbows, my cheeks squished between my fists. "Because I've been dying to tell you about the butterflies I get when Danny smiles."

Pop chuckled and flipped me off. "Little shit."

I smiled and leaned back in my chair, letting out a slow breath as my chest began to ache. "He knows how bad it is now."

"And?"

"And he *knows*." I took another sip of my drink. "He's going to be more careful in the future, I think. And he won't stay longer than three hours without calling."

"That's something at least."

"I understand the caution," I conceded. "We've been pretty insulated here so far, and I think if someone was going to find us here, they would've already."

"Yep."

"So for now I'll stay here so he can do what he needs to do."

"Simple as that, huh?"

"No, I'm going fucking crazy. He knows that I'm capable of helping."

"But you also know that he won't be on his game if he's worried about you."

"And there's the rub," I complained.

"Not an easy situation for either of you."

"Let's be real. It's harder for me."

Pop grinned.

"I mean, come on. I'm far more experienced than Ian, and they brought him with them tonight."

"Glad you didn't mention that when Ian was here."

"I'm not stupid." I rolled my eyes. If I'd said anything of the sort in my cousin's hearing, it would've started a war. My cousin hated that he was two years behind me and was adamant that he was just as capable as I was in all things. The guy was competitive. He'd been struggling to keep up since he learned to walk.

"He might have less experience," my pop reminded me quietly. "But he's still a Vampire."

"Well, I'm fucking immortal, and he isn't," I shot back.

I guess I wasn't as immune as I thought to the comparison.

"Oh," Pop replied. He took a deep breath and smoothed his scruffy beard down over his chin. "Already, huh?"

I shrugged my shoulder and pulled back my lips, showing him my canines.

"Lookin' sharp," he commented.

I snorted. "Really?"

"Seemed like the right thing at the moment," he chuckled.

My clothes grew more damp the longer we sat there, our conversation moving on to less fraught topics like the U-bolt that Pop needed for the tractor before he could use the brush hog attachment to clear out the small field behind the barn. I forced myself not to look at the clock on the stove for as long as I could, but eventually my gaze landed there.

I nearly cursed out loud when I realized Daniel had been gone less than an hour and a half.

"Where do you think they are?"

"Probably gettin' close to the coast," Pop replied. "Want another?"

"No thanks," I said as he put more whiskey in his own glass.

"You want me to get an edible?"

I shook my head. I needed to know how bad things would get without it, and I was a little afraid to have anything mind-altering when I knew Daniel was on—for all intents and purposes—a mission. If something happened, I wanted to be clearheaded.

"Did you know Daniel has his pilot's license?" Pop asked as I stared at the clock.

God bless him for trying to keep me distracted.

"Yep," I replied.

"Good thing to have in the family," he mused. "Maybe he'll take me somewhere tropical."

"Uncle Dalton also has his pilot's license and a plane. Plus, you hate the beach."

"I don't hate swim-up bars," he countered.

"You're so full of shit."

"Did I ever tell you that Dalton took me up one time and let me take over the controls?"

"No!" I raised my eyebrows. "How was it?"

"Felt like I was gonna shit myself," he replied, widening his eyes.

"Well, at least you didn't crash."

"Pretty hard to crash at that altitude when I only had the controls for about a minute," he replied ruefully. "But, damn. It was wild while it lasted."

"Did Mom know you two were fucking around in Uncle Dalton's plane?"

"Hell no," he replied immediately. "She would've killed me."

I laughed. She probably wouldn't have killed him, but she would've berated him for it until the day she died. My mother had married a man whose job was one of the most dangerous in the world, but she still lost her mind if he didn't wear a helmet or did anything else that had the slightest risk.

She always told me she didn't worry about Pop when he was working because she knew his training would bring him through, but she was terrified that he would do something stupid when he was home and get himself killed.

"Do you think Mom would like Daniel?" I asked just as the phone rang.

Pop was out of his wheelchair with a quickness I hadn't seen in literal years.

My heart gave a pitiful lurch as I stood and watched as he snatched it off the wall.

"Halle," he said.

His face lost all emotion as he turned toward me.

"You're in the safe room?"

"Boys are with you?"

"Let me talk to Grant."

His hand gripped the edge of the counter so tightly his knuckles were white.

"Hey, bud," he said, his voice just slightly gentler

than he'd been with my aunt. "How many did you see?" He paused. "Right. You did the right thing."

I moved toward him.

"You know the password?"

"Arm yourselves."

"Yeah, you stay where you are. You don't leave that room unless you hear the password. I'll be there soon."

He went silent again, gritting his teeth so hard that I was surprised I couldn't hear it.

"I'll beat you within an inch of your life if you leave that fucking room."

"All right. Hang tight."

"What?" I demanded as he hung up the phone.

"Dalton and Halle's is under attack," he snapped, limping out of the kitchen.

"What do you mean, under attack?" I asked, following on his heels.

"Exactly what it fuckin' sounds like."

"How many men?"

"Grant wasn't sure. He said he saw maybe ten before he got your aunt and Seamus into the safe room."

"Fuck," I mumbled as Pop opened up the safe in the living room. "Did they get ahold of Uncle Dalton?"

"He's black," Pop replied, handing me a rifle.

"Shit," I whispered, laying the rifle on the couch.

It made sense that Uncle Dalton had cut all communication. It was imperative that they weren't interrupted while they were breaching Adamson's beach house. It was just really fucking terrible timing.

I took another rifle and set it next to the previous one. "I thought they had security."

"They did," Pop replied grimly.

It took less than five minutes before every weapon we owned that was readily available was staged in the living room. Boxes of ammunition were stacked by caliber on the coffee table. The armchair held pistols in neat rows. Rifles covered the couch.

"Pop," I said softly, looking from him to the weapons and back again.

There were only two of us, and one of us spent most of his time in a wheelchair.

Against ten or more assailants.

I was sure of my skill, but I wasn't fucking crazy.

"I'm goin'," he said, brushing his thumb over my cheek. "I'll make some calls on the way, see if I can round anyone up. If you want to stay—"

"Oh, fuck off," I shot back, stepping away. "I need five minutes to get dressed."

"Same," he said, following me down the hallway.

Ignoring the way my muscles screamed and my guts clenched and my head pounded, I stripped down to my underwear and started from scratch. Luckily, when we'd set me up to be kidnapped, we'd moved everything that would look suspicious to someone going through my shit to Pop's house. Kneeling beside the bed, I pulled out the long, shallow plastic bin and threw it open.

First, I tugged on a snug black sports bra. Then, a long-sleeved undershirt. Black trousers. Black socks. Black steel-toe boots. With every piece of clothing, I felt myself falling further into the familiar feeling of both detachment and laser focus.

I tossed the lightweight bulletproof vest on the bed, then the tactical vest, two holsters, two knife sheaths that hung on my belt, and my lucky hoodie. I started threading my belt as I got to my feet, adding the sheaths and one of the holsters.

Then I opened up my phone, found my contacts, and pressed the speaker button.

"Hello?" an unfamiliar accented voice answered.

"Erik?" I wrapped the other holster around my thigh, adjusting the tightness because I'd lost some muscle.

"Who's this?"

"Is this Erik Boucher?" I asked, reaching for the bulletproof vest. It wasn't rated for anything beyond handguns, but it was better than nothing. My heavier vest was still in my locker at Strike.

"It is," he replied slowly.

"My name is Rosemary Whitlock." I pulled on my hoodie.

He didn't say anything.

"Uh...I'm your son Daniel's mate."

"Is Danny okay?"

"As far as I know," I replied, shaking my head. "Look, he gave me your number and told me to call if I ever needed to." Pulling on my tactical vest, I zipped it up the front, making sure that all the pouches were where I'd left them and in easy reach.

"What can I do for you?" The words were immediate.

"Well, Danny is, uh...unavailable at the moment, and I'm in a bit of a pickle."

"Tell me what you need."

It took less than a minute to explain the situation, and then I was on the move.

The pockets on my vest were full, and I'd already chosen my weapons when Pop came striding back down the hallway, his shoulders straight and his expression a mirror of my own.

"Do you think we'll need explosives?" I asked, bouncing on the balls of my feet to make sure everything would stay where I put it.

"You want to explain to Dalton why we blew his property up?" he asked, his hands finding and choosing ammunition by rote.

"I'm bringing some anyway," I replied. "I'll meet you at the truck."

I ran to the lean-to against the back of the barn and undid the combination lock while simultaneously trying to ignore the new way my body responded to my commands. I felt awkward and uncoordinated, my muscles straining to do things they'd done automatically before. I'd been so sick that I hadn't even tried to work out after that morning with the tire, and now I was paying for it.

It didn't help that running made the tightness in my chest feel like a balloon that had reached capacity and was about to pop from the pressure.

I stuffed a couple of small blocks of C-4 and a handful of blasting caps in my trouser pockets, just in case we needed them.

I locked up and ran toward the headlights shining through the side yard. Pop was already inside, his fingers tapping on the steering wheel as he waited for me. Thunder sat in the center of the bench seat, his tongue lolling halfway out of his mouth.

"Go," I ordered as I threw myself inside.

Pop spun in a wide circle and raced back down the road while I pulled the rifle strap off my neck and set it next to the one I was holding at my feet.

"How are we doing this?" I asked, reaching up to pull my hair into a tightly woven braid.

"I'll park at the end of the road, and we'll make our way on foot."

"Pop, how are you going to do that?" I asked reasonably.

I wasn't even sure how he was carrying all the supplies he had. Walking a quarter of a mile up Uncle Dalton's driveway was going to fuck him up big time.

"You got any other ideas?" he asked, barely glancing at me. "You wanna pull up to the door, Rosemary? Knock and see if they'll let us in?"

"Don't fucking snap at me."

"Stop asking stupid questions." He grimaced. "I'll do what needs to be done."

Fuck, I really wished my mate was with us. I tried to regulate my breathing as we raced toward Uncle Dalton and Aunt Halle's property, but nothing seemed to be working. The heat was seriously fucking with my focus. My mouth watered and my throat spasmed as I tried to convince my body not to vomit.

I'd seen Daniel in action. If I'd had him at my back, I would've felt a lot better about what we were walking into. I wanted him close enough to touch. Just the sight of him would've made the fear that clung to me loosen its grip.

It wasn't as if I didn't trust my pop. I trusted him more than any other person in the world, and I knew what he was capable of—but I also knew what his limitations were and that he'd push past them without thinking in order to protect me.

Even if things went well and we took care of the threat, it could end very poorly for my pop. I was petrified that, at the very least, if he lived through this, by the end of the night, my father wouldn't be using the wheelchair part-time anymore.

The drive took us ten minutes. It should've taken closer to twenty. We passed the entrance to the property, watching for signs of sentries, before turning back around and parking in the trees across the road.

"You should post up on the hill," I said, looking at the old sniper rifle propped up on the seat between us as he cut the truck lights. "That'll give you the best vantage point."

"Sure," Pop scoffed. "I'll let you go down to the house by yourself and cover you from a safe distance."

"I won't be alone," I said as first one, then two, then three, four, five people stepped out of the trees.

"Erik fucking Boucher," Pop said, shooting me a look.

"I figured I'd cover our bases," I said, throwing open my door. "In case you couldn't reach anyone."

I hopped out of my seat and grabbed my rifles, slinging one over my back. My hands moved over my vest, checking things were where they should be by habit as I walked toward the newcomers.

I recognized Daniel's brothers instantly. Both of the clean-cut Vampires were standing next to women who looked a little older than me. His father stepped forward, like he couldn't stop himself, as I got closer.

"Rosemary," he said, a smile in his voice.

"Mr. Boucher."

"Please, call me Erik." His eyes widened as Pop stepped up beside me. "Gary Whitlock."

"Thanks for coming, Erik."

"Your father is Gary Whitlock?" Erik said in what sounded like delight. "Gods."

"Ambrose. Beau."

"Good to see you, Gary," Ambrose said with a nod. "This is my mate, Lucy. And that's Beau's mate, Reese."

"You brought your mates," Pop said carefully.

"We weren't too excited for them to leave us behind again," Reese said dryly. "Don't worry. We'll stay out of the way."

"Reese is a hell of a shot," Beau said reluctantly. "She'll post up at a distance."

"And I'm her security," Lucy said proudly.

"Her spotter," Ambrose corrected in amusement.

"Tomato, tomahto."

"Pop's going to be up on the hill," I said, jerking my chin toward the high rise visible on the property across the road.

"Rosemary," Pop snapped in warning.

"Don't fucking start, old man," I shot back, glaring at him.

I had three Bouchers to work with. I wasn't above pointing out exactly why he couldn't be down in the thick of things, and I think he knew it from the look on my face because he didn't say anything else.

There would be hell to pay when we were finished that night, but I'd deal with that later.

Things weren't moving quickly, and everything inside me urged me to start running for the house, but I shoved the instinct down. If we flew in there without a plan, we wouldn't be able to help anyone. Whoever had broken through Uncle Dalton's security team and made their way inside the house had to have been planning for a while.

The only comfort I had was that the safe room was nearly impossible to find unless you knew where to look, but that comfort was slowly fading away the longer those men were in the house and we were across the road. The longer they had to look, the longer they had to find the room, and while they didn't have a way inside, they could easily burn the place to the ground around my aunt and cousins.

I'd drawn the layout of the house on a notebook that the Bouchers had brought with us, and we contributed and discarded ideas for a solid ten minutes before I threw up my hands in frustration.

"Nothing is going to work perfectly," I spat. "I know what you're doing."

"What's that?" Beau asked flatly.

"You're trying to minimize any risk to me," I replied, my voice just as flat. "Which is bullshit. I know what I'm doing, and I'm as immortal as the rest of you. So stop fucking around and let's get in there."

"There's no way to know if your immortality has manifested yet," Erik warned.

"Let's call it an educated guess, then," I countered. "My aunt called us—" I looked at my watch. "Thirty-six minutes ago. How much longer do you think they have before those men get antsy and start blowing shit up or find the safe room and start trying to figure a way inside?"

"We'll breach in this lower window," Erik said after a moment. "That goes into the mudroom, correct?"

"Laundry room," I corrected. "It's off the mudroom."

He nodded. "Ambrose and Beau, you'll go in from

the back. Second story, third window from the right." He looked at me.

"There's an old oak on the other end of the house," I said, pointing to where it was relative to my roughly drawn house. "If you use that to get onto the eaves, it's an easy shot over to the window. That goes into Ian's bedroom apartment. He always leaves that window open because he's a hot sleeper."

Beau eyed me.

"He's my fucking *cousin*," I reminded him.

Pop handed me a little pot of greasy paint. I thanked him with a nod as I opened it up and began to smear it over my cheeks.

"We'll set Lucy and Reese up on the way through," Ambrose said. "You'll need to give us two or three extra minutes."

"We can do that."

"I'll help my pop—"

"I think I can manage to set up," Pop cut me off. He looked at Reese. "I'll be on the eastern side. If at any point you think you've been spotted, lie flat. Don't try to move. I'll draw fire."

"I can do that," she said nervously.

"We brought Ghillie suits," Lucy said with a nod. "We'll be practically invisible."

Erik tossed the notebook in the back of the truck as Pop let Thunder out of the cab, and without any more words, the seven of us split up. Erik, Pop, and I moved toward the eastern side of the property while the Boucher brothers and their mates moved to the west.

"Chance and Danny are out of communication?" Erik asked Pop.

"Went black an hour before Halle called me," Pop confirmed.

"Any idea when they'll come back online?"

"Another hour, maybe," Pop replied. "Could be less depending on what they find."

Erik hummed in acknowledgment.

"I left them a message for whenever they fire things up again."

"Coded?" Erik asked softly.

"Yes."

Then we were silent as we moved further onto the property.

I placed my steps carefully as I led the way. I hadn't seen anyone in the trees, but that didn't mean they weren't there. We just hadn't encountered anyone yet. When we came to the place where Pop would go his own way, he set his fingertips to his lips and then brushed my cheek.

I flashed him the ASL sign for I love you.

Almost immediately, he vanished into the forest, Thunder trotting along beside him.

Erik's hand tapped my shoulder softly to get me moving again.

The minutes ticked away like the *Jeopardy* theme song as we moved toward the window we'd be entering. I hated that Aunt Halle and the boys were sitting in there, probably scared out of their minds. The chance of anyone making it into the safe room was low, but it wasn't zero.

Just as we hit the tree line, something in my peripheral vision made me sway to a stop.

A man in tactical gear picked his way through the brush just thirty feet from us.

Erik gave my biceps a quick squeeze and then disappeared from beside me. As slowly as I could, I leaned toward a tree so I'd blend into the shadow.

Seconds later, the man I'd been watching turned into a larger mass, then dropped slowly to the ground. Erik nodded at me to keep moving as soon as he rose.

Every window in the house was lit up when we reached the detached shop and moved through the shadows that various truck tires and water barrels provided us. The people inside were searching, and they weren't bothering to conserve energy as they made their way through the house.

I was in the lead, so I was the first to see the man leaning against the shop just around the corner. His weapon was held across his chest as his eyes swept the yard.

Go time.

I held my hand up for Erik, then smoothly rounded the corner. In the split second it took for the man to realize I wasn't someone he recognized, I'd shoved his weapon to the side and punched him in the throat. Unfortunately, this man seemed to be able to fight just fine without breathing, and he swung his rifle up. By then, I was too close for him to get it between us. I caught the barrel of the rifle in my armpit, thankful that he didn't seem willing to let it go, and pulled the knife from the sheath on my belt.

Seconds later, I was fighting the urge to gag as I lowered him to the ground, the blood from his neck wound saturating the entire front of me.

Erik was standing just behind me when I went to look for him. His eyes searched me for wounds as I shrugged.

I may not have done it as cleanly as he would've, but I'd still gotten the job done—and silently, for that matter.

There was another man closer to the house that I let Erik take care of. I was still struggling to keep the whiskey in my stomach from making a reappearance. Touching the man had caused my skin to flare with the fire of a thousand hells and my pulse to pound in my temples.

I guess the mating heat didn't differentiate between fucking or killing someone who wasn't your mate.

When we got to the window, Erik bent down on one knee so that I could use his thigh as a stool to reach the lock that had been easy to open for as long as I could remember. The window was two panes that met in the middle or swung inward if you wanted the window open. On a fully functioning window, there would've been a seal between the panes, but in this particular window, Ian and I had shoved a knife through it when I was ten and he was eight, because we were convinced that someday we'd be housebreakers. It had felt very mysterious and cool until Aunt Halle had seen what we'd done to her antique windows.

Long story short, the seal between the panes was gone, and I could easily unlatch the lock between them with a credit card. Sliding the card in beneath the latch, I slowly drew it up, holding my breath as the latch caught for a moment and then let go.

I opened the window slowly, listening carefully for any sound of someone coming to investigate. When no sound came, I pulled myself up to my waist and shimmied my top half inside. Bracing my hands on the top of the washing machine, I pulled my legs inside, cringing as they made a swishing noise as they dragged along.

I'd just landed on my feet next to the ironing board when Erik's head and chest appeared inside.

He was much more graceful as he pulled his body inside than I was. Perhaps he'd been a housebreaker at some point.

Erik lifted his head and winked at me, and I was struck by how much he looked like his son.

Daniel hadn't been lying when he said he had his father's coloring and build, but he'd definitely been understating it.

My father-in-law cocked his head to the side as if asking what the hell I was doing.

Right.

I led him toward the doorway, listening for sounds of the people in the house. There was definitely someone just outside the laundry room, probably standing guard in the mudroom that led to the back door of the house.

Without a word, Erik moved past me. He opened the door swiftly and silently, stepping through it like it was nothing, and almost as soon as I'd made it out of the room, Erik was already wrapping his arms around the man. It was over in an instant.

If I hadn't been around Vampires my entire life—mercenaries at that—I would've been scared as hell at the speed and efficiency Erik was capable of.

We moved through the entire first floor like wraiths. There were two more men downstairs. One at the front door, and one who seemed like he'd been tasked with roaming the house at random. I took care of one with my knife, but the other was too fast for me and a freaking giant to boot, so I let Erik handle him. Fighting fire with fire and all that.

Shaking out my arms, I jerked my chin toward the ceiling, where we could hear more men stomping around. A lot more men. Erik and I had already taken care of five of them, but there were at least double that tearing apart the upstairs.

Grant had counted ten.

Kids were never reliable narrators.

It was a good thing I loved the little punk.

The stairway leading up to the second floor was too open for Erik and me to move on safely, so I led him back toward the laundry room. There was a doorway just off the mudroom that looked like it led to nothing, but actually was a hidden staircase that came out in the huge linen closet at the top of the stairs.

I stopped halfway up and pointed at the eleventh stair, shaking my head. Then I stepped completely over it. I paused and waited for Erik to do the same thing.

They'd built the staircase back when servants weren't supposed to be seen more than necessary, but it had creeped Aunt Halle out, so the Cavendishes rarely used it. Ian and I, on the other hand, had smoked quite a few cigarettes in that tiny stairwell where we knew neither of the little boys would come looking for us. That squeaky eleventh stair had once gotten us caught with the contraband, and we'd been grounded for two weeks.

They never realized or didn't care that grounding both of us, but still letting us see each other, was no punishment at all. We could make our own fun without whatever had been taken away.

God, I hoped Ian and Daniel were okay. I was too preoccupied to look at my watch and see how long they'd been gone already.

Outside the linen closet, I paused again and looked to Erik. He nodded to me. He couldn't hear anything on the other side.

The door caught on the mess they'd made of the closet. They must've already searched it, but somehow hadn't realized there was a door hidden behind a row of shelves. I stepped inside the room and cringed as my boots dug into all the clean linens that covered the floor.

The men were louder now, and we could easily hear their conversations as they called to each other from different rooms. To the left of us was Seamus and Grant's room, and I could hear the men throwing shit around. Glass broke. A loud thump that had to have been one of the bedframes being overturned.

"Steady," Erik said quietly. He paused with his hand on the doorway to the hall.

Once we were out there, we'd be surrounded on all sides. There was no way to hide in the wide hallway that bisected the upper floor of the house. If even one of the intruders was out there, it would be impossible to maintain our cover.

Beau and Ambrose should've already been inside the house, but there was no way to know. Hopefully, they'd gotten inside Ian's apartment and were waiting for a sign from us. If not, Erik and I were kind of screwed.

"I'll go right," Erik said after a moment. He turned toward me and quickly grabbed the back of my head, planting a kiss on the hair just above my forehead. "For luck," he whispered with a wink.

He waited only long enough for me to raise my weapon before he was opening the door wide and stepping out.

The next few minutes were an impossibly loud blur. There were three men in the hallway, and two of them opened fire as soon as Erik had dropped the first. The Vampire behind me was the embodiment of precision. Without even looking at him, I knew the grace with which he moved as he aimed and fired, keeping his body between me and the hallway behind me.

I was a little less precise. I took out the first man and the second, but the third came out too quickly, and I felt a bullet graze the meat at my hip, just below the edge of my vest. It took four shots for me to hit him because I'd automatically jerked when the bullet grazed me, and it messed up my aim.

The hallway behind where I stood was much longer than the one before me, and Erik was firing twice as quickly as more men streamed out of the rooms. He stumbled, and his back brushed mine before he was steady on his feet again. I barely registered the feeling before two more men came out of Uncle Dalton's room and the spare room next to it.

They weren't all coming at once. While Erik and I stood in the center of the chaos, they were strategically sending out one or two at a time.

I swallowed hard as one of the men got a shot off as he went down. It lodged somewhere above our heads.

Then, Beau and Ambrose were there. I could hear

their voices from the other end of the hall as it quieted. In seconds, they were beside me, and Erik had his hand on my shoulder as he covered my back and we made our way toward Uncle Dalton's room.

By the time we were finished, my ears were ringing, and I could barely hear a thing.

I stood in the center of my uncle and aunt's room, barely able to catch my breath.

"Safe room?" Erik asked, looking at the walls.

"It's not in here," I gasped, shaking my head.

"Where is it?" Ambrose asked as the sound of a rifle shot filtered in through a broken window.

The thing about the safe room was that I'd been taught since I was old enough to understand words that it was not to be shared with anyone. Not my teachers, not my doctor, not the police, not the fire department, not my priest—if I'd had one. Absolutely no one outside of Uncle Dalton, Aunt Halle, my mom and dad, Ian, Grant, and Seamus could ever know where the door to the safe room was. All of our lives could depend on it.

So it took me a moment to form the words because everything inside me was screaming not to.

"Downstairs," I rasped, leading the way.

Adrenaline was coursing through my veins as I stepped over bodies and carefully peeked over the railing to the stairs. There was no sound coming from down there, but that didn't mean anything. Someone could've been hiding.

Erik passed me and hurried down the stairs first.

It didn't feel good to be proven right when automatic gunfire came from the media room to the left of the stairway.

"Motherfuckers," Beau spat as he took the stairs two at a time. He reached Erik just as he'd dropped down behind the railing. Thankfully, between the two of them, the shooting stopped.

"You can let go of me now," I told Ambrose through my teeth. His hand felt like it had burned a hole through the skin of my arm.

"Sorry," he said quietly as we followed the others. I turned off lights as we moved through the house, going out of my way to make sure that we weren't lit up like a fish tank for anyone outside to see.

When we reached the center island of the kitchen, I had to force myself to reach beneath the counter and press the minuscule button.

"And turn and go up to the open door boldly, and knock to the echoes as beggars for roses," I said, knocking twice, then four times more.

"What?" Beau asked. "Are you quoting Robert Frost?"

I didn't have to reply because the end of the counter began to swing inward from the floor. As soon as it had swung parallel to the counter above it, Aunt Halle's head came into view, her eyes filled with fear.

"Rosemary?"

"Sometimes during the day I will look at the house and the house will look at me, and the house will weep."

"Yes, it does," she whispered back.

"I can feel it," I told her hoarsely, my throat tight with tears of relief.

"Oh god," she replied. "Come on, boys."

Aunt Halle climbed up the ladder first, her eyes widening when she saw the Vampires with me.

"Daniel's family," I told her, putting my hand on her shoulder so she wouldn't rise into view of the windows. "Stay down there for a sec."

"Rosemary Halle, I wiped your ass."

"And Uncle Dalton taught me to operate," I countered, my eyes on Erik's back as he stared through the window. "Now stay put for a minute."

"Flower?" Grant asked in surprise. He looked around as he crawled out. "Whoa."

"Quiet," I ordered. Erik was watching something, but I couldn't tell what it was.

"Seamus, get out here," I murmured, keeping my voice low. "We need to move."

"Where's Uncle Gary?" Grant asked worriedly.

"He's here," I assured him as we ushered my aunt and the boys along the wall opposite the windows. "We'll see him soon."

"Fucking hell," Ambrose hissed as his arm flew out and slammed both Grant and Seamus closer to the wall. "We've got more."

"How many do you see?" Beau asked.

"Two trucks, you?"

"I see three," Beau called from the other room. "No, four."

"Why the fuck are there more of them?" I asked no one in particular.

I glanced at the kitchen island, which looked completely normal again, but instantly discarded the idea of sending Aunt Halle and the boys back in there. The whole reason we were in the house was to get them out of the situation. That's what we needed to do, and we needed to do it fast before the new men made it inside the house.

"Out the back door," Erik called softly. "Quickly now."

As we shuffled silently toward the mudroom, I could see more than four sets of headlights out front. In a matter of minutes, we'd be surrounded.

CHAPTER 12
DANIEL

"Do you think he'll talk?" Chance asked as we pulled our gear out of the cabin.

"With enough incentive," I replied, ignoring the trembling in my hands as I loaded my rifle.

"He'll talk," Dalton said firmly. "There's an explanation."

"Can't wait to hear his excuses," Chance muttered, with a humorless laugh. "Should be a hoot."

"I didn't say excuses," Dalton countered. "I said an explanation. He's involved for a reason."

"Who gives a fuck what his reasons are?" Ian said angrily.

"Focus," his father said calmly, barely glancing at him.

I wasn't pleased that Dalton had decided to bring his kid along, but I wasn't about to argue about it. If he wanted to get Junior's feet wet on something this important, it wasn't any of my business. I trusted Chance and only Chance to have my back with this.

We'd learned the hard way that the only people we

could trust in this life were our family. I was more than happy to have allies, but when it came down to it, I didn't trust any of them.

"Let's get this over with," Chance said with a sigh.

I followed him as he broke into a jog across the field we'd landed in. We were just over a mile from the Adamson property, and the air was thick and wet coming off the ocean. When we finally slowed to a walk, my entire body was damp from sweat and the moisture in the air. Even my beard had little beads of water that I had to brush away.

Adamson's house was at the top of a small dune, and it was massive. The side that faced the windows was basically an entire wall of glass, but the rest of it looked like any other mansion built in the last thirty years. There were three entry points I noticed right away—the front door and the garage door that opened up to the driveway on the top floor, and a door on the ground floor that led out onto the sand. I was pretty sure there must have been another door on the opposite side of the house from where we were, just by looking at how the house was built, but since we were working with a time limit, I didn't bother to investigate.

We could find the egress points once we were inside.

Posting up in a half circle around the eastern side of the house, we counted seven Vampires patrolling and watching those entrances. There were two black SUVs in the driveway, and the house was lit, but filmy curtains concealed what was happening inside.

"Danny and I have the four to the north," Chance said after a few minutes, his voice lower than a whisper through my comms. "You have the other three?"

"Affirmative," Dalton breathed.

Working with my brothers was always a little bit of a surprise, though why it should be after a hundred years, I had no idea. We knew each other's moves before we made them, and the entire task ended up being far easier than we expected. I incapacitated the Vampire by the driveway entrance by simply knocking him out with the butt of my pistol. Chance choked the next with the strap of the kid's own rifle. When he moved on to the third, he was grinning like he was having the time of his life. Simultaneously, I moved to the fourth, who was a bit more on top of things than the first ones had been, and actually saw me coming. He fought back, but was ultimately pretty ineffectual. He also hadn't called out to his teammates. A rookie mistake.

Unfortunately, he was also huge, and dragging him into the trees to tie him up was a fucking pain in the ass.

"Feels like they're getting younger and younger," Chance said as we stared at the four Vampires tied to the trees.

"They are," Dalton replied from behind us. "Used to be that you had to be thirty to join Command. Now it's twenty, and they make them security guards or admin clerks at the training center. It's bullshit."

I glanced at Ian, who had to be older than twenty.

"I won't work for Command," he said flatly, his eyes dark.

"None of my sons will," Dalton added.

We left the Vampires in the trees and made our way

back to the house. The front door was open, and we walked right in. Moving silently, we made our way through the foyer and checked rooms as we followed voices downstairs to a large room overlooking the water.

There was no security inside.

"They're getting anxious," a familiar grating voice said as we stopped in the hallway. "If we don't get the Bouchers and Dalton fucking Cavendish under control, they're going to back out."

"The Bouchers aren't willing to leave their little compound. Haven't in weeks."

"They took out an entire unit. The humans are worried."

"That's because someone had the bright idea to try to take them when they were all together."

"The brothers weren't supposed to be there."

"They *weren't* there. But they didn't leave the place undefended, and whoever thought they would was a fucking idiot."

"It's over. There's no reason to keep harping on it."

"If you think Erik Boucher and his boys aren't planning something, you're the fucking idiot."

Three voices. Three very familiar voices. I looked at Chance.

No way in hell had we gotten this lucky.

"The Bouchers are hobbled, at least for now. They're regrouping, but we've got time."

"Have you *met* Erik Boucher?"

"It's Cavendish we need to deal with. He's been asking questions, and he's not quiet about it—and he's got that ridiculous company. *Strike*. Gods, he's always been insufferable."

"Hermann doesn't care about Vampire squabbles. He wants results, and he's getting them. He thinks another year, maybe two."

"That's at least twenty-five more mates, yes?"

"At least."

"Well, that's doable."

"Not if Cavendish is telling everyone and their mothers that mates are disappearing."

"He's got no proof."

"His son's mate was held for over a week. Who knows what she heard? We need to take care of that."

My eyes flickered, and I blinked hard, trying to stop them. It was never a good time to see things through a haze of red, but this might be the worst. I needed to keep my shit together.

"If she'd heard anything, we'd already know about it."

"Cavendish sounds like a crackpot, and he won't be a problem for much longer. I want to know when payment is coming through. They've missed the last two, and I'm not putting my head on the line if they're not going to keep their end of the deal."

"They'll pay."

"When?"

"I'll talk to Baudelaire."

I kept my eyes on Chance. Zeke had been right when he'd hypothesized that François Baudelaire was funding the project. He hadn't even put it in his notes because it had just been an idea, but he'd mentioned it to Lucy and Charles before he'd gone back to his unit. Gods, if we sat here long enough, I wondered just how much information these Vampires would spill.

"They shouldn't have killed the youngest Boucher.

You do realize we're fucked now, right? They won't stop."

"So we'll stop them."

"How do you plan on doing that?"

"The Bouchers are off the board for now. Relax, Morren."

"You're wrong."

"We only need twenty-five more, and then we can be through with this entire thing. Eyes on the prize."

"So...fifty," Morren said dully. "Twenty-five Vampires and twenty-five mates. That's fifty."

"You're getting soft."

"I didn't want to do any of this in the first place."

"Yet, here you are."

"Are we done here? I need to be back in Virginia before sunrise. I've got meetings all day."

"We're done. All of us just need to keep things tight and our heads down for a little longer."

"You'll let me know how tonight goes?"

"Yep."

Dalton reached out slowly and pressed his fingers to my arm. When I met his gaze, I nodded.

We barely made a sound as we entered the room.

Adamson was sitting in an armchair, his head in his hands. Morren looked like he was going to shit himself as he stood near the window, and Keihley's eyes narrowed in anger when he realized who'd come to visit.

"Rollins," Morren yelled, taking a step sideways like it would matter.

"If you're hoping for one of those young bucks to come save you, you're out of luck," Chance said cheerfully, his rifle pointed at Morren's chest. "They're a little tied up at the moment."

"You should really train them better," Ian added nonchalantly.

"Who the hell are you?" Keihley asked.

"Fuck off, trash," Ian shot back.

"Dalton," Adamson said, rising slowly from the chair. "What are you doing here?"

"Funny thing, that," Dalton replied softly. "Thought I was coming to show Chance and Danny that my old friend couldn't be involved in this mess. Turns out, we got an education instead."

"You don't understand."

Adamson buckled as a bullet from Dalton's rifle struck his kneecap.

"That's gotta sting," Chance said, making a clicking noise with his tongue. "Uh-uh." He gestured at Morren with his rifle. "You stay right where you are."

"You're fucking dead," Keihley blustered. "I'm a general in the United States Vampire Command. Do you think—"

I looked away as Chance's rifle jerked beside me, but not in time to miss the way Keihley's head exploded.

"We only need two, right?" Chance asked, his tone darker but still eerily cheerful. "I mean, two should be plenty, right?"

"Chance," Morren said. "We don't—"

"You're not going to remind me of your rank like Keihley did, are you?" Chance asked. "Because that might piss me off."

I was struggling to keep myself centered.

These Vampires may not have killed my brother

themselves. They may not have even given the order, but they'd made it possible. They'd sacrificed Vampires and their mates to horrors that I could barely stomach while being driven around by armed security and hanging out in their mansions. They'd spoken about Zeke's death like it was *nothing*.

My mate was in danger because of these motherfuckers. Had been in pain for weeks while I searched for them.

"Danny, how you doing, buddy?" Chance asked as I blinked and blinked.

"I can give you names," Morren said quickly, his face filled with horror. "I can give you everything."

"Yes, but will you?" Dalton replied, his eyes still on Adamson.

"Whatever you want," Morren promised. "I'll tell you everything."

"Right, because you didn't want to be here in the first place."

"I didn't," he said quickly. "I didn't want anything to do with this. I didn't have any choice."

"There's always a choice," Ian barked.

"There wasn't. Once I knew, they would've killed me if I tried to back out. Once I knew, it was too late."

"Fucking coward," I ground out.

"I know." His head nodded so fast he looked like one of those bobbleheads that people put on their dashboards. "I know, but I was forced."

Dalton shot him. "I think one is plenty, don't you?" He looked at Chance.

"More than enough," Chance agreed. Lowering his rifle, he strode toward Adamson. "Come on, little fella. Time to get up."

"You really think this is going to go well for you?" Adamson wheezed as Chance jerked him to his feet. "You broke in and killed two of the top generals in the United States. You think anyone will believe whatever bullshit story you try to spin?"

"Even if they don't," Dalton said, his smile all teeth. "I'll take your head before this is through." He looked to his son. "Make sure there's no coming back for them."

"Yep," Ian said.

I should've done something—helped Chance with Adamson or taken the job from Ian—but I didn't. I wasn't sure that I could keep myself locked down. Listening to the three of them talk about what they'd done so casually had pushed me to the limits of my control.

I led the way back upstairs, ignoring the thumping behind me as Chance dragged Adamson up the stairs. The Vampire was completely unable to walk after Dalton had ruined his knee.

"Let's take one of the SUVs," Dalton said when we reached the front door. He pulled a set of keys from his pocket. "Better than running."

"I'll drive," I replied, catching the keys when he tossed them.

I waited in the driver's seat while Chance searched Adamson and then stuffed him into the trunk. Dalton and Ian disappeared into the woods to make sure that all the Vampires there were still tied up and hopefully still knocked out.

It took us about three minutes to get back to the helicopter, and in that time, Dalton was busy. Bending over the back seat, he tied a tourniquet around Adamson's leg while peppering him with questions. Who had made the initial proposal? How had the three Vampires met Baudelaire? What was the humans' objective? Were there any other Vampires involved? Question after question was voiced, but no answers were forthcoming. At first, Adamson sat silently, but as soon as Dalton tied the tourniquet, he passed out from the pain.

"That mess won't take long to find," Dalton announced as we parked and climbed out of the vehicle. "I'm going to call Arthur."

I just stared at him.

"He asked me to find the head of the snake," Dalton reminded me. "We've found it. I need to apprise him of the situation before he finds out that two of his generals are dead and one is missing."

"Do it," Chance answered for me. "If Arthur wants to party, I'll bring the disco ball."

"You sure?" I asked him. If Arthur was dirty, we'd be fucked. There wasn't a corner of the earth that he couldn't reach. He had the entirety of the United States Vampire Command at his disposal.

Chance nodded.

My brother and I went to the back of the SUV and opened it, lifting Adamson's limp body out, Chance at the head, and me at the feet. Halfway to the helicopter, he fucking let go.

"Whoops," Chance said with a chuckle as my arms wrenched downward and Adamson's head bounced off the ground.

"Stop fucking around," I grunted, my lips twitching.

"He's gonna have a headache," Chance replied, lifting Adamson by his wrists. "What do you think? Should we swing him up?"

"You're so annoying." I tried to hide my smile. Fuck, he was funny. "Just put him in."

We maneuvered Adamson's body across the floorboard of the cabin and left him there. Turning around, I realized Dalton and Ian were still standing next to the SUV, completely frozen.

"That can't be good," Chance said as we set off at a jog back toward the others.

"What?" I snapped as we reached them.

Dalton pressed a button on his phone, and Gary's voice filtered out.

"When you get this, come straight back. Got a call from Halle on the house phone. Do not pass Go. Do not collect two hundred dollars. We're on our way." The message repeated on a loop.

"What does that mean?" Chance asked as Dalton finally snapped out of it and started sprinting for the helicopter.

"Our house is being attacked," Ian said as he threw open the door and climbed into the front seat.

I didn't bother trying to step around Adamson as I climbed in the back. I just stepped right on top of him. The blades began to whirl as I closed the door.

"My mother and my brothers made it to the safe room."

"How the hell did you get that from the message?" Chance asked once we had our headsets on.

"A call from my mom on the house phone," Ian said as we began to rise. "That phone is only used for one thing. Do not pass Go—she's in the safe room. Do not collect two hundred dollars—she has both my brothers."

I braced as Dalton banked right, replaying the message from Gary in my mind.

We.

He'd said *we*. He hadn't said, I'm on my way. He'd said *we're* on our way.

Rosemary went with him.

"Text Ambrose," I ordered Chance. "I'll text Beau."

Chance nodded. "They're closer."

It was the longest flight I'd ever taken. Every minute felt like a year. Neither of my brothers responded to their messages. My dad never answered his phone. My mother's phone went straight to voicemail.

We flew blindly toward Dalton's house. Clutching my rifle, I fought the urge to count my ammunition. I hadn't even fired my weapon at the Adamson house. There was no reason to fidget. It wouldn't get us there any faster. It wouldn't change anything that was happening, as I sat there without a scratch on me.

It hurt to breathe. My head pounded in sync with my heartbeat.

It felt like déjà vu, but this time, I had no control over how fast we got there.

It had been less than a month since we'd gotten the call that, while we were out, our house was being attacked. Then, I'd been afraid for my mother and my brothers' mates, but my mate had been safely seated behind me.

I hadn't realized how agonizing it had been for Beau and Ambrose back then. How completely overwhelming the terror was. My mate was there, in danger, and I was too far away to do anything about it.

Every muscle in my body was locked tight. Sweat dripped off the end of my nose. Nausea wasn't even the right word for the way my stomach churned and cramped. It felt like someone had their hand in there and was twisting a fistful of my guts from side to side.

I'd been able to handle the symptoms up to that point. I'd pushed the discomfort aside, ignored it, pushed through it.

I couldn't ignore it now. With every minute that passed, my fear fed the heat, and it felt like at any moment my body was going to begin shutting down. No one could survive that kind of pain.

Why the fuck had I thought putting any kind of distance between us was a good idea? I knew better. I'd lived through the consequences of it.

I'd just been so sure that Gary would keep Rosemary safe. Between the precautions he'd shown me while Rosemary was sleeping the week before, and his biological need to protect his offspring, I'd assumed that no matter what happened—if anything did—she'd survive it. He'd make sure of that.

I could've never imagined that he would take her off the property.

This was the only reason he would've.

Dalton's mate Halle and their boys. It was the only possible reason that Gary would ever willingly risk Rosemary's safety. He knew he couldn't do it alone. He knew she could help.

He knew he'd never be able to keep her from going.

"How much longer?" I asked, looking out the window.

"Four minutes," Ian answered.

Dalton hadn't spoken once.

"She's fine," Chance said, reaching over to slap my chest. "Only a couple more minutes and you'll see for yourself."

"Don't land at the house," I ordered.

"The closest place to land is a quarter mile away," Ian replied, looking at me in disbelief over his shoulder.

"If we land at the house, we'll barely make it out of the helicopter," I said, leaning forward. I knew Dalton could hear me through the headset, but I wasn't sure he would actually listen.

"We need to go in quietly or they'll be ready for us."

"It could be over by now," Chance said as he watched Dalton worriedly. "Did it say when that message was sent?"

Ian shook his head.

"If we land on your property, someone is going to notice," I warned. "We'll lose any element of surprise we have."

"Dad?" Ian murmured.

Adamson groaned when Dalton took a sharp left and the helicopter swung sideways.

"Shut the fuck up," Chance growled, stomping on Adamson's back. "No one fucking cares."

He pulled a piece of thin rope out of his pocket and leaned down to tie Adamson's hands behind his back. By the time he'd finished, we were just setting down on a grassy piece of land. I wasn't sure where we were, but there were no lights in the distance giving any indication of a house.

I had to throw myself out of the helicopter and land running to keep up with Dalton and Ian through the woods. They leaped over small creeks and circumvented large rocks like they'd run that path a hundred times before and could do it with their eyes closed. By the time they slowed, light was visible through the trees around us.

At first, I thought it was outdoor lights, but as we moved closer, I realized that the front of the house was illuminated with headlights. At least six vehicles were parked out front, and I didn't recognize any of them.

The men were yelling to each other in hushed voices, racing in and out of the house like ants on an anthill.

Then the crack of a rifle shot.

A man in the front doorway of the house collapsed.

Another rifle shot.

Someone near one of the vehicles disappeared behind it.

Three men in the yard began firing at where the second shot had come from.

Another shot, and one of them went down.

"That's Gary," Dalton said, his eyes searching the yard. "I recognize the sound of his rifle."

"Is the other one Rosemary?" I asked, searching the hill.

"I doubt it," Ian said softly. "Someone had to get Mom and the boys out of the safe room."

Everything inside me stilled.

I'd only experienced the sensation once before, but I'd been too young to fully remember it. When my father realized what he'd passed down, he'd done his best to equip me with the tools to keep it in check. We'd had so many conversations about it as I grew, and long after I was an adult.

Up until that point, I'd always been able to hold it back by calming myself down.

Unfortunately, the box that I'd held my emotions in for most of my life was suddenly nowhere to be found.

My father said that when it came over him, it was as if his senses heightened, but everything came through a filter as if his body knew instinctively what mattered and what didn't. All pain disappeared. Tiredness was washed away. Thought narrowed into precise focus.

Like father, like son.

I didn't realize I was moving until I was already upon the men near the SUV. Through a red haze, I cut them down. I didn't even bother with the rifle hanging over my shoulder. The knife in my hand worked just fine.

Chance's voice came from somewhere behind me, but I ignored it.

There was a man inside the SUV. I took care of him too.

Then I strode toward the house.

There were so many of them inside, and they all came to meet me.

My rifle was still on my back, but my pistol was easily accessible in my holster, so I used that as the men raced toward me.

I grunted in frustration as Chance and Dalton ran up the stairs, chasing a few of the men down.

My hands flexed as I stalked through the bottom floor. No more men.

Ian stood next to me, saying something, but I couldn't hear him.

He wasn't important.

Turning, I walked back out the front door. My mate was here somewhere, and I needed to find her. Walking down the side of the house, I searched for more of the humans. Shots peppered around me, but I ignored those too. A bullet wouldn't slow me down unless I let it.

My mate was somewhere on that property, and I was going to find her.

I wasn't sure how many men I faced as I moved toward the back of the property, but there were a lot. They swarmed like locusts on a field of wheat. When one fell, another took his place.

Ian was still beside me, fighting with a skill I hadn't known the young Vampire possessed. It was a good thing that he was so skilled, because I wouldn't have stopped to help him if he got into trouble.

Behind the house were a large shop and two smaller ones. All were dark, but the doors were open and there were men everywhere.

I stumbled as I crossed the yard, but I used the momentum to keep moving forward. There were no helpful shots coming from the ridgeline above the property on this side of the house, and I had to meet every man myself. By then, I was moving slower than I was used to, but it was still effective.

We cleared one shop and had entered the second when Dalton and Chance caught up to us.

We cleared the last shops quickly.

Then there was just silence surrounding us.

"They're not inside," Dalton said so quietly that even I barely heard him.

"Don't touch him," Chance hissed as Ian moved beside him. "Leave him be."

"But—"

"Don't," Chance said firmly.

That's when I heard someone in the woods. I began to jog, barely noticing that one leg was dragging a little with each step. The sound was coming from the area to the west side of the house and moving upward through the trees.

My mate.

I dodged branches and stepped over the ferns and bushes in my way as I followed the sound.

The first thing I saw was Thunder racing through the trees at an angle.

Then from across the property, high on the hill, I heard Gary's voice. He wasn't shouting, but Thunder must have heard him because he picked up speed.

"*Voren*! *Fass*!"

Go. Attack.

I ran to intercept him, and just as I reached the point where I could follow, he leaped like a cat through the darkness and hit what I'd thought was a tree.

The man bellowed in pain as he went down, Thunder's jaw wrapped around his throat.

"THUNDER, *FASS*!" Gary shouted. "*FASS*!"

It was over before the man knew what had happened.

Then all hell broke loose.

I turned and fired as something moved to my left.

Chance was shouting.

Other voices I recognized came from all around me, and I picked my way through them for the voice I was searching for. Men fell one after another. There were so many that I was practically tripping over them.

They filled the forest.

Finally, I stopped.

Moonlight filtered in through the trees, illuminating a long brown braid I would recognize anywhere.

I roared as a large fist wrapped around it and yanked.

CHAPTER 13
ROSEMARY

They had the house surrounded.

We hadn't realized it until we'd made it to the trees, and by then it was too late to turn back. The men in the SUVs had swarmed the yard, and going back that way would've been a death sentence.

Erik and Beau led the way, taking down anything that moved. Ambrose watched our backs.

Aunt Halle and I protected the boys, sometimes with our own bodies.

We were immortal. Someone would have to take our heads to end us for good.

The boys were not.

The bullet wound on my hip throbbed. The one in my shoulder sent shooting pain all the way down my arm.

I was pretty sure there was a hole in my cheek, but I refused to touch it with my tongue, afraid of what I would find.

None of us would leave those woods unscathed. I just hoped that we'd survive it.

As we slowly and quietly made our way toward where Reese and Lucy were hidden, I sent every desperate plea I could think of into the universe. We just had to get outside the perimeter that the humans had made. If we did that, we could find a defensive position and hole up until someone found us.

Pop had made calls to old teammates. Daniel and Uncle Dalton had to be finished soon, and they'd get the message Pop had sent. Someone was coming.

I had to believe someone was coming.

Holding back a scream, I watched as Ambrose fell.

I raised my rifle and fired.

Ambrose rose again. The human didn't.

Daniel's oldest brother nodded at me to keep going.

Setting my hand on top of Seamus's at my waist, I walked forward.

The humans were like fleas, popping up when I least expected them. It wasn't a coordinated attack. Instead, they seemed to be lying in wait until we were nearly on top of them.

My nerves were fried.

Seamus's hot breath shuddered against the back of my neck. He was crying.

The boys had been trained the same way that Ian and I had been. They were proficient in every type of weapon imaginable, and we'd armed them.

But we still forced them to use me and their mother as cover.

Aunt Halle had taken a bullet in her chest near her collarbone while shoving Grant to the forest floor.

I'd been hit in the face while backing Seamus around the trunk of a tree.

And the boys, my poor baby cousins, had to watch.

It was the most heinous thing I'd ever done—making them use us as human shields—and in the few quiet moments, when I had the ability to think, I wondered if Daniel had felt this way when he left me behind. We were protecting them, but I wasn't sure that they'd ever recover from it.

At first, when the humans swarmed us, I didn't realize what was happening. We'd been facing one or two of them at a time for the last ten minutes, and it took me a few moments to realize that the game had changed.

They rose like specters from the bushes around us, and there were so many of them I was struck dumb that the Vampires with me hadn't heard them breathing. These humans were highly trained. They moved like liquid, rising and attacking in one smooth movement.

"*Descendre*," I hissed to Seamus as I turned to meet a human who hadn't even unholstered his weapon.

I felt Seamus drop to his knees and the kick of his rifle as he shot the human.

My guts clenched in fear. By shooting his rifle, he'd become a target to eliminate instead of collateral damage.

"Don't—"

"You won't make it without us," he replied grimly, cutting me off.

There was so much movement around us that I struggled to aim and fire. There were too many of us in the melee, and I was terrified that I'd hit one of the Bouchers or Aunt Halle or Grant. Pulling my knife from my belt, I met the next human that came at us.

I felt feral as I stabbed at his neck and shoulders, struggling to stay on my feet as we grappled.

It took longer than it should have. I was losing too much blood, and between that and the mating heat, my body was slowing down. My arms and legs didn't move the way they should have. My instincts weren't as sharp as normal.

Seamus cried out behind me as the man finally slumped to the ground, and I spun to find him scrambling backward, his pistol in the dirt. A large man was taunting him, the rifle in his hands pointed straight at my baby cousin.

Then out of nowhere, fur that was as familiar to me as my face—even covered in blood like it was—sailed through the air. Thunder's paws hit the man's chest.

"*Fass*," I croaked as the man fell.

He screamed for less than a second before Thunder ripped out his throat.

I stumbled toward Seamus and was yanked to a stop, my head snapping backward as someone wrenched at my braid.

Then I was falling. Panic filled me as I landed flat on my back.

There were people all around, their legs filling my vision. I tried to roll, but was stopped as the human kneeled on my chest.

Get the pistol, Seamus. Get the rifle that human dropped.

"Fass," I wheezed, using up what breath was left in my lungs, hoping Thunder would hear me. I searched my empty sheaths. I'd used and lost my knives and given Seamus my pistol.

The man leaned down, his smile glaringly white in his darkly painted face.

Then, he was gone.

Coughing, I tried to see who had pulled him off me.

"Flower," Seamus groaned, his voice barely a whisper.

I turned my head and found my cousin, half propped against a tree, his eyes wide and terrified.

His hands were pressing against his lower belly where the vest I'd given him ended.

"No," I choked, scrambling toward him on my hands and knees, my arm buckling beneath me.

"It hurts," he whispered, his voice shaking.

"You're okay," I assured him, tearing off my hoodie. Everything around me disappeared as I pressed it against his wound. "You'll be fine."

"I wasn't fast enough," he groaned. "I got him, but I wasn't fast enough."

"You did well," I replied, pressing harder as blood seeped through the sweatshirt.

He was so goddamn pale.

The noise around us died in increments. First, the yelling stopped. Then the shooting. Then the grunts and thumps of hand-to-hand violence.

I didn't even realize when the forest around us was quiet again.

"Seamus," Uncle Dalton called frantically.

"Over here," I called back. "See, your dad's here. Everything's gonna be fine."

"Stop," Erik's voice seemed to come from everywhere. "Rosemary, I need you to back away from the boy."

"What?" I looked over my shoulder. "No, I—"

"Move, Rosemary," Uncle Dalton ordered angrily.

I looked back at my hands, the only thing staunching the bleeding. I couldn't let go. If I let go—

"Please," Uncle Dalton whispered.

That broken word was the only thing that had me scrambling backward. I didn't know what the fuck was going on or why they'd want me to leave Seamus. Had I done something wrong? What the hell was happening?

As soon as I was about twenty feet away, Uncle Dalton rushed forward.

"Oh, fuck," Uncle Dalton said as he dropped to his knees. "How bad?"

I opened my mouth to reply, but the words were stuck in my throat.

I'd failed. I'd had one job, and I failed.

"It's bad," Seamus rasped.

"Ian," Uncle Dalton called over his shoulder. He looked back at Seamus as he pressed on the wound with one hand and pulled something out of his utility pocket with the other. "It's not so bad, bud."

He was a convincing liar.

Seamus nodded, letting out a small breath of relief.

"It's going to hurt like hell when I lift you, though."

"Hurts like hell already," Seamus replied, his lips pulling up a little on one side.

Ian looked me over briefly to make sure I was okay, his eyes widening, then watched as Uncle Dalton lifted his little brother into his arms like a baby. Seamus lost consciousness.

"Take him to Alice," Erik ordered. "She's at our place."

I staggered to my feet as the Cavendish family took off through the woods, Ian leading the way and Grant following at the rear, their rifles at the ready.

The world seemed to be swaying around me.

"Rosemary," Chance called from somewhere behind me. "I need you to stay right where you are."

I spun toward the voice, but before I'd made an entire turn, I saw my mate. He was less than three feet from me, his feet planted, completely motionless.

"Danny," I gasped, stumbling toward him.

Everything would be okay now. He would make everything okay.

"Don't—"

"Stop!"

"Rosemary!"

The voices came from everywhere, all around us, but I ignored them.

It wasn't until I'd wrapped my good arm around his waist and looked up into his face that I realized why they'd tried to stop me.

Daniel's eyes were different. Wrong somehow. The pupils were huge, and the ring around them was light, not the usual dark brown that I'd fallen in love with. His expression was completely blank.

Breath left me in a whoosh as his arms wrapped around me, holding me so tight that I could barely move.

A growl left his throat.

"Danny?" I called softly.

"You're okay," Erik called quietly.

Daniel's lips pulled back from his teeth in a snarl.

"What's going on?" I asked, pushing on his chest.

His arms tightened.

It was as if he couldn't even hear me. His eyes jerked from side to side as he watched the woods around us. His face and beard were covered in blood.

In the distance, the whir of a helicopter's blades broke the silence.

"Ambrose?" Lucy called from somewhere.

"Stay where you are," Ambrose called back. "Don't move."

Then there was silence again.

My eyes were growing a little hazy. I didn't understand what was happening, and I was losing patience and blood. I pinched Daniel's side. He didn't even flinch.

"She's hurt, Arne," Erik said soothingly from somewhere behind me. "She needs help."

Daniel took a step back, dragging me with him.

"I know," Erik said, his voice choked. "But you need to push through it. Look at your mate. She's *hurt*. Look at her."

"Daniel," I whispered, clutching at his shirt as my head grew heavy. "What's wrong?"

I slumped against him, letting him take the full weight of my body. I was so *tired,* and the heat symptoms that had been riding me since the moment he'd left were finally easing.

Thunder's heavy breathing came from somewhere at our feet.

Daniel started to tremble as he moved slowly backward. His heart was pounding.

"Stay here," Beau called out calmly. "You have to stay where we can help her."

"I'm fine," I replied, blinking. I laid my head on Daniel's shoulder. I let the blood in my mouth drain out of my lips, too tired to spit.

"She's losing consciousness," Chance spat. "We've been standing here for fifteen minutes already."

Had it been fifteen minutes? That didn't seem right.

"What do we do?"

"Stand ready," Erik replied quietly. He raised his voice. "Arne, you need to put her down."

"If he doesn't snap out of it, we'll have to take her," Beau said.

Daniel took another step back, a low growl rumbling in his chest.

"Fight it, son," Erik ordered, his voice deepening.

My mate began to shake.

I slid my hand under his shirt, pressing my palm against the warm skin of his back. Yes, that's what I needed. The feeling of his skin against mine. Everything inside me seemed to settle.

It was the opposite for Daniel. As soon as our skin met, he jolted like he'd been shocked and began lowering me to the forest floor.

"Rosie," he called as he gently pushed my hair out of my face.

"You made it," I whispered, watching as his eyes slowly lost the blank look.

"Where are you hit?" he asked, his voice vibrating with terror.

"Hip," I replied, his face going in and out of focus. "Shoulder."

"Daniel?" Erik called.

"Help her," Daniel choked out.

Then there were Bouchers all around me. The pain was constant, excruciating, but I held Daniel's gaze with my own as they pressed against my wounds.

"I'm going to have a scar," I informed him.

"You're going to have a few."

"On my face," I grimaced and then winced.

"It's not so bad," he soothed, his hands shaking as he rubbed his thumb over my temple.

"It's bad," Chance argued. "Think I can see your teeth."

I let out a shocked huff of laughter.

"Gods, Chance," Beau barked. "Shut the fuck up."

"You got this?" Ambrose asked, falling back on his heels. "I'll go get Lucy and Reese."

"Take Beau," Erik ordered as he gently wrapped something around my shoulder. "No one goes anywhere alone."

I gasped and dug my fingers into the dirt, pressing upward. "My pop," I wheezed as Daniel tried to push me back down without hurting me.

"He's fine," Erik assured me, though there was no way he could've known. My pop was out there somewhere in the dark without Thunder to watch his back.

"We need to go get him," I argued, shoving weakly against their gentle hands.

"I'm here," Pop called, breathless.

A few moments later, he stumbled into the clearing, his face so pale that it practically glowed in the dark.

"How is she?"

"She's fine," I replied, coughing as I choked on blood.

"Yeah, looks like it," he said, barely making it to my side before dropping. He landed awkwardly, like his legs had simply gone out from under him.

Thunder scooted closer, nudging Pop's arm.

"Good boy," Pop praised, his eyes still on me as he scratched Thunder's bloody fur.

“We need to get her home,” Erik said as the sound of the brothers and their mates filtered through the trees.

“I can walk,” I said in protest as Daniel gathered me into his arms.

“Let me hold you,” he murmured in my ear.

The rest of the Bouchers reached us just as I realized that my pop wasn’t rising to his feet.

“I’ll meet you,” he said, his voice reed thin. “You go.”

“Pop,” I whispered.

I’d thought that seeing Seamus with a gunshot wound in his belly had broken me, but I’d been wrong. Seeing my pop on the ground, unable to rise, was the final hit that shattered everything inside me into thousands of sharp pieces.

“Unacceptable,” Erik replied. He didn’t wait for permission. He just took two steps, crouched, grabbed my pop’s arm, and yanked him over his broad shoulders.

“All set?” Chance asked, for once, not making any snide comments.

“Careful,” Ambrose ordered as we hurried through the trees toward the house. “Beau?”

“Nothing,” Beau replied.

“Clear here,” Chance added.

They were spread out around us as we moved through the trees, security for those of us unable to fight.

“Good back here too,” Lucy said from somewhere behind us.

“Stay close,” Erik ordered.

"Nah, I thought I'd hang back a little bit," she mumbled to herself.

The driveway and yard were littered with bodies, but the Vampires around me didn't hesitate as they walked past the men on the ground. We converged on a large SUV, and Daniel waited as Beau and Chance tossed everything out of the trunk before climbing in, holding me in his lap. Pop crawled in beside us. Then Thunder.

"I didn't know he could move like that," Daniel said as his family piled into the front.

"He's got hidden depths," I replied groggily as Thunder laid his head tiredly on Pop's hip.

"Never see him comin'," Pop added proudly. He twined his fingers with mine and squeezed, holding them tightly.

"You know, they can slow down," I mumbled. Daniel's body swayed, and me with it, as we flew around a corner. "This shit may hurt, but it's not like it'll kill me."

I closed my eyes, pressing my forehead against the pulse beating in my mate's neck. "I'll be fine. I can handle anything for a while."

"Let's not take any chances," Daniel replied gruffly.

I shrugged and was surprised to find that my shoulder didn't hurt nearly as much as it had. That had to be a good thing. Maybe my body was already healing itself. I'd heard of Vampires and their mates healing faster than humans.

I drifted in and out of consciousness as we raced toward the Boucher property.

"How bad is it?" Daniel asked my pop when they thought I was passed out.

“Not good,” Pop breathed, his thumb smoothing over the back of my palm. “Do you think someone would go get my chair from the house?”

“Of course,” Daniel replied sympathetically.

Then the road changed, and I lifted my head a little as we pulled onto gravel.

“Almost there, baby,” Daniel said.

I hadn’t realized that he’d been tenderly bracing my bad arm until he shifted, and white-hot pain shot down from my shoulder.

The Bouchers swarmed out of the SUV the moment it stopped. The inside lit up as the liftgate in the back opened to reveal Chance standing there.

“Let’s not make this weird,” he said briskly, reaching for Pop.

“Fuck,” Pop groaned as Chance lifted him out of the SUV.

Thunder followed them.

“Now, us,” Daniel said, scooting forward until he could drop his feet to the ground. When he stood, Beau and Reese were there, waiting to see if we needed any help.

“Dalton made it,” Beau announced as we moved toward the front door. “Alice is working on the boy now.”

“She needs to hurry,” Daniel replied as we entered the house.

He was limping. I opened my mouth to ask what was wrong with his leg but got distracted by the view.

The house was beautiful inside. Large and open, it even smelled good. I looked everywhere I could without lifting my head. There was a large stairway off to the side, an antique hutch, and fancy wallpaper with little birds on it. I'd been letting the blood drain out of my mouth, but I sucked it back as we moved over the hardwood floors, trying not to stain them.

"Danny," a sweet voice called out as we entered a brightly lit room. "How can I help?"

I squinted against the light.

"We need to get her clothes off," Daniel replied as he gently placed me on an uncomfortable bed with a railing on one side.

It took me a moment to realize it was a hospital bed.

What the fuck?

I glanced around the room. Six feet away, a small woman was wrapped from head to toe in a green cap and scrubs, ordering the person next to her quietly. Her hands flashed in and out of view. At the head of the bed, my Uncle Dalton stood with his hands on Seamus's head. My cousin's face was covered with an oxygen mask. His skin looked gray.

Beyond them, Ian, Grant, and Aunt Halle stood along the wall. Grant's head was tipped down, staring at the floor. Aunt Halle's eyes were squeezed shut, Ian's arm wrapped tightly around her shoulders.

I met Ian's devastated gaze and held it until he looked away.

Shelves and cupboards lined the room. There was a sink in the corner. A backboard rested against the wall opposite my family. Chance and Erik stood next to it.

"What are you doing?" I gasped as cool air blew over my thighs. I slapped at the hands pulling my trousers down.

"We have to see your wounds," Daniel said, catching my hand.

"Wait."

My cousins were *right* there. So were Daniel's father and brother.

"We can't wait," the sweet voice replied. She lifted her head to look at me, and my mate's brown eyes stared back from a stranger's face.

"Your mom," I whispered, letting my head fall back.

"Yes," Daniel replied, messing with my shirt.

I closed my eyes as cool air hit my chest and then my arms.

"Danny," his mom called, her voice rising an octave. "Erik, come help me."

"Great," I mumbled. "Invite everyone over."

No one paid any attention to me as multiple pairs of hands touched me, pressing and pulling. I could barely feel it anymore. Gauze pressed against my cheek, and then my pop's voice was in my ear.

"Hold on, Flower."

I tried to answer him, but my mouth didn't seem to be working anymore.

Sometime later, it was Daniel in my ear. "Bite, baby."

The scent of his blood filled my nostrils, and I clenched my teeth around his skin.

"It's coming out her cheek," someone murmured.

"She's still getting some," another voice replied.

"Let her take as much as she can."

"I know," Daniel said, his voice still near my ear.

Then there was nothing but a bitchy voice barking orders.

I faded in and out, never once opening my eyes,

even when I felt someone's hands on my face, another set holding my head in place.

Somewhere in the darkness, I stared into Seamus's wide, scared eyes. When I opened my mouth, no sound came out. We just looked at each other, both of us terrified.

CHAPTER 14
DANIEL

"I don't know," Aunt Alice told me for the fiftieth time, her voice less patient than it had been hours before. "Once she's awake, I can check."

"She's already healing," I said desperately, running my hand down Rosemary's arm. "That's good, right?"

"Of course it is," Alice replied. She turned away and walked back to the other bed where Dalton's youngest son, Seamus, lay.

The boy had survived the surgery to remove the bullet and repair the damage. The bullet had entered through the front, but lodged extremely close to his spine. He hadn't woken up, but they knew he would—and thanks to his genetics, he'd be fine. His mother sat in a chair next to his head, her hand on his shoulder. Dalton sat at the foot. Their sons had fallen asleep on the floor just as the sun rose. The younger one's head was pillowed by Thunder's torso. The dog's snores were oddly pleasant in the silent room.

Alice had worked all night, patching the rest of us up. I realized after we'd finished with Rosemary that I'd been slowed down by two bullets in my thigh. I'd barely paid any attention as Alice had dug them out and sewn me up, watching Rosemary's slow and even breaths.

My father had taken a bullet in the chest. Ambrose had a large cut down the side of his stomach. Beau had dislocated three fingers and had a graze wound up the side of his forearm.

All of us were exhausted.

My body didn't even feel like my own. Every muscle ached. The stitches on my thigh barely registered, because everything hurt anyway. It was worse than the mating heat, which had dissipated. That ache had felt clean somehow, purposeful—this ache felt dirty and wrong.

My hands hadn't stopped shaking.

By the time we'd gotten to the house, Rosemary had been pretty out of it. Alice had already been finishing up on Seamus, and it hadn't taken her long to rescrub and get started on my mate, but it had felt like forever.

When we'd taken off her pants, I'd finally seen the damage that the bullet in her hip had caused. A large-caliber round had torn through the muscle. Without the pressure of her waistband, the blood had been hard to contain.

I didn't know how she'd stayed on her feet.

I didn't know how she'd even been awake.

Alice had managed to staunch that bleeding first, her hands moving over my mate with speed and expertise that I'd never equal, no matter how long I'd lived.

Then she'd moved to Rosemary's shoulder.

She'd cursed the entire time.

There was so much damage that she wasn't sure how much function Rosemary would have in her arm.

My mate, who could take me down like it was nothing, who climbed like Spiderman and flipped an old tractor tire when she felt overwhelmed, may never be able to do those things again.

The scar that would bisect my mate's cheek for the rest of our lives felt inconsequential in comparison.

"How's he doin'?" Gary asked Dalton, wheeling himself slowly into the room.

"No change," Dalton replied tiredly.

"Not a bad thing," Gary replied gruffly as he passed the Vampire. "Means he's not any worse."

"I'll take it," Dalton mumbled.

"How's my girl?" Gary asked, stopping at the foot of Rosemary's bed.

"Still sleeping," I replied, my voice hoarse.

Gary grimaced as he looked her over. "She'll be all right."

I nodded tightly. He'd gotten the same information from Alice that I had. Yes, Rosemary would survive, but there was a chance that she'd never fully recover. I was terrified for her to wake up.

And though I knew it was irrational, I was terrified that she wouldn't wake up.

"I'll stay with her," Gary said, rounding the bed. "You go get something to eat."

"I'm not hungry."

"All right," he said, his tone never changing. "Then you go see your mama. She's been sittin' at the kitchen table for the last two hours waitin' for you to come out."

"You'll come get me—"

"The minute she wakes up," he confirmed, cutting me off. "Go on now."

I took my time sliding off the bed, careful not to jostle Rosemary as I went. Alice had inclined the head of the bed after Rosemary puked up blood in her sleep, and my mate started listing to the side as soon as my body was no longer propping her up.

My eyes burned as I gently wedged a pillow in beside her where I'd been lying.

"It's all right," Gary said softly. "Go take a few minutes."

I didn't meet anyone's eyes as I walked out of the room. I had enough emotions of my own to deal with. I didn't want to catch a glimpse of the fear on Dalton's face. I'd already listened to his mate quietly weep for hours.

My mother was in the kitchen, but Gary had neglected to tell me that the rest of my family was there too.

Zeke's mate, Charlie, rose as I entered the room and stepped forward to hug me tightly.

"Thanks, Charlie," I said, patting his back.

He'd been Alice's second pair of hands the night before, handing her what she needed before she could even ask for it. He'd also been the only one to calm Rosemary down when she'd fought the oxygen mask on her face. It was a stark change from the timid, devastated man who had greeted me the first time we met.

"How're you doing?" he asked kindly as he pulled away.

"Not great," I replied, pulling out a chair so I could fall into it.

"She's doing well," my mother said, reaching over to squeeze my hand.

"That's what Alice says," I agreed.

The rest of the table was silent.

"And she's very pretty," Mom added, her lips pulling up in a small smile.

"I thought looks weren't everything, Mom," Beau huffed good-naturedly.

"Oh, you be quiet," she scolded.

"Did you tell your mother I was ugly?" Reese asked, staring at her mate.

"Of course not."

"Then why—"

"Later," Beau said with a grin, leaning over to kiss her.

I looked away. Had Rosemary and I ever had that ease between us? I'd thought we did, but now looking back, I wasn't so sure. I'd left her over and over, and she'd gone out of her way to hide what it was doing to her. She'd been so fucking convincing.

Had all of it been a lie?

"How are you feeling?" my dad asked, watching me closely.

I knew what he was asking, and I held out my hands, which had stopped shaking—mostly.

"Nausea? Headache? Paranoia?"

"Yes, yes, no," I replied. "But my mate is currently unconscious, so I think I get a pass on the first two."

"And you'll tell me if anything changes?"

"Of course."

"What's going on?" Charlie asked suspiciously, looking between us. "Were you wounded?"

"I'm fine, Charlie," I replied. "What have I missed?"

"Adamson's locked in the pool house," Ambrose replied. "He's not talking."

"Of course he isn't," I grumbled.

"Arthur's on his way," my father added. "We called him this morning."

"You think that's the best play?" I asked, glancing around the table.

"I think that by the time I called him, he'd already gotten word of two headless generals and knew one was missing. If we'd waited any longer, it could've looked like we were hiding something."

I nodded, hesitant to argue about it. The day before, I would've pointed out that Arthur had lied to us when he'd said he thought Zeke's death was an isolated incident. I would've reminded them that he'd secretly contracted Dalton to find information, leaving us in the dark.

After last night, I was worried that they'd assume it was the paranoia that my father had asked about.

"Rosemary's awake," Ian called from the doorway to the medical room.

My heart pounded as I lurched to my feet and raced toward my mate. When I made it to her bedside, she was still groggy and scowling.

"Hey, baby," I greeted, slowing as I moved toward the head of the bed. "How are you feeling?"

"Better than you look," she replied. "What the hell happened to you?"

"He was awake all night," Gary informed her.

Rosemary groaned and leaned her head back against the pillow. "Worried about me?"

"Maybe a little," I conceded, leaning close. "You were in pretty bad shape when we got there."

"I was still kicking ass and taking names when you got there," she argued stubbornly, her gaze roaming over my face.

"Fair point."

"You should sit down before you fall down. Here, I'll scoot—" Her words broke off with a wheeze as she tried to use her arms to shift sideways.

"Stay where you are," I ordered quickly, leaning my hip on the edge of the bed, "I'm fine right here."

"Fuck," she moaned, wincing as she lifted her hand to her wounded shoulder. "What the hell?"

"You need to give yourself a little more time," I cautioned. "Just sit still."

"Why the hell isn't my arm working?" she asked, flexing her fingers slowly.

"You can move your fingers," I replied, relief sweeping through me.

"Why wouldn't I be able to move my fingers?" She rotated her wrist just fine, but when she tried to lift her arm, nothing happened. "Fuck."

"Give it some time," Alice ordered, stomping into the room. "Don't ruin all my hard work by popping your stitches."

Rosemary nodded slowly, eyeing my honorary aunt.

"Rosemary, this is my Aunt Alice."

"You're a doctor?" Rosemary asked.

"I am."

"How's Seamus?"

Aunt Alice glanced at the boy in the bed. "He'll be fine."

"Thank God," Rosemary whispered.

Gary and I stood by while Alice checked Rosemary

over, looking under bandages and murmuring to her quietly. When she was finished, she nodded.

"You can take her up to bed," she told me. "She'll heal faster with some peace and quiet."

Rosemary looked worriedly over at Seamus.

"He's just sleepin', Flower," Gary told her, patting her foot.

Alice settled Rosemary's bad arm into a sling, and I helped her to her feet while Gary looked away, so I could wrap the blanket all the way around her bare body before I lifted her into my arms. We'd had to cut all of her clothes off the night before. There wasn't a piece that had been salvageable.

The house was quiet as I carried her to the stairs and up to my room. I wasn't sure where everyone had gone, but I was thankful that we didn't run into anyone. When we stepped inside my small apartment, Rosemary lifted her head from my shoulder and looked around.

"So this is your place," she mused quietly.

"I haven't been here much," I replied apologetically, looking around. The space was pretty sparse. I'd never really decorated because I didn't care what it looked like, but now that I was showing it to my mate, I was a bit embarrassed. While fully furnished, it lacked any kind of personality whatsoever.

"I wasn't at the townhouse much either," she mused as I carried her into the bedroom. "But it still looked like someone lived there."

"You can do whatever you want with it," I offered. "Consider it a blank slate."

"Oh, yeah," she groaned as I lowered her onto the

bed. "I just love to decorate. It's my thing." The sarcasm was thick.

I smiled half-heartedly at the joke and turned to my dresser to get her a shirt.

"Danny?" she called. "What's going on?"

"Nothing. What do you mean?"

When I turned back toward her with a T-shirt in my hands, I froze.

With one arm, she held the thin sheet to her chest. Her entire body was coiled like a spring as she watched me warily.

It was the moment that I'd dreaded all my life. I'd always known it would come. I hadn't been delusional enough to believe that I would be able to hide it forever, but I'd hoped that we'd be further into our lives before my mate became aware.

The knowledge that Rosemary had leaned into the mating bond so easily, had accepted it all so calmly, had only intensified my fear of her learning the truth. Our relationship had started so effortlessly. Part of me had taken that as my due because everything around us had been so fucked up. Like it was the Gods' way of giving me a win when everything else was going to shit.

"Tell me," she said quietly.

I opened my mouth and closed it again, unsure how to begin.

"I know Vampires," she said slowly, her gaze searching my face. "I've seen them in action." She paused and swallowed like she was carefully considering her next words. "I've never seen a Vampire like you were last night."

Every wall that I'd built up, every emotion that I'd

pushed away, every memory of a time when I'd laughed something off instead of being angry, every deep breath I'd paused to take, every warning word or touch that my brothers had given me, every worried look that my parents had shot me or each other, every time I'd deliberately blinked the red out of my eyes as I fought to center myself—it all rushed through me with the force of a tsunami.

The walls silently shattered.

"It's genetic," I choked out, my voice barely audible. I stayed near the dresser.

I wanted to touch her so badly, but I never wanted to frighten her.

"When my father was young, there were warriors who fought bare-skinned."

She frowned.

"Naked," I clarified, as if she didn't already know what I meant.

I was fumbling it.

"Okay," she murmured slowly.

"They were called berserkers," I blurted.

Rosemary's mouth went slack with surprise.

"Most were Vampires," I continued. "Some weren't. They were terrifying on the battlefield. In a time when chain mail and armor were the norm, someone fighting bare was a bit of a mindfuck to their enemies."

"No shit," she breathed.

"Like I said, some were Vampires, some weren't. But they all had one thing in common—they fell into a sort of trance when they fought. Nothing mattered but the battle. Hyperfocus. They didn't get tired. They didn't flag. Not ever. Not even when they were wounded."

I leaned against the dresser and smoothed a hand over my beard, clearing my throat.

"Your dad was a *berserker*?" she sputtered. Her eyes lost a little focus. "I mean, Erik the Butcher is a pretty bloodthirsty name. So I figured that he probably did some shit, you know? I've seen him fight, and the guy can *move*, but—"

"The ability is genetic," I said, cutting her off before she said something offhand that tore my heart out.

Her eyes met mine, and it took a moment before realization set in.

"Oh," she breathed. "Oh, that's what—can your brothers do it, too?"

"No," I replied flatly. I'd been the only one with that particular trait.

"So it's just you then."

"Yes."

She sat there silently for what felt like forever, her eyes pointed toward the floor between us.

"So the red eyes—"

"Yes," I confirmed.

"Does it happen often?" she asked, raising her head.

"No. No, it hasn't happened since I was a child, not until last night."

"But I've seen your eyes. They flicker."

"I've always been able to control it," I explained uncomfortably. "It doesn't go further than that."

"Then why couldn't you last night?" she asked quietly.

I huffed in disbelief.

"Because of me," she said in understanding. "Because I was in danger."

"Yes."

"Is that why you wouldn't let me leave Pop's?"

"Part of it," I admitted. "But only part. I just wanted you to be safe."

"You can't control everything," she countered, gesturing at the bandage on her face. "You realize that now, right?"

That I wasn't willing to admit. My emotions were too close to the surface.

"Why are you standing way over there?" she asked softly, patting the bed beside her. "Come sit by me."

Relief made my legs wobbly as I took the few steps to the bed and sat down carefully next to her. Rosemary had never felt small or fragile to me, and I loved it. I enjoyed the fact that she was strong and capable of doing damage if she chose to. I adored that her body and mine lined up so perfectly. I worshipped the muscles she'd built almost as much as her long, silky hair. But then I'd seen her with that human on top of her, and now I felt like I was finally noticing how much thinner her wrists were, how slender she was in comparison to my bulk, how delicate her long neck was.

"You didn't think I should know?" she asked, reaching out to wrap her hand around mine.

"I would've told you eventually."

"When?" she asked. "After one of our sons showed signs?"

"Before that," I argued halfheartedly. "But there was a lot happening and—"

"You were a coward," she cut in.

"It wasn't that," I lied through my teeth.

"At what point do you think you'll realize that I can

handle a lot more than you give me credit for?" she asked flatly.

"Of course you can."

"Did you think I'd run screaming?"

"I figured it would give you pause," I replied.

"Give me pause?" She snorted.

"I've worked really fucking hard to keep that part of me on a leash," I snapped, irritated that she was acting like this little piece of my DNA was no big deal. "So... yeah. I figured if I told you, it might scare you."

"Wrong."

"You saw me last night. You saw what I turn into."

"*You turn into*?" she whispered in disbelief. She shoved herself to her feet.

"Sit back down," I ordered, reaching for her. "You shouldn't be up—"

"I'm fine." She slapped my hand away. She took one step away and then glared down at me. "Do you want to know what I saw last night? My mate. My angry, terrifying *mate*. I was so fucking relieved you were there. You could've been half-man and half-wolf, and I still would've been ecstatic when you showed up. You know what I thought when I saw you? Oh, thank God, Daniel is here. Everything is going to be okay now."

"I wouldn't even let anyone touch you," I barked, rising to my feet. "I was so out of it that I would've fought them if they'd tried. You were bleeding so much, and I was so fucked up that I wouldn't even let them help!"

Rosemary smiled, and I felt like I'd gotten the wind knocked out of me.

"Do you think I would've done anything differently?" she whispered. "If you were hurt, do you think I would've been thinking any more logically?"

"You don't understand."

"No, you don't," she countered. "There's nothing you could tell me that would make me afraid of you. Not a single thing. I don't care what kind of monster you are. Vampire, berserker, werewolf—you would never hurt me."

"No, I wouldn't," I promised. "Not on purpose."

"How fast did you get to me last night?" she asked, stepping forward to run her thumb over my cheek.

"I don't know."

"How many men did you go through to get to me?"

"Too many to count."

"Exactly." Her lips pulled up at the corners. "That trance, or hyperfocus, or whatever you want to call it? It got you to me when I needed you. Baby, why in the world would you think that was a bad thing?"

I tried to maintain my composure. I stared at the wall. Curled my hands into fists. Clenched my abdominal muscles as hard as I could.

None of it worked.

My breath shuddered out of me in a nearly silent sob.

I'd spent my life hiding that part of me, knowing that humans and Vampires alike would stare at me like I was some wild animal, just waiting for me to lose control. My father had been so adamant that I learn how to lock it down, to never let myself lean into the gift I'd been born with. I understood why. He'd seen friends and fellow warriors lose themselves to the red haze, the feeling of absolute purpose.

But what he hadn't realized, and I hadn't either,

was that when you already had absolute purpose, there was no reason to look for it in the haze.

I'd felt powerful when it happened. Invincible.

But I felt more powerful when Rosemary smiled at me. When she called my name. When her body clenched around mine, and her teeth sank into my skin.

"I love you," Rosemary said, leaning in to brush her lips over mine. "Even when I want to rip your head off and use it like a soccer ball."

I let out a watery laugh and kissed her back.

"It doesn't scare you?" I asked, pulling away the few hairs that had stuck to the bandage on her face. "When I'm like that, I'm not rational."

"Will you use it to protect our family?"

"I think last night proved that I won't have a choice."

"Would you ever hurt me?"

"Never. I'd die first."

"Exactly," she said calmly, her eyes steady on mine.

"I don't think I've ever been more scared in my life," I breathed, looking over her battered features.

"Me neither," she replied softly. "But we made it."

"Yeah."

"A berserker," she mumbled, giving her head a little shake. "Fuck me. I can still be surprised."

"I didn't even try to stop it last night," I replied, swallowing hard. "I didn't remember that it would feel like that."

"What did it feel like?" she asked curiously.

I chuckled in embarrassment.

"What?" she asked, a smile pulling at her lips. "Tell me."

"Like a fucking superpower," I confessed.

Rosemary laughed and pinched my earlobe teasingly. "Not a bad thing to have in a pinch," she said. "But I'm still going to hope you don't need it again."

"Me too, baby."

"Do I look as bad as you?" she asked, picking something out of my hair. "You're filthy."

"You're gorgeous."

"I'm covered in gore."

"We cleaned most of you off last night," I told her.

"Well, no one did you the same favor, clearly. Where's the bathroom?"

Taking her by the hand, I walked her slowly to the shower before I realized she couldn't get in.

"Your bandages," I reminded her with a grimace. "You can't shower yet."

"Shit," she grumbled, looking down at the sheet she'd wrapped around her like a toga.

"Sit down on the toilet," I ordered gently. "I'll take a quick shower and then help you clean up."

"Oh, so you get a shower," she complained good-naturedly. "Nice."

"I'm not going to help you bathe while I'm like this," I countered, pulling off my shirt. "Give me five minutes."

Rosemary hummed in appreciation as I stripped off the scrub pants Alice had given me after she stitched up my leg. "Take your time."

CHAPTER 15
ROSEMARY

I watched as red water sluiced down Daniel's body and swirled down the drain at his feet. His shower was massive, and only half of it was blocked off, so I had an excellent and unobstructed view of my mate as he cleaned off the night before. My heart fluttered as the muscles beneath his skin flexed and moved.

I didn't think I'd ever get tired of looking at him.

"Does anyone else know about the berserker thing?" I asked as he shampooed his long hair and beard.

"Just my parents and my brothers," he replied, his eyes closed. "Why?"

"It seems like a good weapon to have in our back pocket," I mused. "But not if everyone knows about it."

"Oh, so now I'm a weapon?" he asked, his eyes popping open to look at me.

"I mean, you're not *not* a weapon," I teased. "But that makes us a good pair, because no one thinks I'm a weapon either."

He huffed a small laugh as he rinsed his hair.

"Dalton's family knows now too," he said. "They saw me in action last night. I doubt they know any details, though."

"That's fine." I waved him off, even though he wasn't looking at me. "Family should know anyway."

My nails were broken and jagged. Blood had caked dark brown and flaky around the edges of my nail beds. God, I really wished I could shower. Rising to my feet, I shuffled over to the sink and carefully tugged my arm out of the sling so I could wash my hands.

The shower cut off just as I'd turned on the faucet.

"You really don't give a shit, do you?" Daniel asked, stepping in behind me as our eyes met in the mirror.

"That you have a superpower?" I replied, smiling at him. "No. If you couldn't control it, that would be different."

"I couldn't control it last night," he reminded me, tipping his face down to kiss my bare shoulder.

"Danny," I breathed, leaning back against him. "Look at me."

He raised his gaze to mine.

"Don't fucking spiral, all right?"

He stiffened.

Reaching up, I cupped his cheek in my palm and held his face next to mine, our gazes locked.

"If you hadn't gotten there when you did, we were toast," I told him, the memory of all those humans rising from the forest like ants making me shudder. "We were surrounded, and there were too many of them. If we hadn't had the boys and Aunt Halle, it might've been different, but we couldn't go on the offensive because we were too busy playing defense for them."

He turned his head slowly and kissed the center of my palm.

"Don't expect me to judge you for the ability that got us all home alive last night."

"I had some help," he reminded me ruefully.

"Secondary characters," I joked, wrinkling my nose. "You're the main character, babe."

Daniel laughed. "Come on, mate," he ordered, leaning back. "Let's get you cleaned up."

We were quiet as Daniel helped me lose the sheet and sling, then soaped up a washcloth and began to clean me off. The bathroom fan was the only noise in the room as he started with the unwounded half of my face, then my ears and neck. Using a clean washcloth, he rinsed the soap away. Then he grabbed two new cloths and started the process on my chest, arms, armpits, and back. As he worked his way down my body, I let my eyes drift shut.

My body was sore, especially my face. All the talking we'd done had pulled at the stitches in my cheek, and I was actually a little surprised that he was able to understand me because the words that came out of my mouth were consistently slurred and garbled.

Tears gathered in the corners of my eyes as he dropped the next set of dirty cloths on the tile floor and reached for new ones. He was being so incredibly gentle as he washed away the memories and the terror and the evidence of what we'd gone through. Every touch felt like a benediction, his lips brushing over the bruises and scratches he found as he cleaned me off.

"Danny," I whispered as he helped me sit so he could wash my feet.

"What is it, love?" he murmured, looking up from where he kneeled at my feet in nothing but a towel.

"I fucked up last night," I confessed.

"How did you fuck up?"

The fact that he didn't try to argue that I hadn't, just asked what I'd done—no recrimination in his tone—made tears drip down my cheeks.

"I was supposed to guard Seamus," I choked out. "He was counting on me to keep him safe. Everyone was counting on me."

Daniel smiled gently and reached out to wipe the tears from my cheek. "I'm not going to try to convince you otherwise."

I nodded, trying to hold back a sob.

"But I am going to tell you this—are you listening?"

"Yeah."

"When we undressed you last night, there wasn't a single person in the room who understood how you could've stayed on your feet with the wounds you had." His hands wrapped around my ankles and squeezed in emphasis. "You should've been unconscious. At the very least, you should've been down—but you weren't."

I sniffled pitifully, not even bothering to wipe my nose.

"You stayed on your feet, Rosie. You kept going, and no one knows how you did it. I know I can't change how you feel about it right now, but, baby, you didn't fuck up. You fought until the very end to keep that boy safe. Try to remember that when you're feeling guilty for shit that was out of your control."

"Okay," I replied halfheartedly as he went back to cleaning my feet.

"I felt the same way when Zeke died," he continued a few moments later. "Knowing that I wasn't there to protect him?" He shook his head. "That was my job as his big brother. I should've known he was in trouble. Hell, I should've known that he'd found his mate. I hadn't been keeping in touch like I should've. That was on me."

I ran my fingers over his wet hair.

"I won't make that mistake again," he said, dropping the last of the dirty washcloths on the pile. "You got any mistakes that you won't repeat?"

I replayed the night before, going over every move I'd made from the moment Aunt Halle had called the house phone. From picking my weapons to the feel of Seamus's blood squelching between my fingers.

"No," I replied, swallowing back my tears. "No, I don't."

I'd done everything in my power. I'd prepared well with the time I had available. I'd called in help. I'd used my training to the best of my ability. I'd ignored the fear and the exhaustion. I'd kept going even when everything hurt.

Daniel smiled and rose. "Come on, let's get you something to wear."

Getting a T-shirt on without moving my arm was a bit of a pain, and Daniel's sweats were way too big in the waist, but we made it work. I'd just sat down to watch him dress, and I was marveling at the way his ass flexed as he moved, when a disembodied voice came through an intercom on the wall, making me jump in surprise.

"Hey, Danny," Beau called. "Arthur just landed, if you want to be there."

Daniel strode to the wall and pushed a button. "Be there in a few minutes," he answered.

Ignoring the twinge in my hip, I pushed myself to my feet as he pulled on a pair of jeans.

He looked at me in surprise.

I could see the thoughts racing through his expression. He didn't want me to go to that meeting. He wanted to tell me to stay in bed and rest. Contemplated how he could cajole me into doing it. Wondered if it was worth the fight if I didn't comply.

I nearly smiled when acceptance made his shoulders slump just a little.

"I deserve to be there," I said, holding his gaze. "You know I do."

"Fine, but I'm carrying you down there," he said as he turned away to grab a shirt. "You shouldn't even be out of bed."

"Deal," I replied, hiding my smile.

"You need socks," he mumbled to himself.

I was completely bundled up, from a zip-front hoodie to hiking socks on my feet, when Danny carried me downstairs to the kitchen. I wanted to hold my back straight so I looked a little more like a queen and a little less like a waif that he'd just saved, but I didn't have it in me. Instead, I let my head rest on his shoulder, the scent of his skin soothing me. I was so fucking tired, and if it had been anything else happening, I would've happily waved goodbye as he left without me.

Daniel's brothers and parents were in the kitchen along with Dalton, my dad, and a Vampire I'd never met before.

He was of slight build and wore a pair of wire-rimmed glasses. His hair was neatly combed, and his shoulders and back were straight in a way that screamed *military*. Even in dark trousers and a deep blue sweater, he still gave the impression that he was wearing a uniform.

"Daniel," he greeted, barely glancing at me.

"Arthur," Daniel replied curtly. He carefully lowered me to my feet.

"And your mate," Arthur said kindly, almost congratulatory.

"Don't even look at her," Daniel barked. "She doesn't exist for you."

"Arne," Erik chastised.

"Can you blame him?" Uncle Dalton drawled, leaning against the wall. I let out a breath of relief when everyone's attention left us. I grabbed Daniel's hand and gave it a squeeze of reassurance. "Mates are dropping like flies the moment you hear about them."

"I assure you I have nothing to do with the Vampires and mates that are being targeted," Arthur replied stiffly. "I am doing the best that I can with the resources available to me."

The entire room burst into angry chatter.

"Enough," Erik bellowed, silencing the room. "This will get us nowhere. Chance, Beau, bring Adamson to the back patio. I'll not have that motherfucker in my house."

Daniel's brothers left to get the Vampire while we all shuffled outside to the back patio. I shouldn't have been impressed by the manicured lawn and perfectly placed trees and shrubs, considering the inside of the house, but I was. The property I'd grown up on was so different from Daniel's family estate. It would take ten landscapers and a year to make it look anything near what Daniel's parents had going on. Shit, they'd probably have to bulldoze it all and start from scratch.

I turned to look as Dalton helped my dad navigate down the stairs from the house to the cement patio, and a rock settled in my belly. He couldn't get out of his chair.

"You need to sit down," Daniel said, leaning close to my ear.

"I'll meet him on my feet," I countered, shifting my weight a little so my good leg took most of it.

"Stubborn."

"Your family is rich," I muttered, changing the subject. "I mean, I had an idea when I saw the front, but it was dark. This is... whoa." I gestured toward the lawn.

"So is your pop," Daniel replied with a small laugh.

"We've never had to worry about money, but this is another level."

"Does it matter?" he asked curiously.

"Hell no," I said, leaning against his side. "I'm going to get pedicures once a week."

"That's the spirit." He kissed my jaw just as Beau and Chance half-carried and half-dragged the Vampire we were waiting for into view.

He cursed when he lifted his head and saw the commandant.

"Arthur, arrest them all," he blustered. "They took Keihley and Morren's heads. It is a direct attack on the Vampire Federation, article 254, section—"

"Stuff it, Edgar." Arthur spat.

He literally spat in disgust.

I had to hold back a highly inappropriate giggle.

Edgar Adamson's face turned red as a beet as Beau and Chance dropped him hard into a lawn chair.

"Start at the beginning," Erik ordered quietly. "Leave nothing out."

"I don't know what they've been saying, but—"

"Can I just end this now?" Chance asked, nonchalantly unwrapping a piece of gum. "If he's not going to tell the truth, I'd rather go back to my room and watch some porn until I pass out." He lifted his head and glanced around at us. "It's been a long couple of days."

Daniel lifted his hand to his mouth, covering it while pretending to scratch his cheek, but I could see the smile he was hiding.

"I have nothing to say, and you cannot hold me," Adamson said bravely, lifting his chin. "I am a general in the United States Vampire Command. I'm afforded a court-martial judged by my peers."

"Get a load of this guy," Chance said with a laugh. He reached out and ruffled Adamson's hair, making the Vampire practically vibrate with rage.

"You'll tell us everything," Uncle Dalton said calmly. "And if you do so, I'll give you a clean death."

Adamson huffed.

"If you do not," Uncle Dalton continued. "I'll get the information anyway, and it will be far less pleasant for you, but I will have a very good time."

His tone never changed. His expression never faltered. That's what made the words so incredibly chilling.

"Arthur," Adamson said, looking away from my uncle. "I'm afforded—"

"You're afforded nothing," the commandant replied

flatly. "Vampires who turn on their own are put down like dogs. Stop stalling, Edgar. You'll give us the information we need whether you tell us willingly or not."

"It was supposed to be only a few newly mated couples," Adamson said angrily. "Ten at the most."

I shuddered at the irritation in his voice. There was no remorse.

"But the humans didn't find what they needed, so we had to keep providing them with more names."

"What exactly did they need?" Ambrose asked.

"They're trying to replicate the change in DNA when mates become immortal," Adamson replied. "Or something along those lines. I didn't take notes. I'm not a scientist."

My stomach roiled with nausea.

"Who is financing these experiments?" Arthur asked, his fingers gripping the back of a chair so tightly his knuckles were white.

"François Baudelaire," Adamson answered. "He's the only human on the planet who could afford it."

"Zeke was right," Daniel whispered under his breath.

"He was the reason Ezekiel was killed," Adamson told Ambrose. I wasn't sure why he thought he could get a sympathetic or understanding reaction, but he continued speaking even as Ambrose's posture changed. "Your brother was asking questions in places that he shouldn't have been. When he got too close, Baudelaire ordered it."

Daniel's body swayed beside me, but when I looked at his face, his eyes were still clear and focused.

"We didn't even know he had a mate," Adamson said quickly as Ambrose jerked toward him.

Erik stopped his eldest son with a quiet word in his ear.

Beside me, Daniel's breathing had become irregular, and the hand on my lower back had begun to tremble.

"I think I need to go lie down," I whispered, leaning further into his side. "Will you bring me?"

"Go," Erik ordered, looking at us across the patio. "Take care of your mate."

I wrapped my good arm around Daniel's neck as he lifted me into his arms, and I didn't have a single qualm about getting him out of there before he had to hear any more about the reasons they'd targeted his baby brother. I had a feeling that there were few ways I'd ever save Daniel the way he'd saved me—especially with what I would forever think of as his *superpower*—but I could save him from hearing details about the worst thing that had ever happened to their family.

We would get all the information we were looking for secondhand, and there was nothing wrong with that.

"Could you take me to see Seamus?" I asked as we entered the house.

"I thought you wanted to go back to bed," he replied, carrying me toward the hospital room.

"I'll sleep better after I've seen him."

"I was okay, you know," he said, pausing. "I can control myself."

"Of course you can." I kissed his neck softly. "But there's no point in us giving that twisted piece of garbage more of an audience than he already has."

His arms tightened, and he turned his head so our lips met.

"I love you," he said against my mouth.

"Same."

When we entered the room, I was surprised to see Daniel's mom sitting in a chair next to Aunt Halle. Both of their heads swung toward the door as we walked through it.

Seamus was awake.

"My best dude," I called, my breath hitching.

"Hey, Flower," he greeted with a weak smile. "How are you feeling?"

I shifted so Daniel would let me down and then lurched over to his bedside, trying not to cry. "Me? I'm frigging immortal. How are you feeling?"

"Like I got shot in the guts," he said, wrinkling his nose. "Mom said you got hit like three times."

"Yep." I reached for his hand and wrapped my fingers around it. At some point, his had grown bigger than mine, but it still felt like the little kid's that I'd tugged behind me, urging him to keep up with whatever we were doing. "Face—I'm going to look like a badass with this scar. Hip and shoulder."

"I remember the face one," he said carefully, his eyes glassy. "It looked bad."

"Nah," I assured him. "No big deal. I mean, hopefully I'll be able to talk normally once all this shit is healed."

"You sound kind of drunk," he replied. "But I can still understand you fine."

"Oh, good." Reaching out, I smoothed his unruly hair back from his face. "Once you're better, you need a haircut."

"What? I thought you liked long hair on dudes," he joked, glancing at Daniel.

"I hate to break it to you, buddy, but if you grow your hair out any longer, it's not going to look like Danny's. You'll have ringlets."

"I could rock some ringlets," Seamus said stubbornly, leaning his head tiredly back against the pillow.

"I've seen you with ringlets, bro," Grant called from his spot next to Thunder on the floor. "Not a good look."

"He was so cute," Aunt Halle argued. "With his little mullet."

"That's an idea," I teased. "Just let the back grow."

"Yeah, right," Seamus replied, grinning. His expression fell after a moment. "You're really okay?"

"I'm really okay," I confirmed quietly. "You really okay?"

"It hurts," he confessed. "But, yeah. I'm really okay."

"I'm so fucking glad," I whispered with a huff.

His hand tightened on mine. "Me too."

I held his hand for a while longer, even as his eyes started to droop and he fell back to sleep. Aunt Halle and Daniel's mom were talking about random shit I wasn't interested enough in to pay attention. Grant and Ian were both on their phones.

I just stared at Seamus.

I could remember every stage of his life since the day he was born. With Ian and Grant, I'd been too young, but by the time Seamus came along, I'd been old enough to retain it all. The fuzzy black hair that had fallen out in patches, his little chapped lips, the way his fingers had wrapped around my thumb, and I'd sat next to him for hours while he was asleep, fascinated by all the little movements and sounds he made. I could still see him nursing at Aunt Halle's breast, kicking his legs in the bath, his head bobbing awkwardly when he was learning how to crawl, the first time he'd walked across the room. The first few years, when he called me Flowah because he couldn't say his *r*'s. The lost teeth. The scraped knees. The whining and the giggles and the pouting and the arguments he'd had with his brothers.

He was my baby.

I didn't realize I was crying until familiar arms wrapped gently around me and the scent of my aunt's perfume filled my nose.

"He's going to be fine," she whispered into my hair. "Both of you are going to be fine."

"He almost wasn't," I choked out.

"But he is," she replied. "Because of you."

"No, I—"

"Rosemary Halle, don't finish that sentence," she warned, her lips still pressed to my head. "You did everything right. You kept him safer than I could've. As safe as Dalton if he'd been there."

"I tried really hard," I ground out. "I swear."

"Of course you did," Aunt Halle replied incredulously. "No one ever thought any differently. Are you kidding me?"

She let go and backed up enough that I could look her in the eyes.

"You did everything you possibly could, Rosemary, and I better not hear you say anything different." I opened my mouth to reply, then snapped it shut again when she glared. "Seamus was hurt because some assholes wanted to hurt my mate. The only reason we got out of there in one piece is because of you and Gary and the Bouchers. Your uncle would've been so proud if he'd seen you in action last night. I know I was."

"I was shitting my pants," I confessed.

"You and me both," she whispered back. "But that didn't stop us, did it?"

"Nope."

"I love you, kid," she said, pinching my cheek gently.

"Love you too."

"What the hell are you doing out of bed?" Alice bitched as she stepped into the room. "I thought I told you to bring her upstairs."

"I was just about to bring her back," Daniel replied.

"Alice?" Daniel's mom called. She rose from her chair.

She must've seen something in Alice's expression that no one else had, because the small woman nodded her head and then burst into tears. "He's awake," she choked out. "He's asking for Erik."

"Oh, thank the Gods," Daniel's mom whispered, her fingers pressed to her mouth.

She rushed toward Alice and wrapped the smaller woman in her arms, ushering her out of the room.

"Come on, baby," Daniel said, scooping me up off the bed. "Time for you to rest."

"I'll come back down later," I told my aunt and cousins. I met Ian's eyes, worried because he hadn't said a word. Relief filled me when he scratched his nose with his middle finger, flipping me off.

"Much later," Aunt Halle called. "Get some rest."

The house was silent as we moved through it, but Erik intercepted us on his way through the kitchen.

"Good news," he announced as he passed us.

"Tell him I'll come see him in a while."

"You'll have to get past Alice," Erik joked, disappearing around the corner.

I laid my head on Daniel's shoulder and didn't raise it until we were in his dark bedroom and he was setting me on the bed.

"Lay with me?" I asked as he pulled back.

I could've napped by myself. The bed was extremely comfortable, and I knew that he was itching to get back downstairs, especially since his uncle had woken up, but I wanted him with me. It felt like years since I'd felt his body press into mine while I slept, not just a day.

With a silent nod, Daniel helped me slide between the sheets. He carefully situated himself next to me, his hand on my belly, careful not to brush against my hip.

"Your bed's so big," I mumbled, wiggling my toes. They didn't even reach the end.

I didn't hear his response because I fell almost instantly asleep.

I didn't wake up for hours, and when I did, it was because my wounds were fucking throbbing.

"Fuck," I groaned, opening my eyes. I'd somehow managed not to roll over in my sleep, and I was still lying on my back, one arm across my chest in the sling, the other hand tucked up under my chin.

"I ran and got you some painkillers," Daniel said sympathetically. "I had a feeling you'd need them when you woke up."

"Good call," I rasped. "Gimme."

I didn't even bother sitting up. I just let him lift my head a little so I could take the two pills with water from a straw.

"It shouldn't take long for those to kick in," he assured me, lying back down beside me.

"In other news," I said, turning my head to look at him. "The mating heat seems to have disappeared."

"Noticed that, did you?"

"Kind of hard to ignore."

"Don't get used to it. I think it's just dormant while your body is healing. But it shouldn't be as bad when it comes back, since we've completed the bond and your canines dropped."

"And, you know, we're in the same place," I added dryly.

"That too."

"And we're going to stay in the same place," I continued. "Right?"

"I'll even leave the door open when I shit," Daniel vowed in mock seriousness. "My bowel movements are your bowel movements."

"You think you're funny," I countered. "But which one of us will be laughing when I come in while you're on the toilet and sit on your lap to tell you about my day?"

Daniel laughed. "Please don't."

"Doors closed when we poop," I agreed, letting my eyes fall shut.

"It's over downstairs," he said after a moment. "Do you want to hear about it?"

My eyes popped back open. "Yes."

"François Baudelaire financed them to find the secret to immortality. You heard that part."

"Tale as old as fucking time," I grumbled.

"So he approached General Keihley because they had a bit of a relationship already. When Keihley got on board, he pulled in Morren and Adamson. Morren, because he figured he could bully him into doing what he wanted, and Adamson, because he has a human girlfriend who is not his mate."

"No way." My eyes widened.

Daniel nodded. "They've been together twenty years."

"And he's had to watch her age while he stayed the same."

"Yeah," Daniel sighed. "He knew Adamson would be willing to do whatever it took, because if they were successful, then his lover could be changed."

"Fucking hell." The implications were extreme. "But what if he found his mate down the road? That would be a clusterfuck."

"Pretty much."

"There's a human man, last name of Hermann, who is in charge of the human side of things. Adamson doesn't know if he's a scientist or just a strategist, but he's the contact that Keihley had with the human faction. Adamson didn't know how to find him."

"I bet Chance can," I said confidently. We'd had more than one discussion about Chance's aptitude with computers and patterns.

"That's the next step," Daniel said. "Find Hermann."

"Or you could just take out François Baudelaire," I argued. "Stop the money and you stop the attacks."

Daniel smiled. "He's on the list too, baby. But it's not as if he's giving them petty cash to go buy bullets. We have no idea how much money is already in their hands. Killing Baudelaire may not even slow them down for a while."

"Dammit."

"Getting closer," he reminded me, leaning down to brush his lips over mine. "Without contacts in Vampire Command, the humans will be hobbled. Arthur has already talked to the heads of government, and they're going to put out a joint statement warning Vampires not to report their mates, just in case there are any traitors we haven't found yet."

"You think that's a possibility?"

"I think Adamson gave us everything he knew, but I don't trust that he knew everything there is."

"That makes sense."

"Arthur sent out a cleanup team to Dalton's property," Daniel said, propping his head on his hand. "Between the sixty-five men that were killed here and the one hundred eighty-two killed at Dalton's, I think it's safe to say that we've put a dent in the human militia."

"Jesus," I breathed. "One hundred eighty-two?"

"They came ready."

"Not ready enough, since they're dead and we aren't."

"They weren't expecting you." He grinned.

"They weren't expecting the superhero either."

"Gods, please don't say that."

"What, *superhero*?" I teased, making him grimace. "Why? I think it has a nice ring to it."

"If my brothers hear you, they'll never let me live it down."

"Then you'd better be nice to me."

I laughed and then groaned as the movement jostled my shoulder.

"All things considered," Daniel said, running his

hand slowly up and down my side. "I doubt they'll come for us again."

"You don't think they'll be pissed and want to get even?"

"I don't think it's personal for them." He shook his head. "Our mates and Dalton's family aren't worth the risk, not when they can target others who are less prepared."

"So we're safe."

"For the moment, yeah."

"Well, hallelujah."

"But it's not over," Daniel warned, his hand pausing.

"Because we're not stopping," I agreed, running my fingers through his beard.

"Not until they're all dead."

"Humans are the worst, am I right?" I said with a sigh, giving his beard a little tug.

"Oh, I don't know." Daniel nipped at my hand. "I can think of one or two that aren't so bad."

I smiled as he rolled toward me and kissed me deeply. Every movement of his body was carefully calculated not to hurt me, but even though our bodies barely touched, I was still on fire by the time he raised his head again.

"When I can move again, we're going to fuck on every surface in this room," I whispered, making him groan.

"Go back to sleep," he ordered quickly, putting his hand over my face. "Sleep is the best thing for healing."

I didn't even mind the throbbing of my hip as I burst into laughter.

CHAPTER 16
DANIEL

"That's it," I praised, watching Rosemary's back flex and undulate as she rode me. "Harder."

Gripping her ass in my hands, I guided her movements, the sound of her cries filling the room. I grinned breathlessly as her hips started to jerk, pulling against my control, and before she could even reach for my hand, I sat up and lifted it to her mouth.

Her pussy clenched around me as I felt her teeth break the skin of my wrist. Biting down on her shoulder, I let the familiar taste of her roll over my tongue as my orgasm slammed into me.

It never got old.

The taste of her, the smell of her, the sight of her, the sound of her—every day it felt new. Both exciting and comforting at the same time. I no longer worried every second of every day that someone would take her from me. I no longer worried what I'd turn into if that happened.

We'd already faced that possibility and come through it.

Nothing would separate us. Not ever.

Rosemary would fight as hard as I would to make sure it never happened.

"I know I should get up," she said, her words a little slurred as she rolled her hips. "But you're still so hard, and you feel so good where you're at."

"Stay as long as you want," I whispered, cupping her breasts in my hands. "How's your hip feeling?"

"It's fine." She dropped her head back against my shoulder. "Just like the last five times you've asked."

"It's only been three weeks." I slid my hand down and traced the scar on her hip. It was smaller than I'd thought it would be, but still raised and red.

"Three weeks is apparently plenty of time," she replied, lifting off me. "Because I feel great."

I got an excellent view as she crawled away on her hands and knees, but it was better when she climbed off the bed and turned to face me.

Her hair had been so tangled by the time we could wash it that she'd ordered me to cut it. No longer reaching the top of her ass, now it just barely covered her breasts. I missed the length, but I couldn't deny that the new length suited her too. To be honest, I wouldn't have cared if she'd asked me to shave it all off —except for the fact that she'd cried when she'd seen the pieces we'd trimmed off.

"Look." She raised her arm above her head and wiggled it from side to side. "She sells seashells at the seashore. Not even slurring anymore. I'm all better."

"I know," I replied, following her into the bathroom. "But that doesn't mean that you won't still have some twinges."

"If I have twinges, I'll tell you," she shot back over her shoulder as she turned on the shower. "But I haven't."

"I just—"

"How's your thigh?" she asked, raising her eyebrows at me.

"It's fine. Good as new."

"Then why do you keep asking about my hip and my arm?"

"I swear, you just want something to bitch about," I complained as I joined her under the spray.

"Pot, meet kettle."

"I feel like you're picking a fight so that we can make up," I joked, sliding my hand between her thighs. "Is that what's happening?"

"You're the one who started it!" She pinched my nipple, making me jerk back in surprise. "We don't have time for another round. People are going to start getting here in an hour, and I told Reese that I'd help her set up the tables and chairs."

"Why can't Beau help her?" I asked, lifting my hands to her hair to help her wash it.

Fuck, I loved showering with her. Gary's house may have had superior water pressure, but the shower at my place gave us much more room to move, and we'd taken full advantage of it once Rosemary was back on her feet.

"Because it's a bridal shower," Rosemary replied. "No boys allowed."

"He can still help her set up."

"Stop complaining. We'll be in separate rooms for like two hours."

"Maybe I'll see what your dad is up to," I said, running my fingers through her hair to rinse the suds out. "He hasn't been over in a few days."

"You saw him the day before yesterday," she said with a laugh, opening her eyes. "Your bestie probably needs a break."

"Gary loves me."

"Gary loves his daughter," she corrected with a snicker. "You're just what he has to deal with in order to get to her."

"Hurtful," I replied. "Ouch."

"He's doing good, don't you think?" she asked tentatively, turning away to reach for her body wash. "I mean, all things considered."

"Yeah, baby. He's doing good."

She nodded and handed me the soap. As she smoothed it over my chest and shoulders, I lathered it into her skin. It had become almost a ritual since the first time I'd washed her. We didn't always shower together, but when we did, we took care of each other. It wasn't sexual, though sometimes it wandered into that territory. It was more about connection, tactile assurance that each of us was healthy and whole.

"We should probably start looking into plans for the house," I told her, smoothing my hands down her thighs as I kneeled. "And see how long it'll take to clear some trees."

"We don't have to worry about that yet," she replied hoarsely, running her hands over the tops of my shoulders. "Chance thinks he's getting close to finding Hermann. We need to finish that first."

"We can do both," I countered, pausing to let her spread her legs so I could wash the delicate skin between her thighs. "You want to start a family once this is over, right?"

"You know I do," she replied with a shudder as my hand brushed her sensitive clit.

Leaning forward, I kissed the skin below her belly button. "Then we'd better have a house ready when it happens."

I'd barely risen to my feet again when her hand slid between my thighs, gliding slick and soapy over my skin.

"Not so easy to hold a conversation now, is it?" she joked, kissing my chin.

"You sure we don't have time?" I asked, letting my head fall back.

"We do not," she confirmed, her hand circling my cock.

"You're a terror," I complained as she let me go and stepped out of the spray so I could rinse off.

"You love me anyway." She stepped out of the shower and started drying off. "So do you think you want a one-story house or two?"

I laughed and shut the shower off. "I don't care. Whatever you want."

"I'd like a castle," she said, scrubbing the towel over her head. "We can afford that, right?"

"I think a castle might be a little more conspicuous than Gary would like."

"Ah, so you *do* have an opinion," she teased.

"Menace."

It took a lot less time for me to get ready than it did

Rosemary, so when I was dressed, I headed downstairs to help set up. Rosemary may have been healed enough to carry tables and chairs around the house, but that didn't mean she needed to if I was there. The house was a hive of activity when I reached the ground floor, and from what I could tell, all the tables and chairs had already been set up in the living area.

"Nephew," my Aunt Helen greeted, crossing the room to meet me.

"Hey, when did you get here?" I asked, leaning into her hug.

"We flew in this morning. Couldn't miss the party. Now, where is your mate?"

"Ah, I see how it is," I joked. "You're here for Rosemary."

"Beautiful name," she said with a smile.

"Beautiful woman," I added.

"I'm so pleased for you. Beau and Ambrose too."

"Rosemary's still getting ready. I just came down to see if you guys needed any help."

"I think everything is prepared," Aunt Helen said, gesturing at the tablecloth-covered tables. "Your mother has been up for hours."

"Figures."

"Daniel Boucher," Rosemary called from the top of the stairs. "I know what you're doing!"

I laughed as the sound of her feet pounded down the stairs.

"What?" I asked, turning to meet her. "I was ready, so I got out of your hair."

Rosemary looked around the room, her mouth slack. "They're already done?"

"Looks like it."

"You shouldn't have kept me in bed so long," she scolded.

"Baby," I cut in before she said anything else. "Come meet my Aunt Helen."

"Aw, shit," she said under her breath as she started toward us.

Aunt Helen made a sound of amusement in her throat.

"Auntie, this is my mate, Rosemary. Rosemary, my aunt."

"It's really nice to meet you," Rosemary said, shooting me a look before smiling warmly at my aunt and offering her hand. "I didn't realize anyone was here yet."

"Rosemary," Aunt Helen greeted. She clasped Rosemary's hand and held it. "It is very nice to meet you."

The scar on Rosemary's face was very noticeable. I knew that intellectually. But over the past few weeks, I'd started not to even notice it when I looked at her. It was just part of her face, like the freckle on her chin or the little dip in the bridge of her nose or the dimple on her opposite cheek. When the bandage had finally come off and the stitches were out, my mate had stood for a long time looking at herself in the mirror. It was as if she'd been memorizing this new face she'd been given. But after that, she barely mentioned it. There was no self-consciousness, no worry about how it looked.

I'd noticed that because she didn't seem to care that it was there, no one else really looked at it either—and I'd been watching everyone we encountered like a hawk, ready to step in.

We'd been around the same people for so long, people who knew Rosemary, that I was unprepared when Aunt Helen lifted a single finger to Rosemary's cheek and brushed just below the scar.

"You're lovely," she said simply. "You wear it well."

"Um...thank you," Rosemary said, glancing at me.

"Not all of us get to show our scars off so proudly," Aunt Helen said, dropping her hand. She smiled at Rosemary. "But be careful. You'll no longer have the element of surprise when you wear a warrior's mark on your cheek."

She let go of Rosemary's hand and patted my back before walking away.

"What the fuck was that?" Rosemary whispered, staring at my aunt's back.

"Uh...apparently, you're a warrior?"

Rosemary's shoulders straightened. "As if that was ever in question," she replied haughtily. "I've got a fucking warrior's mark to prove it."

"Yeah, you do."

She snickered. "Your aunt is cool as hell, you know that, right?"

"Oh, yeah," I replied as we headed toward the kitchen. "I realized that a long time ago."

"I kind of forget it's there," she confessed.

"Me too."

"Really?"

I shrugged. "I notice the shoulder and the hip more, because I don't want to hurt you when I'm holding you."

Rosemary stopped. "You haven't hurt me."

"Well, I don't want to start."

"Hey, Danny boy," Chance called from halfway down the stairs. "You got a minute?"

"You good?" I asked Rosemary.

"I've been living here for three weeks," she replied, patting my shoulder consolingly. "I think I can walk into the kitchen on my own."

Chance met me at the bottom of the stairs and then led me out into the front driveway. We'd almost made it to the trees when he finally stopped.

"I think I've found him," he said quietly. "I followed the money. It's the only company that's receiving payments and doesn't have any connection to Keihley, Morren, or Adamson. Two properties: a house in Missouri and a warehouse in Arizona. Looking at records, someone is living in the house."

"You got him." I slapped Chance on the back. "Fantastic fucking news. But why are we out here?"

"I didn't want to ruin the day," Chance grumbled, tipping his head back and forth. "You know, the bridal shower shit."

"Wait, you're not going to tell them?"

"I will," he hedged. "Later. After the party."

I debated silently for a moment, then nodded. A few hours wouldn't make any difference.

A car rolled up the driveway, and two men climbed out. I waved at Reese's honorary fathers as they headed toward the front door. I guess *some* boys were allowed. I was definitely going to give Rosemary shit about it later.

"I'll call Dalton after everyone has left," I said, looking back at Chance. "Have him head over so we can set some plans."

"We're getting closer," he replied, rubbing his

hands together. He smacked them together once. "Cool, good talk."

I stood there staring as he strode away.

"Why the hell did you tell *me* now?" I called after him.

"Had to tell someone," he replied, throwing his hands in the air. Without another word, he climbed into his truck and fired it up.

Great, now I'd have to keep it to myself all day surrounded by people, while he was off doing whatever the hell he wanted. I wasn't even surprised.

When I got back inside, all the women were in the living room, and Reese was fluttering around in a short white dress. She was practically glowing as she touched the tables, the flower vases, and the presents. Pete, the man who'd stepped in when she was a teenager to be the adult she needed, wrapped an arm around her shoulders and kissed her head happily.

"What?" Rosemary said, stepping into my view. "What happened?"

"Nothing happened," I replied, lowering my voice in hopes that she would too.

"Spill it," she whispered, glancing over her shoulder. "I know every expression on your face, and something is going on."

I knew with absolute certainty that she wouldn't let it go. After asking for nothing for so long, hiding what she needed from me, carrying the weight of our separations silently, it was as if a switch had flipped in my mate after the night at the Cavendish house. Nothing was off limits anymore. The closeness I'd wanted, the easiness I'd seen between my brothers and their mates, I had that now too. Rosemary told me what she needed when she needed it. There was no hesitation on her part—and she fully expected that to work both ways.

"Come with me." Taking her by the hand, I tugged her toward the stairs and back to our room.

Once we were closed in, she looked at me expectantly.

"Chance thinks he found Hermann."

"No fucking way," she hissed. Her eyes dropped closed, and she let out a long breath. "Where is he?"

"Two properties, two different places to search," I told her as she wrapped her arms around my waist. "But the house in Missouri looks more promising."

"Fuck yeah. When are we going?"

My chest twinged with anxiety.

"Daniel?" she said questioningly. There was irritation in her voice, but worse, there was an almost detached disappointment.

I swallowed back every valid reason I could think of why she should stay home.

"Chance doesn't want to tell anyone until after the party," I said, tightening my arms around her as she started to pull away. "Tonight, I'll call Dalton so we can start planning."

"You can't cut me out of this," she said quietly. "That's not the relationship I want to have."

"I know that," I replied. "I have a feeling we'll be headed south in the next few days."

She nodded solemnly.

"Good," she said, running her hands up my back. "Let's get this shit over with."

"Don't say anything until I'm able to speak with my dad and brothers."

"I won't."

"You ready to head back downstairs?" I asked, letting my fingers tangle in her hair.

"In a minute." She leaned forward and pressed her lips to mine softly. "I just want to be here with you for a little while. Okay?"

We stood there just inside the door, holding each other. When we went back downstairs, she'd be engulfed in women, happy and celebrating Reese. After that, we'd be neck-deep in plans and strategy sessions with my family and hers. But for now, it was just us.

We hadn't had enough time that was just us.

I was really looking forward to when that changed.

"Okay, I'm ready," she said with a sigh as she pulled away.

"You sure?" I asked, sliding my hand down over her ass. "I bet I could fuck you before anyone noticed we were missing."

Rosemary smiled, her eyes lighting up. "After the party, but before you tell your brothers?"

"Deal."

We held hands as I led her back into the hallway and down the stairs, not ready to let go quite yet.

"I love you," I whispered in her ear as we reached the bottom. "And your ass looks incredible today."

"My ass looks incredible every day," she whispered back with a chuckle. "I love you too."

Just as I'd begun to let go of her hand, the front door swung open so hard that it slammed into the wall with a loud bang.

As I turned, Chance came through it, a woman with long dark hair clutched in his arms.

They were both covered in blood.

Shock held me in place for only a moment before both Rosemary and I were moving toward him.

"I found her on the road. Her car was upside down," he babbled, practically sobbing. "Help me."

I'd never seen my Aunt Alice move so fast. She'd rounded the couch and had her hands on the woman before we'd even crossed the room.

"Rena?" Reese wailed in disbelief.

"Please," Chance continued. I wasn't even sure if he knew what he was saying. "Please, you have to help her."

"I'm helping her," Alice assured him. "I'm helping her. Carry her into the surgery."

"She's hurt," Chance said, tears running down his face. "She's hurt really bad."

"Chauncey," Alice snapped. "Into the surgery now!"

"I—" He looked down at the woman, his chest heaving. "My mate."

The words seemed to echo through the room. Even Reese fell silent.

"I cannot carry her," Alice said, reaching out to grip my brother's chin in her hand. "So either carry her into the goddamn surgery or Danny will do it."

Chance lurched into motion just as my father and Ambrose came out of the kitchen at a run.

"Out of the way," Alice ordered, leading Chance and his mate toward the hospital room.

Ambrose followed, but I stood frozen as they disappeared.

Rosemary's fingers slid between mine as somewhere behind us, Reese sobbed. Her other arm wrapped around my waist as she leaned into me.

"Holy Gods," I mumbled, lifting her hand to my

lips. I shuddered as I leaned toward her, fear making my lips numb as I whispered in her ear. "Baby, I don't think she was breathing."

Rosemary's head jerked toward me, her eyes filled with horror that matched my own.

The last of my brothers had found his mate, and I was pretty sure he was about to lose her.

LOOK FOR BOOK FOUR

Coming soon...

AVAILABLE MAY 2026

ACKNOWLEDGMENTS

To my family, who put up with me this summer while I wrote this book. I love you guys so much.

To Michelle, Pam, and Bea, for all of your work in the reader group to keep things lively.

To Donna, who praised my first book in her blog. I wouldn't be where I am without you.

To the readers. So many of you have told me that you don't usually read vampire books, but you read *Vein & Vow* because I was the one who wrote it. Thank you so much. I wouldn't be able to do what I do without your support.

And to Ellie, my friend, editor, publisher, and general problem solver. Love you, dude.

Nicole Jacquelyn started writing before she started elementary school, however she didn't start publishing her stories until her senior year in college. Today, she's the author of the bestselling Aces series, the Fostering Love series, the Kellys series, and The Bouchers series. She loves to read, drinks too much coffee, and lives in Oregon with the coolest children in the entire world.

www.ingramcontent.com/pod-product-compliance
Lightning Source LLC
LaVergne TN
LVHW030916080826
845145LV00013B/2923

* 9 7 8 1 9 6 9 8 7 6 0 2 8 *